PRAISE FOR THE JONATHAN QUINN SERIES

"Brilliant and heart pounding"—**Jeffery Deaver**, *New York Times* bestselling author

"Addictive."—**James Rollins**, *New York Times* bestselling author

"Unputdownable."—**Tess Gerritsen**, *New York Times* bestselling author

"The best elements of Lee Child, John le Carré, and Robert Ludlum."—**Sheldon Siegel**, *New York Times* bestselling author

"Quinn is one part James Bond, one part Jason Bourne."—**Nashville Book Worm**

"Welcome addition to the political thriller game."—*Publishers Weekly*

ALSO BY BRETT BATTLES

THE JONATHAN QUINN THRILLERS

THE CLEANER
THE DECEIVED
SHADOW OF BETRAYAL (U.S.)/THE UNWANTED (U.K.)
THE SILENCED
BECOMING QUINN
THE DESTROYED

THE LOGAN HARPER THRILLERS

LITTLE GIRL GONE
EVERY PRECIOUS THING

THE PROJECT EDEN THRILLERS

SICK
EXIT NINE
PALE HORSE
ASHES

StandAlones

THE PULL OF GRAVITY
NO RETURN

For Younger Readers

THE TROUBLE FAMILY CHRONICLES

HERE COMES MR. TROUBLE

THE
COLLECTED

Brett Battles

A Jonathan Quinn Novel

This one's for Cami and Tori
and all the living you still have in front of you!

CHAPTER
ONE

THE TWO LISTS lay on the table, side by side, black ink on white paper.

The first set of names would be the easiest. Once a man was dead, he was dead.

It was the plans David Harris's boss had for the second set that would be more difficult.

"I want to see their faces," Javier Romero had ordered. "I want them to know what's happening to them. I want them to know why."

"It's risky," Harris argued at the time. "These aren't just normal people. They're professionals. One small error could have serious consequences."

"Then I suggest you make sure there are no errors."

In truth, the idea of bringing the men on the second list to Romero's hideaway excited Harris. It was a challenge, like the way things had been before the incident—as Romero referred to it—four years earlier. Back then, ridding his boss of his enemies had been an enjoyable weekly task. It was something Harris, as trusted advisor and head of security, had done very well, satisfying the occasional call of his mercenary roots.

But since the incident, there had been very little of that, only the promise of one last big project. As the kicker, Romero had promised him a healthy reward once the project was complete. Given the man's wealth and the dollars discussed, it had been more than enough reason for Harris to stick around.

And now the time had finally come, the job that would allow him to get his hands dirty again, if only figuratively.

In another month, two at the most, he'd be gone from here, living his own life however the hell he wanted to, and never having to work for anyone again.

He picked up the second list. Seven names, two crossed out. They were already dead, not by Harris's hand or anyone associated with him or Romero, but by the nature of the work they did.

Unfortunate, but it still left the five.

He smiled.

This was going to be fun.

FOUR WEEKS **LATER**

CHAPTER
TWO

NORTHEASTERN MEXICO

NATE'S PHONE RANG. "Yes?"

"It's going down now." The voice belonged to Kelvin Moore, the ops leader. The pause that followed lasted fifteen seconds. "All right, we're done. You're up, Mr. Quinn. We're clearing out now."

Nate started the van. "Any complications?"

"None." Moore hung up.

Nate shoved his phone into his pocket and dropped the van into gear. Since he'd taken over running his boss's business—temporarily or not was still to be determined—Nate had used Jonathan Quinn's name just to make things easier. Most clients only knew Quinn from his reputation, and had not met him in person, but it was that reputation that kept them calling, so it only made sense to continue utilizing it. Occasionally, Nate would run into a field op who knew Quinn, but so far, though there were a few raised eyebrows, there had yet to be any issues.

"Finally," Burke said, a sly smile pushing his cheek up on one side. He was the assistant Nat had been forced to hire for the job. Daeng, his de facto number two, had been called back to Asia on an emergency, and all the usual freelancers he would have hired to fill in were unavailable. Burke had been the suggestion of the job's broker, and guy named Pullman.

THE COLLECTED

The termination site was a warehouse tucked into the foothills outside of Monterrey, Mexico. The drive from the staging point took four minutes. Per Nate's request, the ops team had left the gate open in the fence surrounding the building when they departed.

"Stick to the plan," Nate said, slowing the van as he drove onto the property. "No conversation. You need me, you get my attention some other way."

Burke waved a dismissive hand. "Yeah, yeah. I got it."

Nate pulled to a stop near the loading dock, and killed the engine. Out of habit, he tugged on his gloves to make sure they were snug on his hands, then nodded at Burke.

Staying inside the vehicle, they moved into the back. As they'd discussed ahead of time, Burke picked up the roll of black plastic sheeting while Nate donned the clean kit—a backpack with all the tools needed to do a proper job.

Nate grabbed the handle on the back door, but paused as he glanced at his temporary employee. "Ready?"

"Of course. Come on."

"Five minutes. No more."

"I know. I know. Let's get this started."

If Nate hadn't already decided this was going to be the only time Burke worked for him, the man's eagerness would have sealed the deal. Nate was a cleaner, and his was a cool, calm business, not something that should be considered exciting. That's when things were missed and mistakes were made.

Per the mission briefing, the building was supposedly secured only by an alarm system that the ops team had disarmed when they first arrived, but as his mentor Quinn always said, "What is supposed to be isn't always what is." A second, undetected alarm was not out of the question, or even security guards who might have hidden while the ops team did their thing.

Alert, Nate approached the door at the end of the loading dock. This, too, the ops team had left unlocked for them. Pushing it open a few inches, Nate moved his ear next to the gap and listened. Dead silence. With a nod to Burke, they slipped inside.

The main warehouse area was a larger room filled with rows of neatly stacked boxes and crates. The overhead fluorescents were off, but a dozen scattered safety lights were still lit, giving the two of them more than enough illumination to find their way around.

The area they were interested in was a quarter of the way down the third aisle. Nate signaled for Burke to wait at the end, then headed quickly between the boxes alone, so he could make sure everything was as expected.

The body lay on three thick layers of cardboard in a nook created within the row of boxes. Nate had been the one who prepared the flooring the previous evening, putting plastic sheeting between the cardboard layers and the floor to prevent blood from leaking onto the concrete. He'd also installed the boxes at the back of the nook, none of which contained the liquid soap or paper plates the rest of the containers held. Instead, each had been filled with a lightweight material that was deceptively strong, and very adept at stopping projectiles. He did a quick scan and spotted the bullet hole in a box just off center, second from the bottom, and was confident the bullet would be inside.

As for the dead man, Nate had no prior knowledge of his identity, nor did he recognize him now. That was often the nature of the job. For whatever reason, someone had decided the man needed to be eliminated. Nate's only concern was getting the body out, and leaving behind no trace that anything happened.

He signaled Burke to join him.

The first thing they did was to roll up the body in the cardboard flooring, then package it all in a double layer of black plastic. It would be heavy to carry, but doable. They then set about pulling down Nate's wall of boxes, and dumping the material from inside onto another piece of sheeting. When Nate reached the box with the hole in it, he found the bullet resting comfortably in the fourth fold of the material.

The damaged box was added to the pile, but the others

they closed and left. In a day or two or maybe a week, someone might wonder why several boxes were empty, but that would be the only clue that something had gone on here.

They carried the discarded materials out to the van, then returned and did the same with the body.

"Piece of cake," Burke said as they were driving away.

Nate gave him a noncommittal grunt. It *had* gone smoothly, and he had to admit Burke had done exactly as they had discussed ahead of time. They had even finished the removal with nearly half a minute to spare. That said, Burke still rubbed him the wrong way, and the guy's chances at being rehired remained zero.

The next step was to make the body and the other items from the warehouse permanently disappear. After that, it would be straight to the airport and a flight back to L.A. that would get Nate home in the afternoon. He'd sleep in his own bed tonight, and then tomorrow Liz would arrive.

He started to smile, but stopped himself. He couldn't think about Liz, not right now. She would only distract him.

Finish the job first, buddy. You can think about her once you get home.

The plan for the body was simple. There was a lot of empty space in this part of Mexico. Nate had chosen a quiet ravine about fifteen miles away from the warehouse. The previous afternoon, he and Burke had dug the grave. Once they dropped the body into it, Nate would cover it with a healthy amount of a chemical powder blend Quinn had developed, and he and Burke would fill the hole with dirt. The chemicals would eat away at the body. Within a day, most visible identifying marks would be gone. Within a week, pretty much any method used to try to figure out who the dead man had been would fail.

The sun was still a good half hour from rising, but the sky in the east was beginning to pale. It was going to be close, but Nate was hopeful they would be done by the time daylight peeked over the horizon.

He checked the odometer. Their turnoff was a mile and a half away. From there, it would be a two-mile ride along a dry, flash-flood wash through a narrow valley.

Nate reached for a bottle of water next to his seat, but paused before he could grab it, his eyes focusing on a point in the distance.

What the hell?

At right about the point where they were supposed to leave the road, there were headlights of at least three cars parked on the side of the highway.

He slowed the van, wanting to give himself enough time to assess the situation before deciding whether it was something to worry about. The situation was not made easy by the brightening sky. It was screwing up his vision, making the ground and anything on it seem even darker than when the night had been in full control.

He checked the odometer again, and looked back at the headlights. No, they weren't close to where he wanted to turn off. They were parked at the exact spot.

Coincidences didn't exist. Not in a cleaner's world, anyway. Believing in them was a quick path to a short career. He had to assume the vehicles were trouble, which meant scratching his primary dump site.

He pulled the van to the side of the road, and killed the lights.

"What are you doing?" Burke asked.

"Not now."

"Something wrong?"

"I said not now."

Before the van could roll to a complete stop, Nate swung the wheel to the left, tapped the gas, and pulled a U-turn. Driving dark, he headed back the way they'd come, his mind switching gears to his backup plan.

"Hey, you going to tell me what's going on or not?" Burke asked.

Nate ignored the question as he flicked his eyes back and forth between the side mirror and the road ahead. If the cars had really been waiting for them, their occupants would be experiencing the same predawn vision issues Nate had been having, which, hopefully, would mean the last they'd seen of his van had been when the headlight switched off. If that were the case, they'd grow concerned and send a car to check what happened. If, on the other hand, they were just there by chance, then the cars would remain where they were.

In twenty seconds, he had his answer. But it wasn't just one car racing down the road. It was all three.

Nate increased their speed.

"What the *hell* is going on?" Burke demanded.

In the mirror, Nate could see the cars slow as they approached the spot where he'd doused his lights. They paused there only seconds before accelerating again.

"We've got company," he said.

Burke twisted in his seat and looked into the mirror on his side. "Who?" He stared at the reflection for a moment. "Those cars back there? How do you know?"

"Because they were waiting at the turnoff."

"No way."

Nate said nothing.

"Probably just some kids," Burke suggested.

"Not kids."

"Who else could they be?"

"Trouble."

Nate pushed the van as fast as it could go, but knew it wasn't enough. At the moment, they had just over a mile's lead, and their lights were still off, but both those advantages would soon be wiped out by the faster cars and rising sun.

They had three or four miles, maybe, a few minutes at best, and then the others would be on them. Their only chance was to reach the outskirts of Monterrey, where they'd have some city to hide in. Roads, buildings, whatever they could find would be better than open countryside. It would be close, but maybe.

"What are we going to do?" Burke said.

"I'm going to drive, and you're going to shut the hell up."

Nate scanned the road ahead. Shapes were starting to appear out of the shadows that had covered the earth. Hills and trees and the still-distant city.

Too distant.

Come on. Just give me something.

Thirty seconds later, he spotted a sign about three quarters of a mile ahead. It was still too far away and too dark to read, but he'd seen its shape a dozen times before—a Pemex gas station sign.

Nate's mind skipped over contingency B *and* C, and went straight to D. Though minor details within contingency D varied from job to job, the nuts and bolts were the same: ditch vehicle, set it on fire, and run.

He checked the mirror again. The gap between the van and the other vehicles had closed to three quarters of a mile. Before he could move his gaze back to the road, a new light flashed in the mirror.

Son of a bitch.

Pulsating now on the roofs of all three cars were police lights.

CHAPTER
THREE

THE PEMEX STATION was on the left. Just beyond it was a road that cut between the station and a row of cinderblock buildings that stretched along the highway for several hundred feet. If Nate could get the van behind those buildings without being seen, the cops might drive straight by and not realize their mistake for several minutes.

"Hold on tight," he said.

Burke grabbed the back of his seat with one hand, and braced his other against the dash.

Now that the gas station was only a few seconds away, Nate had a much better idea of how it was laid out, and could see that instead of having to take a sharp turn onto the intersecting road between it and the other buildings, he could cut diagonally across the Pemex lot and whip behind the row of shops, all without having to touch his brakes.

He waited until the very last second, then yanked the wheel to the left. The van careened across the road, bouncing Nate and Burke in their seats as it hit the uneven asphalt surrounding the filling station. Keeping on as straight a line as possible, Nate aimed the van just to the right of the pumps, then off the curb on the other side.

"As soon as we stop, get out and run," Nate said as he whipped the vehicle around the back of the first cinderblock building.

"Run? Where?"

"Anywhere. As far away as possible. I'll contact you in a

few days."

Out of the corner of his eye, Nate could see Burke nod, but if the other man said anything, it was lost in the squeal of brakes as Nate brought the van to a halt.

"Go!" Nate yelled.

Burke fought with his seat belt for a second, then wrenched open his door and disappeared.

Nate jammed the transmission into Park, grabbed his clean kit, and moved quickly into the back. From the main section of the bag, he removed a can of lighter fluid and a box of matches. He doused both the wrapped body and the package of materials, and removed a match from the box.

Just as he was striking the head against the side of the container, he heard the siren. But it wasn't coming from the highway on the other side of the buildings like he'd hoped. It was quickly approaching the back of the van. Though it sounded like only a single car, it was still one too many.

His ploy hadn't worked.

Cursing under his breath, he threw the lit match onto the plastic covering the body. As the flames ignited, he raced up front, pulled the backpack over his shoulders, and exited through the same door Burke had used.

He kept the van between himself and the police car, and ran as fast as he could, but was sure it would only be a matter of seconds before they saw him. He spotted a break ahead between the buildings. Knowing it was his only chance, he ducked into the gap, and was relieved to see it went all the way to the front. He moved rapidly down the space, crouched down as he neared the end, and eased his head out for a look.

There was another police car, lights flashing, sitting across the entrance to the road that ran next to Pemex. Nate had to fight the urge to jerk his head back as he slowly rotated around and looked in the other direction. The third police car was stopped on the shoulder, about a hundred feet away, on his side of the highway.

He carefully drew his head back into the safety of the narrow alley.

Escaping via the front wasn't going to work, but neither

was returning the way he'd come. He was surrounded. Either he stayed where he was and waited for someone to find him, or...

He looked up.

The roof?

Did he really have a choice? The walls were too close together to effectively spider-walk to the top, but there was a pipe running up the side that looked like it might be secure enough to use as an impromptu ladder. He gave it a jerk, and decided it would hold.

Just as he started up, he heard footsteps. Close, no more than a dozen feet around the front corner, moving in his direction. No way he'd make the top before the person reached the passageway.

He had but one option. He scrambled upward as high as he dared, and wedged himself between the walls and moved as close to the front end of the gap as possible. There, he hung, ten feet up and two feet back from the corner.

The steps approached from the other side, and stopped. Several seconds passed, then the end of a gun and top of a police hat peeked around the corner below him.

That's right, Nate thought. *Come on in for a look, but just keep your eyes down.*

The man's gaze swung from one side to the other across the ground, and seemed to freeze on the spot at the base of the pipe.

Nate's footprints.

The cop moved all the way into the opening, and kneeled down for a better look. A moment passed, then he raised his head, his gaze continuing to move up toward the roof.

A split second before he would have seen Nate, the cleaner dropped from the sky like a stone.

The cop tried to raise a hand in front of his face, but Nate plowed into him feet first before he could, slamming the man to the ground.

Something popped along one of the cop's legs, a knee perhaps, or an ankle bent the wrong way. Whatever it was, the cop wasn't feeling it at the moment. He was out cold, thanks to his head thudding hard against the ground.

"*Lo siento*," Nate whispered, apologizing.

He grabbed the man's gun, and checked the main street again. The two police cars were still there, but now that it was a little lighter, he could see both vehicles were empty. He scanned the buildings in case another cop might be working his way toward him, but there was no one.

Directly across the street was a small dirt field, and on the other side of it were several cinderblock homes. There were no fences around the properties, just more dirt and the occasional patch of grass or brush.

So, go for the roof or take the chance?

Hell, the roof was a chance, too. Perhaps even a bigger one, because he could easily get trapped there.

He glanced at the road again. Nothing.

Option two, then.

He slipped out of the gap, and scooted along the front of the building to his left, alert for any movement. Reaching the end without incident, he snuck a look around the corner, down another road that led back toward the rear of the buildings. There were two cops, fifty feet away. Each had a gun drawn, but their attention was focused in the other direction, as if they expected Nate to come barreling around the back.

Nate glanced toward the highway, intending to pick the best path across the field on the other side, but his gaze strayed to the nearby police car. It was vibrating, its engine idling.

Like coincidences, there was no such thing as luck. "Opportunity, yes," Quinn had once said. "It's up to you whether you take it or not. But no luck."

Consider it taken, Nate thought as he moved silently over to the car and around to the driver's side. He carefully lifted the handle, and eased the door open.

No yells. No one heading in his direction.

So far, so good.

Staying low, he slipped inside, and positioned his foot above the accelerator while grabbing the transmission lever with his right hand.

THE COLLECTED

On three. One. Two.

The moment *three* passed through his head, he sat up, dropped the shift into Drive, and jammed the gas pedal to the floor. As the car jumped forward, he whipped the wheel around and pulled a quick U-turn so he would be heading toward the safety of the city.

The door was still partially open as he finished the turn, so he had no problems hearing the shouts of alarm. He reached out and pulled the door closed just as the crack of a gun echoed behind him, but wherever the bullet went, it didn't hit the car.

He checked his mirror in time to see the men run out onto the highway. They were small and getting smaller fast, but that didn't stop them from firing several more rounds in his direction. Again, none of the bullets hit their mark.

Then the road curved to the right, and the men dropped out of sight.

Nate knew it would only be moments before the other police cars took up chase. He needed to get off the highway and into an area where it would be next to impossible for them to find him.

The good news was that the city was starting to rear up around him. At the first major intersection he reached, he turned right, drove down four blocks, and made a quick left in front of oncoming traffic.

Two more turns, and he was confident there was no way the others would know where he was. A few minutes later, he pulled into an alleyway behind a clothing store and parked the car tight to the wall.

His gloved hands made doing a wipe down of the interior unnecessary, but he still did a check for any hair he might have left behind. Once he was sure the car was clean, he tossed the keys onto the dash so they'd be visible to anyone interested in taking a joy ride, and walked down the alley to the far street.

For the first time since things had gone sideways, he allowed a thought that had been pecking away at the back of his mind to come forward.

The police had been waiting *at* the turnoff for his dump site.

How had they found it? And how had they known what time to be there?

It seemed unlikely that someone had discovered the hole in the ground and reported it. But even if that were the case, the hole wasn't long and narrow like a grave. It was a five-foot-deep square. Odd, perhaps, and they might be curiosity about who had dug it, but jumping to the conclusion that it was criminal in nature was a giant leap.

There really was only one possibility. The cops had been tipped off.

But by whom? The only ones who knew about the pending death of the target were Pullman, the ops team, and Nate and Burke. Well, the client, too, of course, whoever that was. But he or she was unlikely to know any of the operation details. In fact, the only ones who knew about the dump site were Nate and Burke.

That son of a bitch sold me out.

As anger began to build in his chest, Nate fought it back down. He did not have time to worry about the whos and whys right now. What he had to worry about were the hows, as in how he'd get out of town. Given the gigantic fiasco the operation had become, there was no question Monterrey should already have been in his rear window.

Once he was safely away, the next thing he'd need to do was get in touch with Pullman so the broker could handle any damage control that needed to happen. Hopefully the fire in the van had taken care of the body. It wouldn't be the most satisfactory conclusion to the assignment, but the target *was* dead, and Nate had followed procedure, doing all he could to make identification of the body difficult.

Then, and only then, could he start thinking about Burke.

The closest entrance to the US from his current location was along the Texas border. There were several small crossings, but the busy one at Reynosa would be easiest. Busy was good. He could lose himself if he had to. And if anything looked screwy there, he could head east to Matamoros and cross over into Brownsville. Worst case, he could continue over to the Gulf Coast and hire a fishing vessel and work his way north.

The one thing he couldn't do in a timely manner was walk the one hundred and forty miles from Monterrey to the border. But most of the traditional transportation options—planes, buses, rental cars—were out, too. Cops would be watching those. Even if they didn't know exactly what Nate looked like, if they'd been tipped off about the operation, they probably knew he was a *gringo*, too, and would question any Caucasian male traveling alone.

A taxi? Same problem. A quick warning broadcast over their radio, and suddenly the driver would start to wonder about his passenger. Nate could just steal a vehicle, but most of the cars he was passing looked liked they'd be unlikely to make it halfway to the border before giving out.

At the end of the block, a delivery truck turned onto the street, grinded its gears for a moment, and drove right by Nate.

He smiled. That was the solution he was looking for.

There would be hundreds of trucks running between Monterrey and Reynosa, carrying goods bound for the US. If he could get to where the highway started—find the Mexican equivalent of a truck stop, perhaps—he should be able to bum a ride, or, even better, stow away and then hop out when the rig reached the border town.

He consulted a map of the city on this phone, walked four blocks over to a main road, and took a chance on flagging down a taxi for a short ride.

"La Condesa," he told the driver. It was on the outskirts of the city, along the highway to Texas. "*Métele velocidad.*"

NATE WASTED NO time picking out his target. It was a tractor-trailer rig with license plates for both Mexico and Texas, parked in a big lot beside a Pemex station on the side of the road headed toward the border. The trailer was locked up, but there was an area behind the cab surrounded by metal partitions just wide enough for Nate to sit between if he drew his legs up to his chest. It certainly wasn't the safest place to ride, but there were several things he could brace himself against, and as long as he didn't fall asleep or the driver didn't get into an accident, he'd be fine.

He went inside the store attached to the station and picked up some water, all the while keeping an eye out the window in case the driver returned. When he was done, he hung around the side of the building until the trucker finally showed up. As the man was doing a walk around his rig, Nate made his way over to the semi parked in the adjacent spot. He waited there, out of sight, until the driver started to climb into his cab.

As Nate heard the door open, he scooted out of his hiding spot, rushed into the space between the truck and the trailer, and took his self-assigned seat. The engine rumbled and the truck pulled out.

Nate was on his way toward Reynosa.

THE RIDE WAS hot and windy. Nate kept his head tucked down most of the time. With nothing else to occupy his mind, he allowed himself to go over the possibilities of why the job had gone wrong. No matter which scenario he considered, his thoughts always circled back to Burke. There was just no other solution.

His motivation?

Money?

It was the root of all evil, right? And the easiest answer. But even that brought a set of unknowns. Who had paid Burke for the information? And what was that person's motivation?

Was it a friend of the dead man? No, that wouldn't make sense. The person would have wanted to stop the operation from happening at all.

The police? Wouldn't they have been more interested in catching the ops team in the act of killing the target?

Neither choice satisfied Nate. But if not them, then who?

Nate wondered what Quinn would have thought, but immediately knew the answer. Quinn would have never taken the job in the first place.

THE COLLECTED

Pullman hadn't been on Quinn's Preferred Clients list, and Quinn had reached a point in his career where if a job were offered by someone he didn't know, he would have just passed. Nate was not in the position to be as picky. So when the gig coincided with a hole in his schedule, he'd done some due diligence, and found out that Pullman was a mid-level fixer with a decent enough reputation. Nate had seen no reason to turn the job down. It was all experience, he'd told himself. The more he had, the better he would be.

If it was a unique experience he'd been going for—mission accomplished.

He checked his watch. They'd been on the road for almost an hour and a half. Another thirty minutes at most, and they'd be in Reynosa.

His backpack was sitting between his heels and his thighs. He unzipped the top, pulled out the nearly empty bottle of water, and downed the remaining liquid.

As he put the bottle back in his bag, the truck whined loudly, the driver downshifting and reducing speed. A hill, maybe, Nate thought. It certainly wouldn't be Reynosa yet. They hadn't been driving *that* fast.

The truck downshifted again, but the road remained level.

Nate took a cautious peek around the thin metal partition. On the passenger side were the dotted line that indicated the edge of the highway, and the scrub-covered, semi-desert plain. There were no hills or mountains anywhere he could see. He looked to his right. The car in the fast lane next to them was slowing, too, and behind it, he could see the front bumper of the trailing car.

Traffic. Great.

The truck's speed continued to decrease until Nate could have walked faster. Then, with a final hiss of its air brakes, the rig stopped completely.

Nate didn't like it one bit. By his estimation, they still had at least twenty miles left to go before they reached the border. He highly doubted traffic would be backed up this far south. An accident, then?

The truck's engine roared as the semi moved ahead a few feet before halting again.

Nate knew he needed to take a look and get a sense of what was going on. It would be a gamble, but he figured if he stayed low and leaned around the passenger side, there would be little chance someone would notice.

He snaked his head and shoulders around the lower end of the metal partition. He checked the side mirror first to make sure the driver couldn't see him, then looked down the road.

There were at least thirty vehicles ahead of them, inching forward at a mind-numbing crawl. Farther down the road, he could see a few flashing lights, but couldn't tell if they were from police cars or fire trucks or perhaps even an ambulance.

Though part of his mind was thinking that it might very well be an accident, his intuition was saying, *Get out of here.*

Again, the truck moved, this time traveling about a dozen feet. At the front of the jam, another truck also pulled forward, but it was able to keep going, having cleared whatever the problem was. Once it was out of the way, Nate could see three of the emergency vehicles.

There wasn't an ambulance among them. Not a fire truck, either.

Police cars only.

"A roadblock," he whispered to himself.

Even if the cops there weren't looking for *him*, given his unconventional seating arrangements, he would not go unnoticed.

He examined the side of the road. About thirty feet ahead, the highway crossed over a bridge that spanned shallow wash. The scrub grew tall along each bank, while scattered patches of bushes had sprung up down the middle.

It was a better opportunity than he could have hoped for.

He waited patiently as the truck continued to move foot by foot toward the bridge. When the cab finally reached it, Nate grabbed his bag, stepped onto the road, and dropped down into the gulch. Ducking under the bridge, he held his position as the truck and the next few cars behind it passed

THE COLLECTED

by.

No one honked or shouted at him.

He was just starting to think he'd made it without being seen, when he heard a *whomp-whomp-whomp* approaching. Using the bridge to conceal his presence, he looked toward the sky and spotted a helicopter descending toward the road.

It was dark in color and large, and though there were no discernible markings, it looked distinctively official, not private. He crawled farther under the bridge, hoping they were just doing a flyover and he hadn't been spotted, but the rotors continued to increase in volume until their constant beating echoed through every inch of the semi-enclosed space.

Suddenly a voice crackled over a loudspeaker. *"El hombre que está abajo del puente, quédese en donde está. No intente correr, o le disparamos."* The voice then switched to English. "Under the bridge. Do not run. You will be shot."

Even if Nate hadn't understood either language, the message was clear: He was screwed.

More orders were shouted over the speaker, telling the cars parked on the road to move out of the way so the helicopter could land.

Nate moved to the far side of the bridge. Beyond were twenty feet of open space, then a thick growth of shoulder-high scrub shooting up out of the soft sand.

The helicopter sounded like it was nearing the ground.

Now or never.

He sucked in a breath, then raced over to the brush and kept going. He wanted to look back, *had* to look back, but forced his eyes to stay forward.

Go, go, go!

He weaved back and forth through the scrub, trying to build up as much of a gap as possible between himself and the cops who would soon be chasing him, and searched for a place to hide.

Instinctively, he'd been counting off the seconds since he left the cover of the bridge. Thirty-seven turned out to be the magic number. That's when he heard shouts from back near

34

the bridge, and knew they had discovered he wasn't there anymore. Add a few more seconds for them to get organized, and he figured he had, at best, a forty-second lead. Not great, but not as bad as it could have been.

He came to a fork in the wash. To the left, the dry bed rose gently as it narrowed in width. Most likely, it went on for only another fifty feet or so before petering out. The fork to the right, though, continued as it had been.

Knowing the latter would be the direction they expected him to go, he chose the shallower route. Ten feet shy of where the wash disappeared, he found what he'd been looking for. A portion of the sidewall had been cut away by a recent storm, creating an overhang just large enough for him to fit into. If he could pull some dirt on top of him, or cause the overhang to collapse, they might never find him.

As he dropped to his knees and started to roll into the space, a loud roar raced overhead.

"Do not move! You are being covered, and you will be shot dead." The voice from the helicopter didn't even bother with Spanish this time.

To emphasize the point, a bullet slammed into the dirt three feet from Nate's head.

His mind raced, trying to come up with something else he could do. He'd made it this far; there *had* to be some other way out. But the pounding feet nearing his position forced him to realize all his options had been exhausted.

The job was over.

CHAPTER
FOUR

"*IZQUIERDA*," A VOICE said.

Nate was jerked to the left, the plastic cuffs around his wrists cutting once more into his skin.

They walked in a straight line for twenty-three paces before he was yanked to a stop.

He heard a door open not too far ahead. By the sound of the latch, he knew the door had to be sturdy, probably reinforced metal. If it weren't for the black bag over his head, he would have known for sure. Still, he'd trained hard to hone all his senses, and was confident his guess was right.

Once the whine of the hinges stopped, he was pushed forward across the threshold.

Unlike moments before, their footsteps now echoed loudly. A corridor, he guessed—concrete, or possibly tiled, with unadorned walls.

The hallway was surprisingly long. It wasn't until they reached their seventy-sixth step that the man doing all the talking said, "*Derecha.*"

Again there was the quick tug as their direction changed. This time they only went seventeen steps before Nate was stopped again.

Another metallic door clanged. Once the sound stopped, Nate was shoved hard in the back and sent sprawling forward. With his arms secured behind his back, the only thing he could do was twist as he fell to the floor so that he didn't land face first. Instead, it was his hip that took the brunt of the fall.

Behind him, a door slammed shut, and a key turned in a lock. A moment later, he heard the muffled footsteps of his two escorts receding down the way they'd come.

Slowly, he worked his way back to his feet, wincing for a second as the pain shooting out from his hip joined that of the ache in his back caused by a rifle butt that had whacked into him when he was captured.

Using the toe of his shoe as a guide, he found one of the walls, placed his head against it, and tried to work the bag off. Unfortunately, the cord running through the open end around his neck wouldn't loosen to allow the bag to slip over his chin.

He gave up, and used his foot again to work out the boundaries of the room. Five paces wide and seven deep. Against one wall was a thin mattress on a steel cot secured to the ground. This was the extent of the furnishings. There wasn't even a toilet, just a drain on the floor in the back corner.

He half-lowered, half-dropped onto the bed, wondering where, exactly, he'd been taken. He'd initially assumed the police would hustle him off to a holding facility not far from where he'd been captured—Reynosa, most likely—but the helicopter ride lasted much too long for that. When they finally landed, Nate figured they'd been in the air almost two and a half hours, which was also confusing. That was way more time than necessary to fly him back to where the mess had started in Monterrey.

It doesn't matter, he told himself. *You're in jail. That's all you need to know.*

This was the third time in his life he'd been put in a cell. The first was in college, with campus police breaking up a party that had grown out of hand, and Nate acting the tough guy and taking exception to their tactics. Looking back, their detention cell had been a joke. Even with just half of what he knew these days, he could have easily escaped.

The second time had been in Berlin. That cell had been located in the US embassy, his temporary incarceration understandable since he'd driven up to the gate with several boxes of deadly, virus-tainted mints. But he'd known it was going to happen that time. It had been part of Quinn's plan, and the next day Nate was out again.

This time was nothing like the others. This time he had done the one thing no cleaner should ever do. Get caught.

At the very least, the police would connect him to the badly burned body in the back of the van. That would probably be more than enough to get him put away forever. Thankfully, even if he got as far as being sentenced to life, it was unlikely he'd ever serve any of it. Once he was able to make his phone call, he'd get a hold of Pullman, and wheels would be set in motion that should end in his release. And if Pullman failed, Nate could always call Quinn. He was sure his old mentor would figure something out. Until then, though, he would have to deal with these jackasses and their fists and gun butts and whatever else they wanted to use on him to prove how tough they were.

He lay back on the cot and closed his eyes, thinking he might as well get some rest. Though he couldn't see his watch, he knew it had to be right around one p.m., and his last sleep was the hour-and-a-half nap he'd caught the previous evening before he and Burke headed out to the staging point. A little shut-eye now would not be a bad thing.

He wasn't sure how much time had passed when the same voice that had guided him down the hall earlier barked, "*De pie.*"

Nate shook himself awake, and swung his legs off the cot. Before he could stand on his own, two men grabbed his arms and pulled him up.

"Gee, thanks," Nate said. "I couldn't have done that without your—"

He sensed motion a half second before a fist slammed into his gut. His body wrenched forward, trying to double over, but the men at his sides dug their fingers into this biceps, keeping him upright. They forced him across the room and slammed him back against the wall.

Another punch, this one only a inch away from where the previous had landed. Again the men kept him from moving.

A pair of slow and deliberate footsteps entered the room, stopping an arm's length away. Nate could hear the person breathing—not labored, but distinctive. Breathe in, hold, breathe out, hold.

"So this is him," the man said in English. An American accent. New York, it sounded like.

"*Sí*," someone responded.

"About damn time." The voice moved in so that it was only an inch from Nate's ear. "You gave my Mexican friends quite a workout. You're even better than advertised." Pulling way, the man said, "Take the hood off."

One of the guards undid the bag's knot. Once the opening was loosened, the cover was pulled up, taking a few strands of Nate's hair with it.

Standing in front of Nate was a tall, bald man in a dark suit. Like a lot of men with no hair, it was hard to tell his age. He could have been anywhere from forty-five to sixty. Neither fat nor skinny, he wore a scowl on his face that made it clear he was the one in charge.

Behind him was a hard-looking, middle-aged Mexican man in a uniform. There were two others in the room, younger men in police uniforms.

"Are you going to be a problem?" the bald man asked Nate.

Nate didn't respond.

The bald man looked back at the suited Mexican. "Captain Moreno, I'd like a couple minutes alone with our friend here, if you don't mind."

There was a hint of relief in Moreno's eyes. He looked at the two officers and nodded. "We'll be right outside if you need us," he said, and the three of them left, closing the door behind them.

The bald man stared at Nate, his eyes narrowing. "You're younger than I expected."

Nate kept his mouth shut.

"Or is it just that you have a young face?"

Alarms were starting to clang in Nate's head, as he began to realize this was not what he'd thought it was.

"Well, it doesn't matter," the man said. "I'm just finally glad to make your acquaintance, Mr. Quinn."

No, Nate realized. This was much, much worse.

CHAPTER FIVE

LOS ANGELES, CALIFORNIA

AS SOON AS the tone bonged and the seat belt light went out, Liz Oliver stood up and retrieved her bag from the overhead compartment.

For the first time in her life, she had flown business class. That had been Nate's doing. She had told him it was an unnecessary expense, but after the nearly twelve-hour flight from Paris to Los Angeles, she was glad he'd paid the money. Usually when she arrived back in the States, she'd be totally worthless for a couple days. But here it was, just after one p.m. in California, and she felt fresh and awake and ready to go.

Another perk of business class was that she was one of the first ones off, and able to beat the crowd to passport control. Once her booklet was stamped, and the officer said, "Welcome home," she headed straight for the nothing-to-declare exit, her carry-on the only bag she'd brought.

A ramp led out of Customs to an area where dozens of people were jammed off to the left side, craning their necks every time someone new came out like fans watching movie stars walking down the red carpet at the Academy Awards. Liz knew Nate wouldn't be sandwiched among them, though. He'd told her specifically to continue on through the door to the outside, opposite the ramp, and he'd be right there.

Knowing she was going to see him in a matter of seconds sent a spike of anticipation up her spine as she weaved through the crowd and walked out the door. To say she was excited to see him would have been an understatement. It had been nearly a month and a half since he was able to visit her in Paris, and it had started to seem like forever. She'd had her share of boyfriends before, but it had never been like this. Despite the fact they had met each other under false pretense, she felt an intense connection to Nate, and it was obvious he felt it with her, too.

A few feet beyond the door, she paused. While there were several people around, Nate wasn't one of them. Maybe he was at the sidewalk, or waiting at the curb with his car. She headed over. Nate wasn't there either, and neither was his car.

She checked her watch. One fifteen. Her flight was a bit early, but Nate would have surely been tracking her flight online, and would have left home in plenty of time to meet her. He was thorough that way.

Parking. That had to be it. LAX was a crazy, congested airport. No doubt he was having a hard time finding a space.

She moved out of the flow of foot traffic, and kept her gaze fixed on the crosswalk that led from the parking structure. When five minutes passed without him joining her, she brushed it off as nothing. When fifteen more went by, her brows began to slide together, and a frown appeared on her face.

She pulled out her phone. No missed calls. No texts. She dialed his number but was sent instantly to voice mail. Instead of leaving a message, she decided to check inside the terminal again in case they'd mixed up where they were supposed to meet. There was no sign of him.

She called him again. This time when the beep sounded, she said, "Hey, it's me. Where are you? I'm at the airport. Just waiting. Kinda boring here. So, um, yeah, where are you?"

LIZ GAVE IT another hour, then decided Nate had either forgotten today was the day she was coming, or something had delayed him. She didn't want to put too much thought into that last possibility, as, given the nature of Nate's work, it would inevitably have taken her to scenarios she didn't want to consider.

She called him again, and left another message, the fourth. This time she told him she was going to catch a cab and she'd see him at the house.

Fifty minutes later, a taxi dropped her off in front of the gate to the Hollywood Hills home owned by her brother Jake and lived in by Nate.

Quinn, she corrected herself. *He goes by Quinn, not Jake.* She was still having a problem with that. Her childhood was full of wonderful memories of Jake. Until he left, at which point anger and confusion and resentment set in after he basically disappeared from the face of the earth, only to show up again when she was an adult.

Those abandoned years had been painful, a wound that never seemed able to close completely. Intellectually, she now understood why he'd done what he did, not that she would have made the same choices. But he'd played his hand as best he could, and it was what it was. She got that. She even knew now how much he'd always cared about her, but she was still having a hell of time separating the past from the present.

One thing she couldn't ignore, though, was that if he hadn't come back into her life, she would have never met Nate.

She walked over to the pedestrian door in the wall that surrounded her brother's property, and pressed the intercom buzzer.

No response.

She pressed again, and received the same non-answer.

There was a numbered security pad next to the buzzer. She punched in the code Nate had created for her, waited for the click, and entered.

A driveway took up most of the area in front of the house. There were no cars present, and the door to the garage was shut.

Though the house was two stories high, the level she was standing in front of was the top, while the lower level, the one where the bedrooms and the gym were located, followed the slope of the hill down.

There was no doorbell button next to the entrance. If anyone made it that far, it would be only because someone inside had buzzed them through the front gate. There was, however, another security keypad hidden behind a moveable flap of siding directly below the porch light.

Though Nate had shown it to her and given her a code—different from the one for the gate—she had never used it before. She hunted around for several seconds before she found the right spot, then closed her eyes and tried to remember exactly how he'd said the panel opened.

In, to the left, and up, she thought.

She did as she remembered and was pleased when the lower edge of the flap popped out. Moving it all the way up, she exposed the panel. The new code was one she wasn't likely to forget—the room numbers of the first two hotels they'd stayed in together, starting with the hotel in Paris where everything between them had begun.

Twenty seconds later she was standing inside.

"Nate?" she called out.

The silence was total, and she knew she was alone.

Just to be sure, though, she left her bag in the foyer, checked the top floor, and headed down the stairs to the lower level.

"Nate?" she said again.

The bedrooms and the room that served as the gym were all empty. She entered Nate's room. Everything was neat and in its place.

Too neat.

Liz felt fingers slowly squeezing her heart. She walked over to his en suite bathroom. Counters clean and empty, sink and shower bone dry. She grabbed the shower towel and ran a hand up and down it. No moisture at all.

He's not here. He hasn't been here for at least a day or more.

She could no longer ignore the possibility she'd avoided earlier. She knew, despite his assurances to the contrary, that his job often put him in danger. It still might not be that, but...

Please, let him be all right.

She stared at her reflection in the mirror, worried, unfocused eyes locked on worried, unfocused eyes.

She pulled out her phone.

CHAPTER
SIX

SAN FRANCISCO, CALIFORNIA

JONATHAN QUINN FLIPPED over in the water, pushed off the wall, and started a new lap. So far he'd gone up and back forty-eight times. Five more and he'd reach a mile and a half, his goal for the day.

He kept a steady pace, his smooth strokes cutting a path through the pool that instantly sealed up behind him. He tended to be more of a runner, but in the past couple of months he'd worked swimming into his routine, mainly to help strengthen his shoulder and neck after they'd been injured in an unfortunate meeting of flesh and bullet.

It was Orlando who had suggested he try it when they were still in Thailand, mentioning how it would help improve his mobility.

"Plus, you're not getting any younger," she'd added. "The less stress you put on your body, the longer it'll last."

"Thanks," he said sarcastically. He wasn't even forty yet, but truth be told, he could see the birthday in the not-too-distant future.

"Seriously, you've got to think about these things," she told him. "I do."

"You do? For me or for you?"

She gave him one of her patented blank stares. "Me? No. I'm not as old as you are."

BRETT BATTLES

While they were staying at the temple in Thailand, Quinn had taken a boat up the Chao Phraya River every day to a hotel that allowed him to use its pool. Upon returning to the States three weeks earlier, he'd joined a gym with a lap pool not too far from Orlando's house.

Enrolling there had been a strange step for him. The last time he'd belonged to a public gym was during his time as a rookie cop back in Phoenix. Since then, the only time he shared his workout space with people he didn't know was at the occasional hotel while he was on a project. Going back to the same place nearly every day, seeing the same people on the treadmills and weight machines and in the pool made him feel exposed, like he was creating a habit that could be a problem later.

In his business, habits could be dangerous, but the draw of the water was enough to keep him coming back. That, and the fact he wasn't even sure he was *in* the business anymore.

He reached the end of the length, executed another flip turn, and headed back for the second half of the lap.

Forty-nine, forty-nine, forty-nine, he told himself, so he wouldn't forget which one he was on, then let his mind return to what he'd been thinking about—the business and his place in it. It was the same topic he'd considered the day before, and the day before that, and the weeks before that.

For years he'd been one of the best cleaners in the espionage world, the person in-the-know clients would go to when a body needed to disappear. Quinn was efficient, discreet, and reliable, with a highly developed ability to see details where others would see nothing. Using him on a job was as close as possible to a guarantee that there would be no blowback.

A year ago, he'd occasionally wondered how long he'd be able to keep doing the job, but hadn't given it any serious thought. A lot had happened since then, most notably his mother and sister being targeted because of the man he'd become. He'd been able to keep them from harm, but that didn't mean he hadn't been severely shaken by the events, or ashamed of his own arrogance at thinking he'd built adequate barriers to keep them safe.

The months in Thailand—despite the interruption of having to deal with an old job that had flared back to life, and getting shot in the process—had helped him work through those feelings, and learn how to live with them.

That was all fine and good, and a necessary step, but what they hadn't done was help him decide what was next. Should he leave the business completely? He had more than enough money to retire on and live the rest of his life with Orlando and her son Garrett without worry. Or should he jump back in? Do what he had been good at? What he knew he was still good at? Was he ready to just stop? And if he wasn't, what about his family? Would they ever be in danger again?

He knew it should be easy to walk away, but it wasn't.

It also wasn't easy to stay.

Another flip turn.

Fifty, fifty, fifty.

QUINN SHOWERED, TOWELED off, and headed over to his locker.

As he was dressing, his phone vibrated once. He pulled it out and saw that someone had called while he was in the pool. The surprising part was who.

Liz.

His relationship with his sister was still a work in progress. There were years of damage yet to be undone, all of which were Quinn's fault. Things were improving, but, until now, they had not reached the point where she would call him. It was always the other way around. The times when she did want to reach him, it was either via email, text, or she would call Orlando.

He navigated to his voice mail and pressed the link to her message.

"Call me as soon as you get this. I don't know if I'm just overreacting, or there's a problem, but—" A pause. "Just call me."

There was no missing the panic in her voice.

Quinn hurriedly pulled on the rest of his clothes, and made his way to the exit. As soon as he stepped outside, he called his sister back.

"Jake?" she said, answering before the first ring was complete.

"Is everything all right?"

"I, I don't know. Um, uh…"

"Slow down. Take a breath. Tell me what's going on."

"It's Nate. I think he might be missing."

Quinn paused on the sidewalk. "Why do you think that?"

"I can't find him."

He closed his eyes, and grimaced. Every since it became clear the relationship between Liz and Nate was more than a fling, he'd been worried something like this was going to happen. Nate's work meant there would be times he wouldn't be reachable. It was the nature of the job, and Quinn was sure there was no way Liz could fully understand that, and would at some point feel hurt because of it.

"Liz, it's probably nothing," he said. "Sometimes projects take a bit longer than expected, that's all. I'm sure he'll call you as soon as he can."

"No. You don't understand. He was supposed to *meet* me. He didn't show up."

Quinn cocked his head, surprised. "Meet you? Where?"

"Los Angeles. I flew in a couple hours ago."

"Where are you now?"

"I'm in your house. He's not here, Jake. I don't think he's been here for days."

"And you were *supposed* to meet him?"

"Yes," she said, annoyed. "We've been planning this for weeks. He's the one who flew me out. He was supposed to pick me up at the airport, but he wasn't there. So I came here, and he's not here, either."

Quinn started heading toward Orlando's again, walking quickly at first, then breaking into a run. "You tried calling him?"

"Half a dozen times. Straight to voice mail. What's going on? Where could he be?"

"I don't know. I haven't talked to him in a while. Look, Liz, sit tight, okay? It's probably nothing. Let me see what I can find out, and I'll call you back."

"When?"

"As soon as I know something."

He could hear her breathing rapidly on the other end. "What could have happened? Do you think…do you think…"

"I don't think anything," he said, knowing where her mind must be going. "Just relax, okay? I'll call you soon. I promise."

He thought he heard her say something, but it was low and unintelligible, then she hung up.

Without breaking stride, he called Orlando.

"Hey," she said. "You all—"

"I just talked Liz."

Orlando's light tone disappeared. "What's going on?"

"She was supposed to meet Nate in Los Angeles today."

"Yeah, I know. She emailed me a couple days ago. Said they might come up here next week."

She had failed to share that information with Quinn, but that wasn't surprising. "He didn't show up."

"What?"

"He didn't meet her at the airport and he's not at home, either. She thinks he's missing."

"He's probably just stuck on a job."

"Probably, but…"

They were both silent for a moment before Orlando said, "But he would have at least let her know."

"Yeah. Listen, I'll be there in a few minutes, but can you—"

"Make some calls? Not while I'm talking to you."

The line went dead.

QUINN SPRINTED THE rest of the way back to Orlando's place, and yanked open the front door. Mrs. Vu was standing at the entrance table, sorting the mail. She whirled around, gasping in shock as he entered.

"Sorry," Quinn said. "Where is she?"

The old Vietnamese woman hesitated only a moment before pointing up the stairs. "In office." As Quinn started across the foyer, she pointed at his feet. "Shoes. Shoes."

He ignored her, and ran to the stairs.

"Shoes!" she called after him.

He paused halfway up, just long enough to pull each shoe off, then continued to the second floor. Behind him he could hear Mrs. Vu scoff. She and her husband took care of the house and helped with Garrett. Undoubtedly, she was already heading for the vacuum, and would have the stairs spotless in a matter of minutes.

Orlando's office was located at the front of the house. Quinn skirted around the top of the banister, and raced over to the open door. She was sitting at her desk, her phone to her ear. Looking up, she raised a finger, telling him to hold on.

"Uh-huh...Yeah, I understand...Thanks. I appreciate it." She hung up, and said to Quinn, "Isaac Parker."

Parker was a middleman, a job broker who put together projects for clients who wanted to maintain distance from the actual work.

"And?"

"Nate's not working for him."

"Have you reached anyone else?"

"Two others. Simmons and Van Dorn. Was going to try Tan—" She paused. "What am I thinking? Daeng."

"What about Daeng?" Quinn asked.

"Nate's been using him a lot lately."

"He has? How do you know that?"

"Someone had to keep an eye on things here when you were doing your soul searching."

"You were there with me."

"Yeah," she said, lifting the corner of her laptop. "And there's this little thing called the Internet. Perhaps you're familiar with it."

He tried to keep from glaring at her as he pulled out his cell and selected Daeng's number.

Three rings, then a sleepy, "Hello?"

"Daeng? It's Quinn."

THE COLLECTED

"Kind of early to be calling, don't you think?"

Quinn glanced at his watch. It was four-twenty in the afternoon. "Depends on where you are."

"Everything depends on where you are." Daeng let out a long yawn. "It's all right. I needed to get up anyway."

"Are you back in Bangkok?"

"Yeah."

Quinn did a quick time calculation. It would be six twenty a.m. there. "Nate wouldn't happen to be with you, would he?"

"Nate? No. Why would he be here?"

"Haven't you two been working together?"

"Yeah, but I had to come home to deal with something."

"So you're not helping him on a job right now."

"No, I'm not. What's going on?"

Quinn filled him in. "It's only been a few hours, so it's possible he's just tied up, but it's not like him to let Liz arrive without getting word to her that he wouldn't be there."

Daeng was silent.

"Are you still there?" Quinn asked.

"Yeah. I was just thinking."

When Daeng didn't continue, Quinn said, "Thinking what?"

Daeng hesitated, then said, "Not important."

Quinn let the silence hang for a moment. "When did you leave L.A.?"

"Five days ago."

"Do you know if he was going to be working on a job while you were gone?"

"Yeah. He had something lined up."

"Who hired him?"

"He didn't tell me. The gig came in after I booked my flight, so he knew I wouldn't be helping him."

Which meant Nate's ethics would keep him from sharing the information, a habit Quinn himself had drilled into his former apprentice.

"Any idea who he got to replace you?"

"He was making some calls, but not having any luck at

52

the time. He did say the broker offered to set him up with someone if he couldn't find anyone."

"He said a broker? Not a client direct hire."

"He said broker."

"Okay, that's something. Can you think of anything else?"

Daeng said nothing for several seconds. "No. That's it as far as I can remember."

"Thanks. If you do come up with something, call me," Quinn said. "Doesn't matter what time."

"I will."

Quinn hung up, and looked at Orlando. "Not Daeng. But Nate did have a job set up through a broker. That'll narrow things a bit."

She nodded without looking up from her laptop. After a moment, the printer whirled to life and spit out two sheets of paper. Once it was done, she closed her computer and stood up.

"All right, we'd better hurry," she said.

She handed him one of the printed pieces of paper. As often happened, they were on the same wavelength again.

In his hand was one of two tickets for a flight to Los Angeles.

CHAPTER
SEVEN

BANGKOK, THAILAND

WHAT DAENG HADN'T told Quinn was that the thing he'd come home to deal with turned out to be nothing. The message he'd received from Ton a week earlier had concerned a Burmese refugee kid, one Daeng had personally helped get onto the right path. According to the note, the boy had been arrested by the Bangkok police for drug trafficking, an offense punishable by death.

When Daeng couldn't get ahold of Ton right away to get more details, he had caught a flight home the next day, knowing the arrest had to be some kind of mistake because there was no way the kid would get mixed up in something like that. And he was right. Only it wasn't the police who'd made the mistake, it was Ton. The kid was not in jail and had no idea what Daeng was talking about when Daeng tracked him down.

Relieved but frustrated, Daeng had called Ton to try to figure out where the miscommunication had occurred, but Ton was still not answering his phone. Daeng had then checked around and learned that the man had gone northeast to Issan to visit family. That didn't explain why he wasn't answering his mobile, though. As a member of Daeng's loose organization of misfits, Ton was expected to have his phone on him at all times. Not about to travel out to the countryside himself, Daeng wasn't going to do much about it until Ton called him back.

Over the following few days, Daeng had become so preoccupied with checking in on his network of people and businesses, and making sure everything was still running smoothly, that he'd shoved all thoughts about Ton to the far reaches of his mind. He knew they'd get things cleared up soon enough.

Maybe that had been a mistake.

He headed into the bathroom with his mobile phone, turned on the speaker function, and tried Ton once more. As the line began to ring, he applied shaving cream to his face. Receiving no response, he punched DISCONNECT, finished his shave, and jumped in the shower.

In less than five minutes, he was dressed and making another call as he walked through the house.

This time the line was answered with a grunt.

"Yai, wake up," Daeng said.

Another grunt.

"Come on. I need you."

"Who is this?" Yai asked, his voice a slur.

"Who do you think it is?"

There was a rustle on the other end. "Daeng? Sorry. It's kind of early, you know?"

"Yeah, and I'm already up and dressed."

"Oh…um…what's going on?"

"When was the last time you talked to Ton?"

"Ton?" Yai seemed confused for a moment. "Little Ton? Or Big Ton?"

"Little."

"Uh, I don't know." Yai paused for a moment. "Well, he did tell me he was going away."

"When was this?

"If you hold on, I can check the time on his text."

"Wait, he told you by text? Not on the phone or in person?"

"Yeah."

"When was the last time you actually talked to him?"

Another few seconds of silence. "Maybe a week ago. It was a Friday, I think."

"Did he say anything about visiting his family then?"

"No. Not that I remember. Why?"

"Have you tried calling him since?"

Daeng could almost hear Yai shake his head. "I didn't have any reason to."

"What about a number for his family in Issan? Do you have one?"

"He should have his mobile. Just call that."

"I *have* called his mobile. He's not answering. But I need to talk to him now."

"Okay, okay. Um, let me think." Yai fell silent for several seconds. "Dom might know. She's been hanging out with him on and off for a while now."

"Get ahold of her. Tell her to call me."

"Sure, of course." A pause. "You want me to do that *now*?"

"Yes," Daeng said. "Now."

While he waited for the girl to call him, he cut up a mango, and started to eat it. Two slices in, his phone rang, only it wasn't Dom. It was Yai again.

"She's not answering," Yai said.

"You tried more than once?"

"Yeah. Three times. Maybe she sleeps deeper than I do."

Maybe, Daeng thought. *Then again...*

"You know where Ton lives, right?" he asked.

"Sure," Yai said.

"Meet me there in twenty minutes."

"It's going to take me a little more than—"

Daeng hung up.

TON LIVED IN the rooftop apartment of a building near Silom. Yai was waiting out front when Daeng's taxi pulled to the curb.

"You go up yet?" Daeng asked.

Yai shook his head. "Just got here."

"Come on, then."

They went inside and took the scuffed-up elevator to the seventh floor. From there, they had to climb the stairs one more flight to Ton's place—a four-room structure built right in the middle of the roof. It had a wide wooden patio at the front, and a jumbled storage area behind.

A plank pathway led from the stairwell door along the edge of the roof to the home's side entrance. Daeng knocked when they reached it, but, as he expected, no one answered.

He tried the knob and was surprised to find the door was unlocked. He glanced back at Yai, who also looked confused.

"You armed?" Daeng whispered.

Yai reached around to the small of his back, and pulled a gun out from under his shirt.

Daeng's intention had been merely to find a way inside, where he was sure they'd find some way of contacting Ton's family in Issan, but as he opened the door, he instantly knew a call to the countryside would be unnecessary.

The smell of death rushed through the opening as if it had been waiting for someone to let it loose.

"Shit!" Yai said, blinking his eyes and twisting his head away.

Daeng looked around, and spotted several old rags by the back corner of the house. They were dirty, but better than nothing. He retrieved them, gave a couple to Yai, bundled together the two he'd kept, and pressed them tightly over his nose and mouth.

Yai looked surprised. "We're going in?"

Daeng answered by doing just that.

They found Ton and Dom in the living room, sitting side by side on the couch, their throats slit. A swarm of flies hovered around their bloated corpses like auras. Their eyeballs and tongues seemed to be trying to jump out of their head.

Yai groaned twice before rushing out of the room.

Daeng could hear him just outside the front door losing whatever was left in his stomach from the previous night. Daeng didn't have the same problem. Even before he'd started working with Nate removing all sorts of bodies, he'd seen more than his share of the dead. Instead of running out, he moved closer, looking for any clues as to who had done this and why.

But whoever slashed Ton's and Dom's necks had left no calling card.

"THIS IS VERY disturbing," Christina said.

Daeng remained silent, letting the woman process what he had told her.

They were in a storage room at the back of a restaurant Christina owned near Khao San Road, just one of dozens of businesses the American woman had around the city. She'd been in the Thai capital for decades and was known in certain, very exclusive circles as someone who got things done. She and Daeng had used each other's services many times over the years, and she had always exhibited a level of protectiveness over him, not quite as if he were the son she never had, but close.

"And you're sure about how long they've been there like that?" she asked.

"As sure as I can be," he told her. Given the condition of the bodies, Daeng was certain Ton and Dom had been dead for at least a week, which would have been right around the same time Ton had sent Daeng the message to return to Bangkok. Perhaps even *before*.

She stared at an empty shelf, the hint of concern on her face. Without turning back to him, she said, "Someone *was* asking about you."

"What? Who?"

"I didn't talk to them directly. They spoke to one of my people, who then put them in contact with your organization."

"With Ton?" he asked, already knowing the answer.

She hesitated, then nodded.

"When?"

"Thursday last week."

A day prior to the message Ton had sent Daeng.

"Who was it?"

"Like I said, I didn't speak to them, so I don't have a

name."

"But you can call whoever it was they talked to and find out."

"Do you really think a name will get you anywhere? If this person is responsible for the deaths, the name was undoubtedly fake."

"It's a place to start."

Five minutes later he had a name—Thatcher—and, in an unexpected bonus, a cell phone picture taken by Christina's man as Thatcher left. Thatcher was in profile and far enough from the camera that his facial features were slightly blurred.

But he did have one distinctive feature: a bald head.

CHAPTER
EIGHT

A SOUND, A smell, then nothing as Nate passed out again. Over and over, the sequence repeated.

A constant droning, like an air conditioner in the background.

Black.

The overpowering smell of sweat.

Black.

A door slamming.

Black.

A vibration.

Black.

Voices, talking to him but making no sense.

Black.

Then the prick of a needle in his arm.

And black, deeper than before. Oh, so deep...

CHAPTER
NINE

LOS ANGELES

BETWEEN THEM, QUINN and Orlando had seven messages on their phones when they deplaned in L.A.

Each was from a freelancer who had worked with Quinn and Nate in the past. All had received calls from Nate within the past week, checking on their availability, but to a man they had been previously booked and therefore unavailable. The most disturbing part was the bookings. While two of the men had actually gone out on jobs, the other five had been put on paid holds for projects that ended up not panning out, so they had basically earned their fee for doing nothing.

"I don't like this," Quinn said as they waited for the shuttle that would take them to the rental car lot. "We need to know who hired them."

By the time they had their car and were driving away from LAX, they'd finished calling everyone back. Though the contact name changed from job offer to job offer, the descriptions of the projects the men had been put on hold for were remarkably similar. Calls to the two men who'd actually gone out on assignments confirmed another suspicion. They, too, had been contacted about being put on hold, but had turned the offers down because of their prior commitments.

It was clear someone had purposely tied up the people Nate would have normally hired.

Quinn took La Cienega north toward the hills. Just after they passed Wilshire Boulevard, his phone rang.

He checked the display before putting the call on speakerphone. "Daeng?"

"Have you heard from him?" Daeng asked.

"Nothing yet."

There was a pause before Daeng spoke again. "Something's happened here. I'm not sure if it's connected, but it might be."

"In Bangkok?"

"I believe I was tricked into returning home." Daeng explained about the message he'd received that turned out to be untrue, about the man who had sent him the false information being murdered, and about the guy calling himself Thatcher who had been looking for Daeng just before all this had happened.

Quinn's concern had already increased after learning about the other freelancers. Now, it skyrocketed. "Any idea who this guy was or what he wanted?"

"No. Haven't been able to find out anything else about him. I'd be willing to bet he's not even in the country anymore. A friend did get a picture of him, though. It's not very good, but it's better than nothing."

"Send it to me."

"Hold on." Daeng was quiet for several seconds. "On its way."

Before Quinn could even reply, his phone beeped with the incoming message. "If anything else comes up, let me know right away."

"Screw that. I'm flying back," Daeng said. "On my way to the airport right now. My ticket's for L.A., but if you think I should go somewhere else, tell me."

Quinn was pleased to hear it. Though he hoped Daeng's help would turn out to be unnecessary, it would be nice if he were close, just in case. "L.A.'s fine for now. Call when you land."

"Will do."

As soon as the line went dead, Orlando took the phone

from him and accessed the photo Daeng had sent.

"I don't recognize him," she said.

"Show me."

She held the screen out so Quinn could take a quick glance.

As Daeng mentioned, the profile shot of the bald man in question wasn't the best. Quinn took a second look, and finally shook his head. "Me, either."

"I'm going to send this around, see if any of our regulars know who he is."

Quinn nodded but said nothing, his dread growing by the second.

IT WAS STRANGE pulling up to the gate of his house after more than eight months since the last time Quinn had set foot inside. In some ways, it felt like the place didn't even belong to him anymore.

Orlando jumped out and punched the code into the keypad, triggering the gate to roll open. Before Quinn could even pull the car to a stop in front of the house, Liz hurried out the door.

She looked drawn and pale, her eyes bloodshot.

The moment he climbed out of the car, she rushed over and threw her arms around him, her head pressing against his shoulder. Momentarily caught off guard, he hesitated then returned her embrace, telling himself she was only looking for comfort, not trying to show him any affection.

"Have you heard from him?" she whispered anxiously.

"No," he told her. "But we've been checking with a lot of people. I'm sure we'll find out where he is soon."

"He was supposed to meet me at the airport. He was supposed to be there waiting."

"I know, and I'm sure that's exactly what he had planned to do."

"Then where is he?" She looked up at him. "Why isn't he here?"

He knew those weren't really the questions occupying her thoughts. They were only masking the what-ifs.

What if he's in trouble?

What if he's hurt?

What if he's dead and never coming back?

"Let's go inside," Orlando said, putting an arm around Liz's shoulder.

Liz let herself be pulled away from her brother, and they all entered the house. Orlando guided her to the couch, and the two of them sat down.

Quinn glanced around the room. Everything looked pretty much the same as when he'd last been home. There were a few different books in the bookcase, and a dark gray hoodie draped over one of the chairs, but that was about it.

Liz had left the blinds drawn across the back wall. He walked over and pulled them open, letting the late afternoon sunlight flood in through the floor-to-ceiling windows that overlooked the city.

As he walked back, he said, "Liz, we're going to have to ask you a few questions. Are you up for it?"

"Of course," she said quickly. "Whatever you need."

He smiled, hoping to relax her a bit. "When you first came into the house, did you find anything unusual?"

She thought for a moment, then shook her head. "No. Nothing."

"Have you moved anything?"

"Some soap in the bathroom." A pause. "A glass in the kitchen. That's it. Oh, and I lay on Nate's bed for a little bit. But I didn't put anything away, if that's what you're asking."

"The gym?"

"I only looked in. I didn't touch anything."

Quinn looked around. "Where are your bags?"

"Just one bag, a carry-on. It's down in Nate's room. I can go get it if you want." She started to stand.

"It's all right," Orlando said, putting her hands gently on Liz's shoulders and easing her back down. "It's not important."

Quinn knelt in front of his sister. "You're doing good. This is helping. Now I need you to do me a favor."

"Of course. Anything."

"Orlando and I are going to check around the house, see if Nate left something that'll help us contact him. I'd like you to stay right here. All right?"

"I...I can help," she said.

"I know you can. But it'll go faster if only Orlando and I do it. We know what we're looking for."

She stared at him, her eyes pleading for something to do.

"He's right," Orlando said calmly. "The most important thing right now is to let us do what we do best."

Liz took in a deep breath. As she let it out, she nodded. "Okay. You're right. I just..." She pressed her lips together for a moment, then said, "I'll wait here."

"Thank you," Orlando said.

"If you need me, though, let me know."

Quinn gave her arm a gentle squeeze, and rose to his feet. "We will." As they walked out of the living room, he whispered to Orlando, "Downstairs first."

Though Nate had basically taken over Quinn's house, he had not claimed the master bedroom. It was still occupied by Quinn's furniture and belongings.

Nate's room was the largest of the guest bedrooms. The only addition to the furniture that had already been there—the bed, dresser, and two nightstands—was a small wooden table in the corner Nate must have been using as a desk. On top of the table were a laptop power cord, a pad of paper, and a pen.

Quinn ran his fingers over the pad, checking for indentations made by the pen. Nothing, just as he had expected. Nate had been trained better than to do something that stupid.

"Where does he keep his computer?" Orlando asked.

Quinn shook his head. "Don't know."

"What about when you were living here?"

"I never asked him. That was his business. Maybe he put it—"

"Please tell me he wouldn't have taken it with him."

"Absolutely not. He would have taken a field computer." Leaving your main computer at home base, and taking ones you could afford to lose when you traveled was standard procedure. Something both Quinn and Orlando did without a second thought.

"What about data backup?" she asked. "Was he using your system?"

"He was before, so I assume he still is. You want to try to see if you can access his backup while I search for the computer?"

She was already headed for the door before he even finished speaking. "If you find it, bring it up."

"Really? I thought maybe I'd just sit down here and play Solitaire on it for a while first."

She paused in the doorway. "Solitaire? You couldn't have said something like Halo? Or *Call of Duty*? Or even, I don't know, Tetris?"

"Weren't you on your way to do something?"

She grunted a "huh" and disappeared into the hallway.

The first thing Quinn did was run his fingers underneath the desk to make sure there wasn't a hidden compartment. He then methodically searched the rest of the room for potential laptop hiding spots. He removed drawers from the dresser, checked the mattress and box springs, and even looked for any structural changes his former apprentice might have made to the room, but he came up dry.

Next, he entered the small walk-in closet. Inside were shirts and jackets and sweaters and several boxes filled with the stuff Nate had moved in from his old apartment. Quinn looked through each box, patted down the clothing, and felt along the shelf that ran around the top. Still no computer.

Though he was frustrated, he was also pleased that Nate hadn't just left it someplace easy to find.

Okay, then. Where?

He scanned every corner of the closet, and did the same in the bedroom.

Not in here, apparently.

He thought for a moment. If it were him, he would have simply used one of the three secured safety boxes he'd built seamlessly into the walls. One was in his bedroom, one in the gym, and one upstairs just off the living room. Even if someone were able to figure out where they were located, and dislodge the small wall portions covering them, there was still each safe's door. If the correct code was not input on the touch screen the very first time, the contents would be flash fried, rendering anything inside—especially a computer—worthless.

Quinn had only shown Nate the hiding place upstairs, and had never given him his code. He probably should have done that. Nate was the one living here now, after all. It would have made sense for him to stick his computer in a space that was designed to protect it.

Quinn walked into the hallway, and looked first one way, then the other.

I'm Nate. So I'd put my computer...

He looked left again, back toward his room and the stairs.

I'd put it...

He swiveled his head to the right, toward the gym.

I'd put...it's not possible, right? I mean, he couldn't have.

Quinn stared at the gym, walked down the hall, and went inside. The safety box in this room was along the baseboard, behind the stationary bike. He pushed in and up on the molding in exactly the right spot, and the board popped away from the wall. Underneath was the safe door with the touch screen embedded in the middle. A tap of his finger brought the screen to life. He input the first number of his code, and immediately stopped. The number had turned green. This was the fail-safe. Since it would only allow a single input before destroying everything inside, the numbers would appear in a specific color. Red meant everything was fine, but if they were green, you were inputting the wrong code.

Son of a bitch, he thought. Nate had actually found the box *and* changed the code somehow.

After fifteen seconds of no additional numbers being input, the screen reset. This time Quinn tapped in the emergency master code, a string of digits that would open the box one time only. When the door swung open, he reached inside. There were half a dozen passports from different countries, all with pictures of Nate; several small bundles of cash, also from different locations; and a GLOCK 9mm pistol. But no computer.

Quinn went into his bedroom, and quickly discovered that Nate had taken over that safe, too. This one held some documents, and another pistol, but still no computer.

Returning upstairs, he jogged past the living room, and stopped where it transitioned into the kitchen. Orlando was at the breakfast table, her own field laptop open.

"Did you find it?" she asked.

Quinn lowered himself to his knees. "Still looking."

"Find what?" Liz said from the couch.

"Nate's computer," Quinn said, then realized that was one question he hadn't asked. "You haven't seen it, have you?"

She shook her head. "No."

Quinn opened the baseboard, and input the master code.

Bingo.

He pulled Nate's computer out of the safe. "Got it."

Orlando looked up, surprised. "Don't just sit there. Bring it here."

As he carried it over, he made a mental note to discuss with Nate how he had managed to find the other two hidey-holes and gain access to all three without rendering them useless. His protégé was getting good, maybe too good.

Orlando set to work on Nate's laptop. It took her nearly fifteen minutes to get through the security, which, by the frown on her face, was obviously longer than she'd thought it would have taken.

Quinn watched from behind as she looked through a list of recent files, then opened his email.

After several minutes, she said, "There."

Quinn scanned the message on the screen. A job confirmation for a cleaner named Quinn. He knew Nate had been using his name, but it still felt...odd.

"It says the project should have finished yesterday morning."

"No location," Orlando pointed out. "But it couldn't have been too far away if Nate was going to be back in time to meet Liz today. If I know him, I'm sure he planned on returning last night so he wouldn't chance being late picking her up."

Quinn nodded, knowing she was right.

The message was signed P, and the sender's email address was just a string of letters and numbers.

"P," Quinn said to himself. "Are their any other emails?"

Orlando sorted the messages by sender. There were three more. Two were also signed P, but one, the very first message Nate had received, had a name.

Pullman.

"That doesn't sound familiar," Quinn said.

"I think I've heard it before," Orlando told him.

"You have?"

"Give me a second."

She switched back to her own computer, her fingers flying over her keyboard. After about forty-five seconds, she said, "Yeah. This has got to be him." She typed for a few more seconds, then smiled smugly. "And I'm right. Again. That email address traces right back to his location." Another keystroke and a picture appeared on the screen.

Quinn leaned forward to get a better look. The image was of a man around forty with receding brown hair and pale skin.

"Who is he?" Quinn asked.

"Mr. Timothy Pullman is a broker who works out of Chicago."

"Is that so?"

"Yeah. Mid-level jobs usually, with the occasional stretch to something a little more ambitious."

"You have a number?"

She smiled. "I do."

THEY DECIDED ORLANDO would make the call. Quinn was conferenced in on his phone, his mic on mute.

"Mr. Pullman?" Orlando said.

"Who's calling?"

"My name's Newsome. I was given your number by a mutual acquaintance. That is, if you *are* Mr. Pullman."

"And which acquaintance would that be?"

She let a few seconds of dead air fill the line. "Are you or are you not Mr. Pullman? I'd rather not waste my time."

This time Pullman paused. "Fine. I'm Pullman. So who's this person who's giving out my number? And what do you want?"

"Good. So I'm talking to the right person. I was given your number by a cleaner named Quinn. He's actually why I'm calling. I hired him for a job that he was supposed to show up for two hours ago. He's not here, and I haven't heard from him, so I'm calling— "

"I don't know anyone named Quinn."

Orlando and Quinn exchanged a glance.

"This was the number he gave me as a backup in case I needed to get ahold of him."

"Sorry. Don't know why he would have done that. I can't help you."

"Maybe he's using a different name. Have you hired a cleaner recently?"

"Lady, I don't talk business with people I don't know. But I'll tell you this much. I haven't run an op in over two weeks. Now, if you don't mind, I've got to go."

He hung up.

Orlando immediately jumped on her computer, and a few minutes later, she and Quinn were booked on a flight to Chicago.

CHAPTER
TEN

NATE'S HEAD BOUNCED against the wall, jolting him awake.

His eyes flew open, but once more, the only thing he could see was the black cloth bag over his head. He braced himself, thinking someone was going to shove him into the wall again, but instead, he realized he was rocking back and forth, the room he was in moving.

What the...

He tried to concentrate to figure out what was going on, but his thoughts would only hold for a moment before wandering off again.

As the swaying slowed, he could feel his consciousness beginning to slip away. He fought to hold on. He knew it was important. He knew he had to—

The black nothing engulfed him again, but not before he registered one last detail—the sound of a large engine winding down.

CHAPTER
ELEVEN

CHICAGO, ILLINOIS

THE PLANE LANDED at Chicago's O'Hare International Airport at five fifteen a.m. Within thirty minutes, Quinn and Orlando were heading into the city in the car they'd arranged for ahead of time from a local contact. Waiting for them in the backseat was a bag of items they couldn't bring with them on the plane—two SIG SAUER P226 pistols, extra preloaded magazines, lock picks, duct tape, and a syringe filled with liquid sleep.

Using the GPS on her phone, Orlando directed Quinn to a quiet industrial street on the southeast side of the city.

"That's it," she said, pointing at a two-story brick building a quarter of the way down the block.

Quinn drove past, made a U-turn, and parked at the curb.

The building in question was dark. From the research Orlando had done while they waited for their flight, they knew the lower half was used by a company that made novelty buttons and bumper stickers. It was the top floor, though, that Quinn and Orlando were interested in.

That was where Pullman lived.

His place had large loft windows across the front that were covered by heavy, dark curtains. Too bad, Quinn thought. It would have been nice to get a look inside.

He examined the rest of the block, then pointed at a

building two down from Pullman's. "That's one."

Orlando grabbed the bag from the back, and they exited the car. There was a narrow alcove entrance at the left edge of the building Quinn had singled out. From inside their bag of tricks, he removed the set of picks, and had the lock opened in seconds.

As he'd hoped, on the other side of the door was a staircase leading to the second floor. There was also a standard alarm keypad mounted to the inside wall. On it, a red light blinked rapidly. Orlando disabled the system by using a set of custom-rigged wires that linked the keypad to her phone, where an app she had written herself to override dozens of different types of security systems did the rest of the work.

Free to move around, they headed up the stairs, located the access to the roof, and were soon standing outside again. From there, it was simply a matter of jumping a three-foot gap onto the next roof, then stepping over an even smaller opening onto the roof of Pullman's place.

There they paused while Orlando extracted from the bag the two SIGs and matching sound suppressors. She handed one set and a spare mag to Quinn, and prepped the second pistol for herself.

Once his suppressor was in place, Quinn removed from the kit the small metal cylinder that contained the syringe, and slipped it into his pocket.

"Ready?" he asked.

She gave her suppressor a final twist. "When am I not?"

TIMOTHY PULLMAN WAS freaking out. He had never received a call from another broker like the one he'd had late the previous evening.

Sure, it could have been legit, but he didn't believe that for a second. Would Quinn really have left Pullman's number as a contact? Did anyone ever do that? He'd never heard of it before.

In the hours after the call, he'd moved through his apartment, sitting down on the couch or the bed or a kitchen chair, but never for more than a few seconds before his nerves made him stand back up and walk around again.

Fucking money, he thought. *You're an idiot, idiot, idiot!* He should have never taken this job. He should have thought about it more when it was offered to him, but he hadn't been able to see through the piles of cash, and the dangled possibility it would lead to more.

Lead to more. What a joke.

While his client had dutifully come through with the payment, the man had also conveniently fallen off the map. The timing of which, *incidentally*, coincided with the job going to shit.

The hit hadn't been the problem. The target was dead. There was no question of that.

But the cleanup?

Something had gone seriously askew, and Quinn—who Pullman had been hearing for years was the cream of the crop—had disappeared without a trace. That might not have been so bad if police hadn't discovered the body in an abandoned van just outside Monterrey. And *that* might not have been so bad if the body had been unidentifiable. Unfortunately, with the exception of a well-placed bullet hole and a few burn marks from a fire that had been quickly extinguished, the dead man was apparently in perfect condition. The police had no problem identifying him as a powerful Mexican senator, and former United Nations official.

If word got around about how disastrously things had gone, Pullman would have a hell of a time drumming up any new business. But it wasn't business, or even the potential lack thereof, that had kept him awake all night.

It was the phone call.

"I was given your number by a cleaner named Quinn," the woman had said.

Whoever she was, she wasn't some broker waiting for Quinn to show up. Pullman was sure about that now. So who, then? Probably more importantly, who did she represent?

His biggest fear was that the senator had ties to the

northern Mexican drug cartels. It hadn't been mentioned in any of the news reports, but he knew all those political types, especially in that part of the world, had to have their hands in someone's pocket. What if the senator's cartel friends had already discovered that Pullman had been involved in the assassination?

Perhaps *they* had captured Quinn, and tortured Pullman's name and number out of him. That stopped him pacing for a moment.

Jesus. If that were true, he was toast.

Those bastards weren't just dangerous, they were unrelentingly vicious, and wouldn't be content to just kill Pullman.

Not long after midnight, he'd retrieved his Colt .45 pistol from the safe in his room. Being on the administrative end of projects, and never having to go out into the field himself, he'd only used the gun a few times at a firing range, with less than spectacular results. But he felt better having it in his hand as he continued carving a path across his floor.

He next wondered if there was a way they could figure out where he lived.

He'd always been careful never to let *anyone* know where his place was. Even his family had no clue. And when he craved companionship, he paid for a few hours of Jessica's time in a cheap motel room across town.

The phone call. Could they pinpoint his location through that?

He didn't think so. He'd paid good money for some equipment that was supposed to prevent anyone from doing that. Granted, it wasn't quite top of the line, but the guy who sold it to him promised it was more than adequate.

More pacing, more questions.

Run?

Don't run?

Threat?

Not a threat?

At 5:57 a.m., he still had no answers.

At 5:57 and five seconds, the floorboard behind him

creaked.

PULLMAN STOOD NEAR his couch, staring at the wall, a cannon of a gun dangling from his hand. Quinn and Orlando, having already checked the rest of the apartment and confirming there was no one else present, watched him from the shadows across the room.

Finally, Quinn gave Orlando a nod, and he moved forward, making it to within ten feet of the man before the floorboard groaned.

Pullman started to turn, his gun rising. Quinn took two quick steps forward and grabbed the gun. A *boom* filled the apartment as Pullman pulled the trigger, the bullet flying over Quinn's shoulder and into the ceiling.

Quinn wrenched the gun out of the man's grasp, tossed it behind him, and slammed the butt of his SIG into the side of Pullman's head.

Pullman wheeled backward, a shout of surprise and pain escaping his lips. Quinn followed right after him, this time whacking an open hand against the man's ear.

Pullman jerked in response, his hand flying up to protect himself as he cried out again.

Quinn grabbed him by the shoulders and shoved him at a stuffed chair next to the couch. When Pullman's legs hit the seat, he crumbled backward.

"Please, please," the broker said, his hands raised protectively in front of his face. "This is all a mistake."

"You're damn right it is," Quinn said. "I am *not* a fan of being shot at."

"I'm sorry. I'm sorry. I didn't mean to…Look, I didn't realize who he was. Okay?"

Quinn cocked his head, his eyes narrowing. "Didn't realize who *who* was?"

"The senator. Um, uh, Lopez. Right? That's his name, I think…Yeah, yeah. Senator Lopez. I swear. I didn't know."

Senator Lopez? Who the hell was this guy talking about?

He glanced at Orlando. She shrugged, as confused as he was.

76

As he turned back, Pullman started to push himself out of the chair.

"No one said you could get up." Quinn knocked the broker back down. "Tape," he said to Orlando, his eyes never leaving Pullman.

There was a loud rip, and a second later Orlando came around his side, a loose end of duct tape in one hand and the roll in the other.

Pullman pushed back in the chair. "Wait! Wait! I told you I didn't know."

"Arms at your side," Quinn ordered.

"Please!"

Quinn pointed his SIG at the man's shoulder. "Take them down or I will."

Pullman dropped his arms.

"Take off your shirt."

"What?"

"Take it off."

"Okay, okay," the man said. He pulled off his shirt, revealing an abnormally hairy chest.

"Drop it on the floor."

As soon as the man did, Quinn grabbed him by the nape of the neck and pulled him forward several inches so Orlando would have room to work. Orlando stuck the end of the tape to the broker's chest, then wrapped it around the man's body several times, pinning Pullman's arms tightly to his side. Once that was done, Quinn pushed the man back, and Orlando wound more tape around the chair, creating a web that would keep Pullman where he was. She then ripped off a small piece and stuck it over the man's mouth.

Pullman yelled in protest, his voice leaking from the bottom of the strip.

"See, that just pisses *me* off," Orlando said.

She tore off two more pieces. The first she put over the lower half of the man's mouth. The other, longer strip she wrapped under Pullman's jaw and up the side of his face so that it held down the ends of the other two.

"Yell again," she said.

Pullman stared back, silent.

"You heard her," Quinn told him.

Pullman gave a halfhearted yell. This time his voice was sufficiently muffled.

"Better," Orlando said.

Quinn leaned forward a few inches. "You brought this on yourself. If you hadn't tried to shoot me, we might have had a nice, pleasant conversation. But you just couldn't help pulling the trigger, could you?"

Pullman mumbled something.

"I'm going to let that pass, but from now on this is how it's going to work. Your mouth stays shut unless I give you permission to speak. Understood?"

Pullman nodded.

"I'm going to ask you a few yes-or-no questions. A nod for yes, a shake for no. Easy, right?"

Another nod.

"Excellent. All right, something simple first. You are Timothy Pullman, correct?"

Pullman stared at him for a moment, his eyes widening ever so slightly.

"Before you answer," Quinn said, "some of these questions we already know the answer to, so we'll know right away if you lie to us, and that won't make us very happy." He raised his gun a few inches to ensure the message wasn't too subtle for the man.

Pullman looked away.

"So, Pullman, right?"

A nod.

"Good. Then we're in the right place. It would have been pretty embarrassing if you were the wrong asshole, don't you think?"

The broker looked like he wasn't sure if he should nod or shake or what.

Quinn raised his hand, his palm out. "Rhetorical." He smiled. "Yes or no. You put together an op that supposedly finished two days ago."

A nod.

"Did this Senator Lopez have something to do with the job?"

Yes.

"The victim?" Quinn guessed.

Pullman hesitated.

"Remember. Only the truth."

Pullman's head moved up and down.

"So you think we're here about him? Maybe we're not too happy that he's dead?"

Pullman nodded.

"And that's where you're wrong," Quinn said. "Partially, anyway. We *are* here about the project, but we couldn't care less about Senator Lopez."

Pullman looked confused.

"You've been straight with us so far. I can see it in your eyes, so don't screw it up now."

The man immediately shook his head.

"Good. The person we're interested in is one of the people you hired. The cleaner. Quinn, right?"

A quick, decisive nod.

"See, here again is an example of something that could have made things a lot easier. When my associate called you last night, you could have told us the truth then. If you had, we wouldn't have had to come all the way out here to see you." Quinn paused. "Please tell me you regret not being a little nicer."

Pullman nodded with enthusiasm.

Quinn clicked his tongue against the roof of his mouth several times, then said, "All right. I'm going to take the tape off your mouth now, but your lips stay sealed unless you're answering a question from either me or my friend. Got it?"

Yes.

Quinn smiled, and ripped off the long piece that went under Pullman's jaw. The broker's eyes widened as he let out a grunt.

"Sorry about that," Quinn said. He removed the two pieces from over the man's mouth. "There. Better?"

Pullman started to speak, then thought better of it, and

nodded.

"Another easy one. The Lopez job, is it over? Or did it get extended?"

"Over," Pullman croaked.

"When?"

"Like you said—almost two days."

"So, on schedule."

A nod, tentative.

"Then where is Quinn?"

"I don't know. The job went...bad."

"Explain bad to me."

"The police found the body before it could be disposed of."

Quinn hid his surprise. "They caught your cleaner?"

Pullman hesitated.

"Answer the question."

"I don't *know* the answer. I'm not sure if they arrested him or not. I tried to find out, but it's like he disappeared."

"What are you talking about?"

"There was some kind of manhunt in the news after they found the body, but I'm not sure if they caught anyone."

A manhunt? That did not sound good. Quinn didn't want to ask the next question but he knew he had to. "What about other bodies? Any found around the same time but not officially connected together?"

"No. Nothing reported."

Despite the fact it didn't mean much, Quinn was relieved by the answer. "All right. Let's start at the beginning. Who was your client?"

"The man I talked to went by the name of Mr. Brown."

"Did this Mr. Brown belong to a particular organization?"

"He never said. But he used the right passwords to prove he was legit. And the payments appeared on schedule."

"How was contact handled?"

"Over the phone."

"You never met him in person?"

"No."

Playing something he knew was more than just a hunch, Quinn retrieved his phone and accessed the photo Daeng had sent him. He showed it to Pullman. "Do you recognize this man?"

At first Pullman shook his head, then he stopped and squinted. "I'm not sure. He looks kind of familiar."

"Familiar how? You've met with him? You've talked to him?"

"I don't know," Pullman said defensively. "It ain't a great picture. Could be hundreds of people who look like that."

True enough, but the fact that Pullman hesitated in saying no outright made Quinn more convinced that what happened to Daeng was connected. He put the phone away.

"Your client. I assume you have a number for him."

"Yes, but…" He paused. "It's disconnected now."

"You've called it?"

"A few dozen times since yesterday."

"Give me the number."

Pullman's gaze flicked past Quinn, across the room. "It's in my phone over by my computer."

"I'll get it," Orlando said.

While she did that, Quinn said, "Where did the job take place?"

"Monterrey, Mexico."

"This Senator Lopez—is he really a senator, or is that just a nickname?"

"Really a senator."

"In Mexico?"

"Yes."

"Tell me about the job and what happened."

In fits and starts, Pullman began telling what he knew.

"Wait," Quinn said before he got too far. "Quinn's assistant. What was his name?"

"Uh, Burke."

Quinn had never heard of the guy. "Do you know how he got the job?"

"I…recommended him."

81

"*You?*"

"Well, actually, the client did. I just passed the name along."

That was also disturbing. "All right. Let's go back to the job."

Pullman told them the rest, finishing up with learning that the Mexican authorities had discovered the body, and that he could no longer reach his client.

"What's your password?" Orlando asked.

"My what?"

"Password. For your computer."

"Why?"

Quinn raised the gun.

"Uh, uh, it's Jessica36b."

"God, that better not mean—" Orlando stopped herself with a disgusted groan. "Never mind."

Quinn could hear her disconnecting the man's laptop and shoving it into her bag.

"What are you doing?" Pullman said. "That's mine. I need that."

"It *was* yours," she said.

"But my work. Everything's on there!"

"I'm sure you have a backup somewhere," Quinn said. He stood up. "A little advice. You might want to lie low for a while."

"Hold on. Are you going to leave me like this?"

"Thanks for reminding me."

Instead of unwrapping the tape, Quinn pulled out the cylindrical container, unscrewed one end, and slipped the syringe into his hand.

"Whoa, whoa, whoa!" Pullman protested.

Quinn stuck the needle into the broker's arm.

"Hey! What the hell?"

"You're going to have a nice headache when you wake up," Quinn said. "You'll want to take some aspirin and drink plenty of water. But the good news is, you won't have to worry about that for another twenty-four hours, at least."

"What did you...give...me?" The man's voice was

already losing strength.

"Sweet dreams, Mr. Pullman."

CHAPTER
TWELVE

NATE'S EYES SHOT open as he gasped for air.

Before he could even register that he was soaking wet, another wave of water slammed into him.

He gasped again.

Close by, someone laughed.

He twisted his head toward the noise, and saw a big man with scraggly blond hair and a goatee, a foot long and braided. He grinned at Quinn, an empty bucket in his hand.

"You up now. Good," the man said. "No fall back asleep, okay?"

The man wagged a finger at Nate, exited the room, and shut the door.

It wasn't until he was alone again that Nate realized the bag was no longer over his head.

He turned to look around to get a sense of where he was, but had to stop and squeeze his eyes shut as a wave of nausea swept over him. Nearly half a minute passed before he could open his eyelids again.

This time, when he scanned the room, he kept his movements slow to prevent another attack. He was in a space that couldn't have been more than ten feet square, enclosed by stone walls broken only by the single door. No windows, he realized, and no drain in the floor. Which meant this wasn't the same room he'd been in when he met the bald man.

He turned his attention to the metal chair he was sitting in, and quickly discovered that it was attached firmly to the concrete floor. Straps across his chest and lap held him in place. In addition, cuffs around his ankles were connected to the chair's legs.

Apparently, his captors hadn't realized that his lower right leg was artificial. Of course, without patting down the area where it met his stub or taking his pants off entirely, there was no reason why they would. The limb was wrapped with a synthetic exterior that created the look and feel of a real leg.

Missing this detail was a mistake he hoped they didn't rectify. His leg was more than just a means of helping him get around. If he could get to the secret compartment in the calf area, then he might have a chance.

The other partially good news was that even though his wrists were still cuffed together, they were now on his lap instead of behind his back. More comfortable, and easier to use if the chance arose.

He leaned his head back and tried to recall the last thing he clearly remembered.

Quinn, he thought. *The bald man had called me Quinn.*

From the aches and pains he felt, he could tell he'd taken a beating, but as for more memories, he was a blank.

No. Wait.

He closed his eyes. There *was* more. A burst of sound…and…and…*vibrations*. A jolt, too. What the hell had that been?

Moved. Yes, that had to be it. I was moved.

It was the method used he was having a hard time identifying. It had been distinctive, he was sure about that, something he should have been able to identify, but the answer remained elusive.

Pieces, that's all he had to figure out what was going on. The run for the border. The police who hadn't taken him to an official jail. The bald man. The noises. The vibrations.

And then there was the job itself.

Unfortunately, the pieces that bound everything together were still missing, and he wasn't going to figure anything out just sitting there.

He refocused his mind.

Priorities.

Number one: Get free.

Number two: If possible, find out what is going on, but not at the sacrifice of the first goal.

Number three: Once free, find that bastard Burke.

What he'd do with that asshole once he had him was something he could figure out later. At the moment, the thought of ripping Burke apart limb by limb was pretty damn appealing.

The door opened again, and the big blond man with the stupid grin reentered. Only he wasn't alone. Coming in right behind him was the bald man.

I guess it's time to play.

The big guy was carrying another bucket of water. He set in on the floor as the bald man closed the door. The two of them then stepped in front of Nate.

"Have a good rest?" the bald man asked.

The less said, the better, Nate knew, so he didn't answer.

"You were out for quite some time."

Nate kept his expression blank.

The man looked at his watch. "Unfortunately, I am unable to chat right now, but I just wanted to say that I'm glad to see you're up, and if you need anything, don't be afraid to ask Janus, here." He gestured to the other man. "You and I will talk later, Mr. Quinn."

He dipped his head an inch, in what amounted to a farewell bow, and left the room. Janus stayed.

"Brought you more water," the man said, picking up the bucket. "Thought you might be thirsty."

He tossed the contents at Nate.

This time the water was freezing and filled with bits and pieces of ice that pelted Nate in the face and shoulders. Nate turned his head just in time to avoid a chunk stabbing him in the eye.

Janus laughed loud and deep, almost doubling over as he did. "Cold, huh? Good for skin." Another laugh and he, too, was gone.

What Janus hadn't noticed, though, was that as Nate's body reacted to the shock, he'd automatically shoved up on his feet, tilting the chair backward a quarter of an inch as the bolts holding the front two legs down gave a little under the pressure. Nate had sensed it immediately, and had used his toes to slow his descent back to the floor so the movement wouldn't be noticeable.

He remained motionless for the first three minutes he was alone. Finally, when he felt his visitors wouldn't be returning right away, he rocked back again. He went up a quarter inch before the bolts caught. On his next try he used more force, moving higher. He kept at it, each time gaining a fraction of an inch, until finally he heard one of the bolts pop.

Instantly, he dropped the chair to the floor and eyed the door, expecting Janus to come rushing in. He counted off seconds, stopping when he reached the four-minute mark without the door opening.

He finally allowed himself to glance at the floor. Because his chest was strapped to the chair, he couldn't lean far enough forward to see the front legs. Also, if he'd heard right, the pop had come from the right side, so even if the bolt had come loose and fallen to the floor, it would have been difficult to detect with his faux foot.

Keeping an eye on the door, he rocks slowly back. While the left front leg of the chair still caught on its bolt, the right side was definitely free.

The door started to open. He quickly put the legs back down, and hoped to God the bolt was hidden by the chair or his own legs.

Janus entered. Instead of a bucket, he had a Taser.

"We go for a walk," the man said. "You will be good boy, yes?"

Nate stuck to the same script he'd been reading from since his captivity began and kept his mouth shut.

As Janus approached him, he touched a button on the side of the Taser. An electronic hiss emanated from the device.

"See this? You don't want me touch you with this. Not

feel nice. I guarantee. So you be good boy."

Nate kept his face blank as Janus circled around behind the chair.

Don't look down. Don't see the bolt.

Janus undid the straps across Nate's thighs, released the one around his chest, and backed away.

"Unbuckle your ankles," he said.

A smart move, taking away the possibility he might get kicked or punched in the process. But it also gave Nate the opportunity to find the bolt. As he leaned down, he searched the floor, but couldn't see it.

"Faster," Janus ordered.

Nate undid one ankle, then the other as he continued to hunt for the piece of hardware.

There it is.

It was directly behind his right heel. As he started to reach for it, Janus pushed him on the back, sending him sprawling from his chair.

"On your feet."

Silently cursing himself, Nate slowly rose. As he did, he kept his head down like he was tired, and glanced back at the chair. The bolt was still there.

"Let's go," Janus said, underlining his order with a test zap of the Taser.

Nate took a single step forward, then halted.

"Keep moving," Janus told him.

Nate turned toward the other man. "I don't feel very—"

Before he could finish, he saw the Taser shoot toward him. Nate acted like he was going to throw up and dropped to the floor, Janus's weapon slicing harmlessly through the space where he'd just been. He shot his arms forward, grabbed the bolt, and brought it down to his chest as the Taser touched his back.

For the next several seconds, he jerked and jolted on the ground, the electric pain seemingly touching every nerve ending as he lost control of his body. When the hissing stopped, he continued to spasm for several seconds, playing out the last of the Taser's effects.

Nearly a minute passed before Janus said, "I tell you to be good boy. Now, get up."

Nate felt a pain on his chest. Not electrical from the Taser, more like a bruise. The bolt, he realized. He'd been thrashing against it. He put his hand over it and curled it into a loose fist as he shakily pushed himself back to his feet.

"No more stupid move, okay? Now go."

Nate walked out of the room into a narrow passageway. As Janus closed the door, Nate slipped his potential weapon into his pocket.

CHAPTER
THIRTEEN

"**THE CLEANER HAS** arrived?" Romero asked.

"Yes," Harris replied. "He proved a bit of a challenge, but nothing that couldn't be handled."

"I don't care about any difficulties. He's here. That's all I need to know."

"Yes, sir."

Truth was, Quinn's capture had been more than just a challenge. If Harris hadn't forced that idiot Moreno to continue the search and set up roadblocks after the cleaner got away in Monterrey, Quinn would have been in the wind, and they may have been staring at that one small error Harris had warned about at the start.

He had expected the taking of the cleaner to be difficult, just not *that* difficult. After all, Quinn's abduction had been the hardest to set up. As a cleaner, the man was in charge of his own work, and not a part of the official ops team, which meant he called his own shots and hired his own people.

To achieve their goal, Harris needed to get someone close to Quinn to feed information to the group of police officers Moreno had put together. The problem wasn't who that person would be. That was easy. Harris simply trolled the lower levels of the freelance world and plucked someone more interested in money than loyalty. Burke had served his role well.

Getting Quinn to hire Burke, though, was another issue. Harris's research had shown that the cleaner had a small group of operatives he'd consistently worked with over the last few years. Jamming their schedules had been a necessary first step before even offering the job to Quinn.

The hardest person to deal with in Quinn's select little group turned out to be a man named Daeng from Thailand. According to several sources, Quinn had been using him a lot as of late. When Harris tried to find a way to contact Daeng and put him on the same kind of hold as the others, the people he talked to said the man only worked for Quinn, no one else.

Harris decided it was time to get a little actual dirt on his hands, and followed a lead back to the man's home country, where he was able to finally figure out a way to get Daeng out of the picture. It had been a while since he'd killed anyone, but he hadn't forgotten how. More importantly, the ploy had worked.

Daeng was moved out of the way, Burke was hired, and now Quinn was here.

"The shooter?" Romero asked.

The shooter was the only one on the list left to pick up. "In progress, sir."

"So he'll be here...?"

"Tomorrow."

In contrast to Quinn, taking the shooter had been the easiest to set up, so Harris had saved him for last.

"You will inform me when he arrives," Romero said dismissively.

Harris tilted his head in acknowledgment, but it was a wasted gesture. Romero was no longer paying him any attention.

CHAPTER
FOURTEEN

SAN PAOLO, BRAZIL

M<small>AURICE</small> C<small>URSON</small> C<small>OULD</small> not believe his luck. For four years, he'd been persona non grata in the secret world. The only suitable employment he could find for someone with his particular skill set was as a bodyguard for rich losers.

But the asshole clients weren't the worst part. It was the other bodyguards who really annoyed him. While there were a few ex-military types who Curson could respect, he was convinced the majority had all come straight from gyms where they'd spent their time lifting weights, taking steroids, and mostly likely watching that stupid Kevin Costner-Whitney Houston movie over and over. Smoke blowers who acted like they'd come straight out of the Secret Service and knew best what to do in any situation. Only none of them had been in the Secret Service.

In Curson's old career, he'd done jobs in over thirty different countries, had killed, been shot at, and successfully protected people a hell of a lot more important than the latest winner of *American Dumbass*. These other guys? They wore it as a badge of honor any time they knocked a member of the paparazzi to the ground.

Amateurs. A whole mess of idiotic amateurs.

That's why when he'd been offered the gig—an actual, honest-to-God black ops situation—he had jumped at the chance. To hell with the fact it meant backing out of a previous commitment. And it didn't even matter that it wasn't a trigger-man position. He didn't care. He was back *in*, and, hopefully, if he played his cards right, he'd never have to go back to that other crap work again.

The op was pretty straightforward. A snatch and grab. The target: a Brazilian economist who was stirring up trouble and needed to be convinced to adjust his thinking. While Curson would have preferred to be on the snatch team, he was content to be in charge of getting the package from the op site to the safe house—in effect, a glorified driver.

Two days of planning, a dry run, and he and the other team members were ready. Hell, he'd been ready for years. It was all he could do to keep the smile off his face as he sat in the appropriated ambulance, waiting for the target to be brought to him.

Four years in the cold—exiled for a mistake that could have happened to anyone—were finally behind him.

Goodbye, Mr. Stoned Movie Star. I'm really back in the game now.

"Sixty seconds." The voice came over the comm in his ear.

This was it. The grab had been made and they were on their way.

Maurice climbed out of the ambulance and walked around to the back. He checked the street, confirmed it was as deserted as it had been before, and opened the rear doors.

"Thirty seconds."

He climbed inside, ready to accept the package.

The three-member snatch team appeared at the back right on time, the target propped up under one of the men's arms like a passed-out drunk. Working quickly, they transferred the Brazilian onto the gurney inside, and Curson buckled him down.

"Set?" the team leader asked.

"All set," Curson told him.

"He's all yours."

The men disappeared down the street.

THE COLLECTED

As Curson checked the buckles one last time, he realized his cargo didn't appear to be breathing.

Oh, crap.

He checked the target's pulse, or tried to, because there was none.

Oh, God, no.

The snatch team had delivered him a stiff.

He immediately began CPR.

"Come on, come on," he implored the lifeless body.

No response.

He glanced at his watch. If he didn't leave now, he'd be behind schedule.

Dammit!

He tried another go at CPR, but there was no bringing the man back.

Dammit, dammit, dammit!

He knew this would somehow become his fault. His grand reentry into the realm of secrets and spies thwarted before it could even get going.

He took a deep breath. *Be a pro. Finish the job.*

He climbed out of the back, circled around the vehicle, and got in behind the wheel. Sticking to his preplanned, less-trafficked route, he reached the turnoff for the safe house just inside the time range he'd been given.

During the whole drive, he'd been thinking about the dead man in back. He'd explain everything to his client. Tell him the target had arrived DOA, and that he'd even tried multiple times to resuscitate him. They'd have to believe him. They'd just have to.

He turned down the driveway, rehearsing in his head what he was going to say. But as he approached the isolated house, thoughts of his explanation vanished. Parked directly in his path were two sedans, their occupants standing outside, guns drawn and pointed at him.

He looked in his mirror, intending to back out of there as fast as possible, but a third car was pulling across the driveway, blocking his exit.

Oh.

Crap.

CHAPTER
FIFTEEN

CHICAGO

PULLMAN WAS RIGHT about the phone number he had for Mr. Brown. Disconnected.

"A burner," Orlando said. "Probably already dumped in a landfill."

Quinn nodded. "What about this Burke guy? Is he missing, too? Because if he isn't, I would very much like to talk to him."

They stopped at the next coffee shop they spotted, and took up residence at a table near the front door as early morning commuters lined up for their shot of espresso.

Orlando first made a pass through the documents on Pullman's computer. It didn't take her long to turn up the list of people who'd been hired for the Lopez project—each name accompanied by contact information. She turned the screen so Quinn could see. He recognized only one of the names from the ops team, but it wasn't someone he'd worked directly with before. Below the team were two more names: QUINN and BURKE.

"I say we give Mr. Burke a call," he said.

Orlando punched the number into Pullman's phone. "Ringing."

He watched her, hopeful, but it soon became clear no one was going to answer.

After disconnecting, she handed the phone to Quinn and moved Pullman's computer to the side, aiming the screen at him. "Maybe one of the others will answer," she said. She pulled her own laptop out of her bag.

Quinn went straight to the last name on the ops team list. Kelvin Moore was the team leader, so, theoretically, he'd be the one with the most information.

The line rang three times, then, "What the hell is it now, Pullman?"

"Mr. Moore?"

A long pause. "Who is this?"

"My name's Jonathan Quinn."

"Quinn? The cleaner? Bullshit. You don't sound like him at all."

"The man you worked with in Mexico is a colleague of mine who also goes by the name of Quinn."

"What kind of crap is this?"

"My friend hasn't checked in yet, and I'm trying to figure out—"

"Brother, you have called the wrong number."

Moore hung up.

Quinn called back. The line was answered and immediately disconnected. A third try received a message telling him the subscriber was out of calling range.

He tried the other names on the list. Two of the numbers played back the same out-of-range message, but the last was answered.

"Pullman?" A woman's voice.

"I'm looking for Bob Rooney," Quinn said.

"This is Bobbie."

Bobbie? Wait. "Bobbie *Harbin*?" he said.

Silence.

"Don't hang up. It's Jonathan Quinn."

"That name's been thrown around a bit lately."

"I know, I know. The guy who was in Mexico with you. He's my partner. Uses the same name."

"That's…weird."

"Long story."

"How do I know you're you?"

"Baton Rouge. Crawfish dinner. Cajun karaoke."

Orlando looked over for a second, one eyebrow raised.

Bobbie grunted a half laugh. "Okay, okay. Just don't go into any details. I barely remember that night, which I think is probably for the best."

"What's with the Rooney?"

"A little trouble under the old name. Thought it best to change it up. What the hell are you calling me for? And why are you on Pullman's phone?"

Ignoring the second question, he said, "I'm hoping you might have some information."

He could sense her hesitation. "What kind of information?"

"I'm sure you heard things didn't end up going so well on the job you just finished."

"I might have run across something about that."

"Then you know the body was found."

"Yeah. I guess your partner isn't quite as good at his job as you are."

"My partner is excellent at his job," Quinn said quickly.

"Currently, there seems to be some evidence to the contrary."

Bobbie had always been one to see the world in terms of black and white, while Quinn operated in the grays. He said, "He's missing, Bobbie. He hasn't been heard from since he last talked to you all. I want to know if there was anything unusual you might have noticed."

The line was silent for a few seconds. "Nothing that comes to mind. I'm sorry your friend is missing, but—"

"What about Burke? The guy who was working with him?"

Another pause. "I only saw him twice, and neither time for very long. I did get kind of an odd vibe from him, though, like he wasn't the kind of guy I'd want to hang out with."

"Did he say anything unusual? Anything that stands out?"

"I did see him on his phone behind the motel where we

were having our planning meeting once. He didn't see me at first, but when he did, he wrapped up his call pretty quickly. As he walked past, he shook his head and said, 'Family drama. What are you going to do?'"

"Was he lying?"

"Sure he was," she said. "But we all do that. I just figured he was lining up another gig, and didn't want to share the information."

"Anything else?"

"No. That's it," she said.

"Okay, thanks, Bobbie."

"Quinn."

"Yeah?"

"I *am* really sorry your partner's missing. If you want my guess, either the police have him and aren't talking, or he died trying to get away. Watch your step. It's probably something you don't want to get pulled into."

"Call me if something comes to mind," he said, then hung up.

"Bobbie?" Orlando asked.

"Bobbie Harbin. You remember her?"

"Hard to forget a five-foot-ten skinny blonde. What's this about crawfish and karaoke?"

"A bad night."

She gave him a skeptical half smile. "Define *bad* for me."

He laughed. "Not as bad as you're thinking."

With a roll of her eyes, she returned her attention to her computer. "I've located Burke's phone."

Quinn pushed out of his seat and came around so he could look over her shoulder.

She had her cell-phone-tracking software up. In one window was a map pushed in close on two intersecting roads. In the middle, a small blue circle pulsated, indicating the phone's location.

"Mexico?" Quinn asked.

"Yeah, but not Monterrey. Imuris."

"Never heard of it."

"It's in Sonora. South of Arizona. I was able to pull a twenty-four-hour history. The phone hasn't moved."

"Dumped?"

"It's an empty lot, so either that or he likes camping out."

Quinn frowned, disappointed. "He could be anywhere now."

"Or," Orlando said, "he could have gone someplace he knows well."

"And where would that be?"

"While the program was running down the phone's location, and you were still chatting with your ex-girlfriend—"

"Never was my girlfriend."

"Ex-lover, then."

"Not that, either."

"We'll just call it a one night stand."

"No we wo—"

"*While* you were still on the phone," she said, "I did a little digging on Burke. The guy's still new to the business. Takes whatever comes his way. It's obvious no one's taught him how to effectively cover up his information."

"And?"

"Seems our Mr. Burke is from Tucson, Arizona. Which is only about one hundred and ten miles due north of Imuris."

Quinn frowned. "He wouldn't."

"No. *You* wouldn't. *I* wouldn't. This guy, I'm not so sure."

"Who do we know in the area?" he asked.

Orlando thought for a moment. "Doesn't Kim Lakey work out of Tempe?"

QUINN AND ORLANDO flew to Phoenix, where they waited for their connection to Tucson.

As they sat near the gate, Quinn kept expecting to see someone he knew. Of course, that was ridiculous. If he had seen anyone, he probably wouldn't have even recognized the person. It had been a long time since he'd called this city home. He'd been a rookie cop then, thinking his career path was set. It wasn't, though, thanks to Durrie, his mentor. Phoenix was where their paths first crossed, Durrie both saving his life and changing its path forever.

In an attempt to distract himself, Quinn pulled out his phone and called Liz. She didn't answer. He left a message saying he and Orlando would probably be back in L.A. that evening, then he started scanning the other passengers again.

It wasn't until they were finally back in the air that he was able to relax a little. There were just too many ghosts in Phoenix, of things and events and the actual dead. Sitting there for the short layover had been more than enough to reconfirm that it was a place he needed to avoid as much as possible.

They met Kim Lakey on the west side of Tucson, in the parking lot of the Waffle House off Star Pass Boulevard.

"Good to see you guys," she said as she climbed into the back of their car, setting the gray canvas backpack she'd been carrying on the seat beside her.

They exchanged handshakes. Though Kim looked large compared to Orlando, she was only five foot three and a hundred and ten pounds. In their world, she was a jack— someone who was good at a whole range of things, and easy to slot into pretty much any support position that might be needed.

From the backpack, she pulled out the weapons they'd requested, handed them up front, then said, "Shall we go for a drive?"

Kim had been able to get to Tucson and do some hunting around before their flight had arrived in Phoenix. She confirmed that Burke had a townhome in the area, and that someone was inside.

The guy's place was located among a sea of tan, pueblo-style townhomes in a complex west of the city. If it weren't for the numbers next to the doors, it would have been nearly impossible to tell one unit from the next.

"Park there," Kim said, pointing at an open spot with the word VISITOR painted over the asphalt.

Once out of the car, she led them along a wide path

through several of the buildings, slowing when they reached the point where the pathway ended at another road.

"On the right," she said. "Four down on the other side."

Quinn glanced over. Like all the other places, there was nothing remarkable about Burke's townhome. The only thing slightly different was that curtains had been pulled across all the windows.

"How did you establish someone was inside?" he asked.

"Saw them peeking around the curtains a couple times. Couldn't see the face, though."

They walked across the street to where the path continued, taking them out of sight of Burke's place, and stopped again.

"Well?" Orlando asked.

"He knows things didn't go as planned in Monterrey," Quinn said, "so he'll obviously be running scared. If it is him inside, I doubt he'll just open the door if we knock."

"How many ways in and out?" Orlando asked Kim.

"Two doors, the front and a sliding glass one in back. Since he's between two other places, he only has windows on the front and back on both floors. Unless he barricades himself inside, it'd be an easy flush."

Quinn thought about it for a moment, then nodded. The simplest plans were often the best. "You play instigator," he told Kim. "We'll play rear guard."

IT WOULD HAVE been better if Quinn and Orlando could have climbed over Burke's fence and hidden on his porch, but, with the sun still out and the person inside undoubtedly on edge—and potentially armed—they thought it best to play it safe.

What they did instead was position themselves on the pathway that ran along the back wall enclosing Burke's small patio area. Once they were set, Quinn called Kim. "We're ready. Give him something to think about."

There was a delay of several seconds, and then they heard the distant pounding as Kim knocked, hard and decisive, on the front door. She paused for five seconds before pounding again. When she knocked a third time, Quinn heard the sliding glass door on the other side of the wall ease open.

He tensed, ready to act.

A footstep on concrete, then a thud, like something had been bumped into. And breathing, rapid, almost panting.

Whoever was on Burke's patio was scared out of their mind.

This time, instead of knocking, Kim rang the doorbell twice in a row.

Quinn heard a quick intake of breath, and then the person on the other side ran from the house to the fence. Hands wrapped around the top, and there was a *whack* against the other side as a foot or a knee slammed into it. A loud grunt of exertion, and the person's head and shoulders popped over the top.

Not Burke.

Not a man at all.

A young woman with long sandy blonde hair and a desert tan.

She worked her way up until she could bend over the edge at the waist. That was when she saw Orlando.

With a yell of surprise, she dropped back down onto the patio.

Orlando beat Quinn over the top by half a second, and grabbed the girl's arm just before she ran back into the house. The girl tried to break free, then started to yell.

"Leave me alone, you bitch! I know what you—"

"I think you need to relax," Quinn said, coming up fast on her other side, flashing his gun.

The sight of the weapon had the desired effect. The girl's jaw went slack as her eyes widened in fear.

"Anyone else here?" he whispered.

She continued to stare at the weapon.

"Hey," Quinn said. "Is anyone else inside?"

She blinked, and shook her head.

"Then why don't we go in where it's cooler?" he suggested.

As he stepped toward her, she moved backward into the house. Once inside, Orlando closed the glass door and repositioned the curtain so no one could see in. "I'll do a check." She headed for the stairs.

The doorbell rang again.

"Have a seat," Quinn told the girl.

Not taking her eyes off him, she backed all the way to a black leather couch, and sat down.

"Stay right there, and everything will be fine. Okay?"

She nodded.

Quinn went over and opened the front door.

"Success, I see," Kim said.

"Appreciate the help." He glanced back to make sure the girl hadn't moved.

"You need me for anything else?"

"Nope. We've got it now. Thank you. If you want to wait, we can give you a ride back to your car."

"Don't worry about it. Just do what you have to do. I can get back on my own. And Quinn, keep in touch. It's been a while since we've worked together."

After they shook hands, Quinn closed the door and headed back to the living room.

"Second floor's clear," Orlando said, descending the stairs.

When she reached the bottom, she headed off to check the rest of the ground floor, but Quinn knew she wouldn't find anyone. The girl had been too scared to lie about being alone. Wherever Burke was, it wasn't here.

"What's your name?" Quinn asked, lowering himself into the matching leather chair next to the couch.

Her jaw moved a few times as a few incoherent syllables stumbled out of her mouth.

"Take a breath. It's okay. You're going to be fine. Come on, like this. In," he said, breathing in deeply. "And out." He pushed the air back out again. "Your turn. In." Her intake was not quite as smooth as his. "And out." The air moved out of her lungs in a mad rush. "Again, slower this time." She tried again, her breathing better. After the third time, she was almost back in control. "Better?"

A hesitant nod.

"Good. What's your name?"

"Ellie," she said, a tremor in her voice.

"All right, Ellie. I just want to ask you a few questions. Nothing's going to happen to you. I promise."

Her gaze flicked to his gun, then back to his face.

"Here," he said. He tucked the gun between his leg and the arm of the chair, where it was out of sight, but retrievable in a hurry if the need arose. "Better?"

She chewed on her lower lip, and nodded once.

"All clear," Orlando said, walking back into the room.

Ellie jumped at the sound.

"Don't worry," Quinn said. "My friend's not going to hurt you, either."

"How about some water?" Orlando suggested as she headed toward the kitchen. "I'm going to have some."

"Um, yeah. Okay," Ellie said. "There are, um, cold bottles in the refrigerator. In the door."

"I'll take one, too," Quinn said.

Quinn waited until Orlando returned. Once they had all taken drinks, he said, "Ellie, do you live here?"

"Uh-huh," the girl said. "Well, I mean, I have my own place, but I'm here a lot. When Doug's home, anyway."

"Doug Burke?"

"Yes."

"He owns this place?"

"Uh-huh."

"So where's Doug now?"

She looked frightened again. "I'm not sure. He said he was going to the store, but that was like two hours ago. I thought he'd be back by now."

Quinn tried hard to keep the disappointment from showing on his face. He had a bad feeling the man wouldn't be coming back at all.

"Was Doug upset about anything?" he asked.

"He's been a little keyed up since he got back, if that's what you mean."

"And when was that?"

"Yesterday. Hey, if you're looking for him, I'm sure

he'll be back any minute. But whatever you think he's done, you're wrong. Doug's not like that."

"Like what?"

"I don't know. Like someone you'd have to point a gun at." She glanced at where he'd hidden the pistol. "He works for the United Nations. UNI-something. You know. The group that works with kids? He travels around all the time, doing what he can to help them. He's a good guy."

Everyone in Quinn's world had his or her own cover story. His was international banking. It seemed, though, that Burke had chosen something that would not only explain his absences, but also make him look like a hero at home. Quinn knew Orlando must be seething inside. Unlike Burke, she actually did a lot of work for those in need on her own time.

"I have a question," Orlando said, her voice remarkably calm.

Ellie looked over.

"I noticed the suitcases upstairs. Are you going on a trip?"

The girl's demeanor turned noticeably icy as she answered. "In the morning. We're flying to Australia for two weeks."

"That sounds like fun. Sydney?"

She nodded.

Quinn picked up a picture from the end table. It was Ellie and a man he assumed was Burke on a deep-sea fishing boat. Both were smiling. "Another trip?"

"Cabo," she said. "A few months ago."

He set the photo back down. "What kind of car does Doug drive?"

"Mustang. One of those new ones."

"Color?"

"Silver gray."

CHAPTER
SIXTEEN

IF THERE WAS one lesson Douglas Burke had taken to heart when he first started working ops, it was always be aware of your surroundings.

He knew he wasn't a great shooter, or strategist, or even spy. He was adequate, which was okay. For the two years he'd been in the business, his satisfactory skills had kept him employed enough to live a nice life when he was home in Tucson. Hell, he'd been able to buy a decent townhouse, had a cool car, and was even able to score a hot girlfriend.

But he knew, given his shortcomings, if he wanted to survive, he needed to stay alert.

He hadn't lied to Ellie. He had fully intended on returning from the grocery store. Since they were planning to drive all the way to Los Angeles for their flight to Sydney, he wanted to pick up some snacks for the road. A ten-minute drive to the store, fifteen inside, ten minutes back.

The detour in his plans happened as he drove through his townhome complex to his assigned parking spot. His route took him on the road that passed his place. It was just before he drove by that he saw the woman. Short and thin and brunette. If she'd been taller and had a bigger chest, she might have been his type, but that's not why he noticed her. She was walking by his place and glancing up at it.

On a normal day between jobs, it probably wouldn't have registered as anything unusual. But this wasn't a normal day. The events in Mexico were still fresh in his mind, and though he didn't have a complete picture of what had gone down, he knew enough to be worried that it could turn into a problem for him.

Hence the trip to Australia. Out of sight, out of mind.

Instead of parking in his regular spot, he found one near the community pool, and snuck back on foot. Across the street from his place were two adjacent townhomes that were currently unoccupied. He hopped over the fence into the patio area of one, picked the lock, and went inside.

Each of the townhomes had rooftop decks, one of the amenities that had helped him decide to buy here. He made his way through the empty townhouse and up onto the deck. Staying low, he moved to the front edge, then lay down and looked out at the street.

His place looked unchanged. Ellie had left the curtains closed like he'd told her to, which wasn't surprising. He'd scared her into thinking that a psycho ex-girlfriend of his was back in town and trying to find him. He had laced the tale with stories of trashed apartments and disabled cars and public rants. He knew Ellie would want no part of that.

He scanned the street, but there was no sign of the woman he'd seen.

Maybe he'd just overreacted. Just because she'd looked at his place didn't mean she was trouble. Ten minutes passed with still no sign of her.

Okay, I was *overreacting*, he thought, relieved.

He pushed himself back to his feet, intending to head downstairs, but as he was turning to leave, he caught sight of someone standing near the end of the pathway that weaved through the homes about a quarter block from his place. From his position, he could only see a hand and partial profile, but it was enough to make him suspicious.

Carefully, he worked his way down the row of townhomes until he reached the one on the corner above the unknown person. Lying down again, he inched out until he could look straight down.

His stomach clenched.

It was the woman.

He watched her for a minute, then pulled back, suddenly afraid she would sense his gaze and look up. There was no question why she was there. The entire time he'd observed her, her eyes had been trained on his place.

As far as he was concerned, there were only two people who could have sent her to look for him: Pullman, who'd want to know what the hell had gone wrong; or the man who'd called himself Mr. Blair. Of the two, it was Blair he worried about most.

Though he'd done exactly what the man had asked—delivering the information about the cleaner's plan—Burke now thought that Blair had only been playing him, and hadn't actually intended for Burke to get away. Ironically, it was Quinn who had preserved his freedom, by buying time and ordering Burke to take off.

I'm a loose end.

Burke looked in the direction of his place. "Sorry, Ellie," he whispered. "Gonna have to take this trip alone."

Four minutes later, he was back in his car, heading for the freeway.

CHAPTER
SEVENTEEN

LOS ANGELES

ANGER WAS AN emotion Daeng had learned to control during the time he'd spent as a monk at the temple in the Thai countryside. It would still occasionally rear up, but only in the most extreme situations. Years before, the crackdown in his mother's homeland of Burma that saw many of his brother monks murdered had not only been one of those situations, but the one that had pushed him out of the saffron robes and into a life where he could have a more direct hand in dealing with the injustices being thrust upon the Burmese people.

Now, being coaxed away from Los Angeles by lies so that he would not be in a position to help his friend was another. He let it simmer inside for the entire return trip from Bangkok, knowing it was best to let it run its course. It wasn't until the plane began its descent into LAX that he finally allowed himself to close his eyes in his well-practiced ritual. In his mind, he pictured a box rotating just below his ribs. As it turned, it sucked in more and more of his anger, until finally the last wisps of it were gone. As he closed the box and stored it away, he could feel his body relax. Opening his eyes, he was calm again, his anger a memory now, but one he could grab on to and use to focus as needed.

He waited until he cleared passport control before he called Quinn. No answer, just voice mail.

"I'm here," he said, leaving his message. "I'll head over to your place and call you again when I get there."

He arranged for a rental car, then drove across town and up into the hills.

Quinn had told him Liz would be at the house. Daeng had heard plenty about her from Nate, and had seen several pictures, but the two had never actually met. So, not wanting to walk in and scare her, he pushed the buzzer on the gate intercom.

When she didn't respond, he had no choice but to enter the code. He parked in front of the garage and knocked on the door. Still no answer. Apparently, she'd gone out, so he let himself in. It was good to be back at Quinn's house. Nate had been letting him use the second guest room, so it was almost like coming home.

"Hello?" he called, just in case she hadn't heard him knock. "Liz? It's Daeng. Nate and Quinn's friend. Hello?"

He was answered only by silence.

He set his bag by the stairs so he could take it downstairs later, and went into the kitchen to start some coffee. The flight was a long one, and his internal clock was all screwed up from going back and forth.

It wasn't until he'd pulled a mug out of the cabinet that he noticed the piece of paper on the table. He went over and picked it up.

"THIS IS WHAT I want you to do," Quinn said to Ellie. "Take your suitcase and go home to your place."

She looked at him, the area between her eyebrows wrinkling. "But…he's coming back. Our trip."

"Do you feel safe here?"

She pulled back a few inches. "You're going to hurt him, aren't you?"

"I never said that. I just need to ask him a few questions."

Her eyes suddenly lost focus as she tilted her face down. With a half laugh, she looked over at Orlando and shook her head. "I'm such an idiot. There wasn't an ex-girlfriend."

"You thought I was his ex?" Orlando said.

She frowned as she looked back up. "Never mind." She stood up. "I'll go. If you see him, tell him...Tell him if he wasn't lying to me, he knows where to find me. And if he was..." She shook her head and said, "Screw it."

Once she'd retrieved her suitcase and left, Quinn pulled out his phone and took a picture of the photograph of Burke and Ellie on the boat. He asked Orlando, "You didn't happen to see a ticket for their flight, didn't you?"

"If he printed them out, they'd probably be in his carry-on up in his room."

Quinn ran up the stairs, and returned a few moments later with several pieces of paper.

"You think he's stupid enough to still go?"

"Let's find out."

He led the way back to the car. Just as he was climbing in, his phone vibrated. He pulled it out and saw that he already had one missed call.

"Hello?" he said.

"It's Daeng. I'm at your house."

"Oh, crap," he said. "I forgot to tell Liz you were coming. Please tell her I'm—"

"She's gone."

Quinn had been about to start the car, but paused. "Gone?"

"She left a note. It says, 'Jake, I can't stay here. Don't call me unless you find him. I need to think about things. Liz.'"

Quinn grimaced. It was just as he'd feared. She was going to get hurt all over again, and, ultimately, it would be his fault.

"Snap a photo of it and message it to me, okay?" he said. He wanted to make sure it was her handwriting.

"No problem," Daeng told him. "I *could* go out and look for her if you want."

Quinn glanced at the tickets Burke had printed out. "No. It's better if we just leave her alone. I actually have something else I need you to do. I'm going to send you a picture of a guy named Douglas Burke. He's scheduled to fly out on Qantas for Australia tomorrow night, but I have a feeling he's going to try to move up his reservation. Get back to LAX. If you see him, detain him. I don't know if he's driving in or flying, but he'll have to go through the international terminal. We'll get there as quickly as we can."

"GOOD AFTERNOON," THE female attendant said as Daeng walked up to the Qantas Airlines check-in counter. "Passport, please."

"Actually, I'm not checking in," he said, putting on his friendliest face.

"Oh. Well, then, what can I do for you?"

"I hope I'm not too late. I'm supposed to meet someone who *is* flying out today, and give him these papers." He held up a manila envelope he'd picked up at an office supply store on the way to the airport and stuffed with several pieces of blank paper. Written on the outside was: DOUGLAS BURKE. "Is there any way for you to tell me if he's already checked in or not?"

"No problem. Name?"

He set the envelope on the counter so she could see it. She typed in the name, then studied her screen.

"Oh," she said after a few seconds. "I see he changed his reservation to today."

"Yeah. He was supposed to leave tomorrow. That's why I had to rush."

"Well, he hasn't checked in yet, but his flight doesn't leave for another five hours, so you have plenty of time."

Daeng put on his best look of relief. "Thank God. I was told the plane was leaving at seven p.m."

She smiled. "No. Just after ten."

"That's good. Well, except now I have to sit around and wait." He grinned and shrugged.

"Better than missing him, though, right?"

"That's true," he said, picking up the envelope. "Thanks."

At the back of the Tom Bradley International terminal

was a balcony level with several restaurants that overlooked the check-in area. Daeng went up, bought a bowl of chicken udon soup from the Japanese place, and took a seat at the front edge of the balcony, with a view of the Qantas counter.

For the first hour, it saw very little action. Then, just a little after six p.m., traffic started to pick up. First the line was a constant half dozen, then a dozen. By seven p.m. it had almost doubled again, and new staff had come on to direct people to the different stations as they opened up.

He still hadn't seen Burke.

At a quarter after seven, Quinn called.

"We just landed," he said. "Any news?"

"You were right. He changed to tonight's ten-o'-clock flight. But so far, he hasn't checked in."

"All right. We're on our way over to you."

"I'm sitting at the—" He paused, his eyes narrowing as he looked at a man who'd just joined the end of the line.

"Daeng? Are you there?"

"I think I see your friend."

"Are you sure?"

"Hard to tell from where I'm positioned. I'm going in for a closer look, but you'd better hurry."

"Five minutes," Quinn said, and hung up.

Daeng dumped his empty bowl in the trash and rode the escalator back downstairs. As he approached the line in front of Qantas, he saw his instincts had been right. It was Burke.

The guy was wearing a baseball cap and sunglasses despite the fact he was inside, but the jawline was the same, as were the ears and the mouth. He was nervous, too. He kept looking over his shoulder, scanning the crowd. He even paused on Daeng for a moment, but quickly moved on, obviously dismissing the former monk as a threat.

By the way the line was moving, it would be at least ten minutes before Burke's turn. Daeng moved down to the end of the aisle nearest the front doors, and casually stood where he could keep an eye on the man.

Quinn and Orlando joined him three minutes later.

"Where?" Quinn asked.

"Qantas line, about midway, in the baseball cap and glasses."

"Subtle," Orlando said.

"Yeah, wouldn't have been my choice," Quinn agreed. He watched Burke for a moment. "Here's what I'd like to do."

"GOOD EVENING. PASSPORT, please," Maddee James said.

The passenger placed his passport on the counter. "My reservation was for tomorrow, but I switched it earlier today," he said.

"No problem, sir," she told him, hoping he was right. It had been a long day already, and the last thing she wanted was to deal with a passenger who thought he'd changed his flight but actually hadn't. It had happened before and it was never any fun.

She input his name into the system, and smiled. He was indeed on tonight's flight. She printed out his boarding card, tagged his bag, and handed the card and passport back to him.

"Security check is in the back and to the left. Have a nice flight, Mr. Burke."

It wasn't until he grunted a thanks and walked off that she remembered his name from earlier. He was the person that cute messenger was looking for. She had a second to wonder if they'd been able to find each other before the next passenger walked up.

"Good evening. Passport, please."

QUINN WATCHED FROM the back end of the aisle as Orlando moved in beside Burke, and Daeng took up position behind the man.

Subtly, Orlando angled her path so that Burke had to move more and more to his right. As they took the turn toward security, he was almost up against the wall. That was Quinn's cue.

He moved in quickly, a broad smile on his face, his arms open wide. "Doug!"

He enveloped Burke in a hug before the guy even knew

what was happening.

"Great to see you again," Quinn said loudly, then whispered, "If you try to draw *any* attention, we will kill you here and leave you to die."

Both Orlando and Daeng moved in close so Burke would know they were there.

"Do you understand?" Quinn asked.

Burke swallowed hard. "Yes."

Quinn let go and took a small step back. "Let us help you with your stuff."

Daeng grabbed Burke's carry-on, while Orlando took his passport and boarding card.

"I've got a plane to catch," Burke said.

"Maybe. That depends on your answers to a few questions."

"What questions?"

Quinn smiled. "Why don't we go outside where it's a little quieter?

CHAPTER EIGHTEEN

JANUS LED NATE down a long dark hall to the room with the washbasin and toilet. It was the second time he'd been taken there since he came into possession of the bolt. This time, though, there was a clean shirt and pair of pants hanging from a peg on the back wall.

"Wash up," Janus said. "You want to look good for later."

Nate held his cuffed hands in the air, silently asking how he was supposed to do that.

Janus smirked, then pulled a pair of cutters out of his back pocket and snapped the plastic tie in two. For half a second, Nate thought about making a move, but Janus quickly stepped back into the doorway, out of range.

"Now wash," the big man said.

With Janus keeping an eye on him, Nate used the toilet, removed his shirt, and cleaned up, using the soap and washcloth next to the sink. It felt good to get some of the grime and old sweat off, but he knew it was just temporary. Unlike the room he'd been held in, this one didn't seem to have any climate control. The air was thick and humid. Even as he was drying off, he could feel sweat forming on his skin again.

He grabbed his shirt, but before he could pull it back on, Janus said, "Uh-uh. Change."

The big man nodded at the clean clothes. Nate hesitated. If he wanted to avoid revealing his prosthetic, the pants were going to be a problem.

He grabbed the shirt—a brown button-up with short sleeves—and pulled it on. When he was done, he turned back to Janus and took a step toward the door.

"Pants, too," Janus said.

Nate looked at the pants he was wearing, then at those hanging on the wall. They were both jeans.

Realizing his only possible way out was to break his silence, he said, "What difference does it make? They're the same."

If Janus was surprised to hear his voice, he didn't show it. His look took in both pairs of pants. He shrugged. "Change."

"I'm not going to change. They're the same damn pants."

Janus's ears grew red as his face tightened in anger. "You will change."

"You want me to change? Fine. But I'm not going to do it with you standing there watching me."

"Change."

"Privacy, and I will."

They stared defiantly at each other for several seconds.

Finally, Nate said, "What do you think I'm going to do? Steal the soap? Here." He grabbed the bar and tossed it at Janus. "Better?"

Janus frowned, took a quick look around the room, and nodded. "One minute." He pulled the door closed.

The first thing Nate did was remove the bolt from his pocket. He then pulled his pants off, but before donning the other pair, he bent down and opened the seam on the calf of his artificial leg. As much as he now wished there was a weapon embedded inside, that was one option his leg didn't have. Traveling as much as he did, his prosthetic already made him a target for extra attention from airport security, so he couldn't afford to take that kind of chance.

What it did have, though, was a small space he could use to stow the bolt. It was meant for a memory card, or a note or photograph, so it would be a little snug, but he was pretty sure the bolt would fit.

There was something else in the storage space, too. A button designed to be pushed in just these kinds of circumstances. His leg had a heart-rate monitor, which, in turn, had a dead-man switch. Unless the switch was turned off each time he removed his leg, an emergency signal would be activated if the leg was not attached to his stump for more than an hour. To help cut down on the chance of it being discovered, the signal was passive and needed to be pinged. In addition to the dead-man switch, there was also a way to activate the signal without removing the leg—a button at the top of the storage area.

He searched for it with his fingertip, found its grooved top, and pressed it.

Knowing he was running out of time, he jammed the bolt inside, sealed up his leg, and quickly pulled the new pants on. He was just buttoning the top when the door opened again.

"Happy now?" he said.

Janus grunted. "Hands."

Nate held out his hands, wrists together.

Once Janus had secured them with another plastic cuff, he said, "Let's go."

THE NEXT TIME Janus took Nate from his cell was several hours later.

They went back down the long corridor, passed the toilet without stopping, and out a door into a large, open courtyard.

The area was rimmed by a high stone wall spackled with decades—if not centuries—of dirt. The ground was also covered with stone, big square slabs with more than the occasional weed growing up between the cracks. What was beyond the walls was impossible to see. The only things visible were scattered clouds across a dusky sky.

At the far end of the courtyard was an old wooden table surrounded by several empty chairs. On the table were burning candles and two settings of plates and silverware. At intervals along the courtyard wall beyond the table were eight unsmiling men, dressed in fatigues, and armed with automatic rifles.

"Go," Janus ordered, pointing with his chin toward the table. "Take seat near right end."

Nate tried to imagine what could possibly be going on here, but he hadn't a clue. It was just all too strange.

He took his assigned place and looked at Janus, wondering what he was supposed to do now.

Janus smiled, moved around the table, and took a chair on the opposite side that had no place setting.

They sat silently as the sky continued to darken. The whole time Janus stared blankly at Nate.

It was just over thirty minutes when a door somewhere behind Nate opened. This was soon followed by the *clack, clack, clack* of someone striding across the courtyard. Nate resisted the urge to turn and look. The new arrival finally came into view as he moved around to the chair at the end of the table and sat. Not surprisingly, it was the bald man.

"Good evening, Mr. Quinn," he said. "How is everything? I trust you've been treated well?"

Nate looked at him but said nothing.

"Still the silent routine, I see." He looked past Nate. "Janus, I think we're ready."

"Yes, sir."

Janus rose from his chair and headed off to the right.

"You can call me Mr. Harris," the bald man said, smiling. "It is my pleasure to have someone of your status at my table this evening. I assume you're hungry. The chef has prepared baked swordfish. One of my favorites."

A door opened.

"Ah, excellent."

Several footsteps approached the table, and soldiers in the same fatigues and the men with the guns set plates in front of Nate and Harris.

In addition to the fish, there were grilled vegetables and fresh fruit. Nate tried to keep his face blank, but inside he was salivating at the sight. He hadn't eaten since before things went wrong in Monterrey.

Another soldier placed a glass of water beside Nate's silverware.

Harris picked up his fork. "*Bon appétit.*" He speared a piece of his fish and put it in his mouth. As he chewed, he looked back at Nate. "Don't you like fish?"

Nate raised his bound hands.

"Of course," Harris said. "Janus!"

Janus appeared at Nate's side, and freed Nate's hands again.

Nate wanted nothing more than to shove everything into his mouth, but he took his time, acting only semi-interested in what had been served.

"It's become my habit to have a meal with each of our guests on his first evening here," Harris said. "One of my little joys, I guess you'd say." He took another bite. "Last night you arrived a bit too late, but you're here now. That's what counts."

Each of us? Nate thought.

Harris cut away another piece of the swordfish. "This is delicious, isn't it?"

The one-sided dialogue continued throughout the meal, with Harris commenting on everything from the food to the weather to the stars that now sparkled above them.

When they finally finished, he said, "I want you to know how much I admire your career. A man with your reputation is rare indeed. You are a true artist, you know that?" He smiled. "But all things come to an end." He pushed back from the table and stood up. "Well, I wish I could stay, but our last guest arrives tomorrow, and I need to oversee the preparations. Have a good night, Mr. Quinn."

THE CELL JANUS took him to was not the same one he'd spent the day in. His new living quarters were located down a hallway housing several rooms. Each had a heavy door that was locked in place by a levered handle. The handle controlled a double metal-rod system attached to the outside of the door. In the locked position, the rods fit snuggly into slots in the ceiling and on the floor, literally barring the door from opening.

The room itself was a bit larger than his last, and came

complete with a mattress on the floor and a rudimentary toilet in the corner. The stone walls were worn and blackened with age, and while there were still no windows, there was a rectangular vent low on the door that allowed fresh air to drift in.

The only light came from a dull bulb screwed into a socket crudely attached in an upper corner. The wire wasn't visible, so Nate assumed a hole must have been drilled through the rock.

He lay down on his mattress and stared at the ceiling. So far, he'd been captured, knocked around, transported *somewhere*, bound to a chair where he was dunked in water, and then treated to a gourmet meal. Even odder, perhaps, was that even though he'd been asked a few questions here and there, there had really been no interrogation.

It just didn't add up.

"Hey."

Nate sat up. The voice had been a distant whisper, or maybe not even a voice at all. Perhaps it had just been the groan of the building.

"Hey, new guy."

No groan could put words together like that.

Nate crawled over to the door and leaned down to the vent. "Who's there?"

"Who are you?" the voice asked.

Before Nate could respond, another voice whispered, "Shut up. You know they can hear everything we say."

"So what?" the first voice said. "New guy, who are you?"

Nate hesitated for a moment, then whispered, "Quinn."

"Holy shit. The cleaner?"

He paused again. "Uh-huh. Who are you?"

"Lanier. Remember me? We've worked together before."

Lanier?

It took a second before the name clicked. An ops guy, good at logistics, wasn't he? They *had* worked together once or twice, but Nate knew the man was thinking of the original

Quinn, not him.

"Sure," he said. "I know who you are. Who's the other guy?"

"Berkeley, another ops guy like me, and scared shitless."

"I'm not scared," Berkeley whispered, his voice a bit more distant than Lanier's. "I just think we need to be smart."

Berkeley's name was also familiar. "Either of you know what's going on?" Nate asked.

"No clue," Lanier said. "I'd just finished this gig in Panama and the next thing I know, I wake up here. That was a week ago."

"A week?" Nate said, surprised.

"Berkeley's been here even longer. A week and a half."

"Almost two," Berkeley said, obviously not wanting to be short-changed.

"And they haven't told either of you why?"

"Other than the first day we each got here, the only guy we've seen is that big son of a bitch Janus," Lanier said.

"And the first day?"

"Same thing that happened to you tonight, I'm guessing. Dinner with Mr. Baldy."

"He said his name was Harris," Nate said.

"That's consistent, anyway."

"So you've been in your cells since then?"

"They haven't even let us take a shower."

"Anyone question you?"

"No."

"Seriously?"

"Kind of freaky, isn't it?"

It wasn't just kind of freaky, it was *all* kinds of freaky.

"Did Harris tell you anything?" Lanier asked.

Nate repeated what he thought were the key points from Harris's monologue, and added, "He did say another guest was coming tomorrow."

"That'll make five."

"Five?"

"Yeah, there's another guy in a room somewhere down the hall. They take him in and out a lot. I get the feeling he's been beaten up pretty bad. Never responds when we call out to him."

Five people, at least two of whom Nate was tangentially associated with. No, at least two of whom *Quinn* was associated with.

For the first time, he felt there might be a chance to fit the pieces of the puzzle together. How and in what order was still an unknown, but a little light was creeping in.

He put his lips near the vent. "Lanier?"

"Yeah?"

"How many—"

A door down the hall opened, and Janus shouted, "Be quiet! Time to sleep."

His heavy, booted feet pounded quickly down the hall, stopping right in front of the vent.

Something hit Nate's door. *Bam! Bam!*

Nate jumped back, his ears ringing.

"No talking," Janus said.

Nate waited, hoping Janus would walk off and he could get more info out of Lanier, but the big man seemed to have decided to take up residence outside his door.

Eventually, Nate crawled back over to the mattress, but it was a long time before he finally fell asleep.

CHAPTER
NINETEEN

HARRIS PACED BACK and forth across his room. Despite his outward appearance earlier, his dinner with Quinn disturbed him.

The purpose of the face-to-face meals was to show the men they'd taken that there was no hope. The soldiers, the controlled meal, the relaxed façade of the man in charge—all meant to reinforce that message.

But there was something troubling about Quinn.

While the others had put up stoic fronts, Quinn seemed almost relaxed, like he knew something Harris didn't.

For the first time, the thought that perhaps they should have just killed Quinn and the ops team crossed his mind, but he quickly pushed it aside.

Damn Quinn!

Instead of getting into the cleaner's head, it was like the cleaner was starting to get into his. That would never happen.

He poured himself a glass of whiskey.

Fun, remember? It's going to be fun.

He toasted that thought, and poured himself another.

CHAPTER
TWENTY

"I'M NOT GETTING in there," Burke told them.

They were standing next to Daeng's rental car in the parking structure near the international terminal.

"Fair enough. A question first," Quinn said.

"I'm telling you, I'm not getting in."

"If you give me the right answer, you won't have to."

Burke looked at him warily, but said nothing.

"We know you were part of the termination in Monterrey," Quinn said. "And that you were assisting the cleaner, Quinn. So what happened?"

Burke hesitated. "What do you mean?"

"That's the question, Doug. You answer it right, and you can walk away."

Burke held Quinn's gaze for a second. "Did Pullman send you? Or…"

"Or who?" Quinn asked.

"No one. Never mind."

"Or who?"

Burke shook his head. "I was just testing you."

"You're a horrible liar. Do you realize that?"

Before Burke could even respond, Quinn's fist slammed into the man's gut.

Burke let out a groan as he doubled over and clutched his stomach.

"What the hell?" he said, panting.

Quinn opened the car's rear door, and shoved the bastard

into the backseat. While he climbed in next to Burke, Daeng swung around the car and bookended the guy on the other side. Orlando slipped into the driver's seat.

Quinn grabbed Burke's shoulder and shoved him against the backrest. "See, this is what not being helpful gets you."

Burke stared at him, not even attempting to hide the fear in his eyes. "Who are you people?"

"Well, we're not with Pullman."

Burke's eyes widened. "Shit."

"Come on, Doug. Tell me about Monterrey."

"Look, I did everything your boss wanted. If you couldn't catch him, that's not my fault."

Keeping his face neutral, Quinn said, "And why wouldn't that be your fault?"

"I...I told you where we were going to be," he pleaded. "If you hadn't had cop cars waiting right there, Quinn would have never known anything. It's not my fault. It's *your* fault you couldn't pull it off. The guy is good, man. He outsmarted you."

It took every ounce of Quinn's will not to punch Burke senseless. "What happened after he saw the lights?"

"He turned around and made a run for it," Burke said, as if it were obvious. "Ask your people. They know what happened."

"Where did he run to?"

"To that building he ditched the van behind. Where do you think?"

"And what did you do then?"

"I ran like hell."

"Together?"

"No. He...he told me to leave first."

"So, he didn't get out of the van?"

"What are you talking about? Of course, he did. I saw him steal one of your..." Burke's voice trailed off. "You're...you're not with Mr. Blair, are you?"

Quinn tapped Orlando on the shoulder. "Let's go."

"Hey, wait a minute," Burke said as she started the engine. "Hey, come on. I'm being cooperative."

THE COLLECTED

Quinn's hand shot forward, his fingers wrapping around Burke's neck. As he squeezed, he said, "No, we're not with Mr. Blair, either. We're with Quinn."

Burke began to shake.

THERE WERE VALLEYS and canyons in the hills behind Malibu that, despite being within a few miles of over a million people, were surprisingly unoccupied. Quinn directed Orlando to one he'd used in the past.

"Here," he said, after they'd traveled deep into the ravine.

Orlando pulled to a stop and shut off the lights, plunging them into a darkness the nearby city no longer knew. The only illumination was from the star-filled sky and the glow of Los Angeles to the north and east.

Quinn climbed out first. "Let's go," he told Burke.

"No way," Burke said.

Daeng pushed him in the back. "Do as you're told."

"You're going to kill me," Burke protested. "Like hell I'm going to make it easy."

"We might," Quinn admitted. "But again, it's up to you."

"Oh, no. I'm staying here. If you're going to shoot me, shoot me in the damn car."

Quinn reached in and grabbed the man by the front of his shirt. With Daeng once more shoving from behind, he dragged Burke outside and dropped him on the ground.

"Up," Quinn said.

Burke rose reluctantly to his feet.

Quinn waited until Orlando and Daeng had joined him before he said, "We're going to take a little walk."

Burke looked like he was beginning to accept what he assumed was the inevitable, and made no further protest.

In a loose line, they hiked up the side of the ravine until they reached the top. They could see lights in the distance from a few homes closer to the beach, and the flat blackness of the Pacific Ocean.

"On your knees," Quinn said.

"Please. No," Burke pleaded.

"On. Your. Knees."

Daeng pushed down on the man's shoulders, and Burke dropped to his knees.

"Please. Please," he said. He was starting to cry. "I'm sorry, okay? I'm sorry."

"What happened?" Quinn said. "From the beginning. And don't leave anything out."

"Okay. Sure, sure. Um...we picked up the body, and, uh, uh, were taking it to the place where, uh—"

"No. How did you get the job in the first place?"

"M...Mr. Blair arranged it."

"You knew ahead of time?"

A pause, a nod.

"Tell us."

"He contacted me a couple weeks ago. Said there was a job he'd get me on, and would triple whatever pay I was usually offered."

"And for this you had to...?"

"Keep tabs on the cleaner. They wanted him. I just needed to tell them where to be."

"So you sold him out."

"I, I mean, I thought that, well, I was given the impression that...he'd done something wrong." He looked momentarily at each of them then focused back on Quinn. "Hey, it was going to happen whether I helped or not."

Slowly, Quinn got the rest of the story out of him. How Nate was supposed to have been captured, about how he spotted the ambush, about the chase, and about how, as far as Burke knew, Nate had gotten away. By Nate's continued absence, though, Quinn and the others knew he hadn't.

"Tell us about Mr. Blair. Did you ever meet him in person?" Quinn asked.

"One time, when he first came to me."

"Describe him."

"About as tall as you, maybe. Bald. Decent shape."

Quinn glanced at Daeng and nodded. Daeng pulled out his phone, brought up the picture of Mr. Thatcher in Bangkok, and held it in front of Burke's face.

"Is that him?" Quinn asked.

"Yeah. Yeah, that's him," Burke said, surprised.

Quinn said nothing for a moment. They now had confirmation that this had been more than just a job that had gone bad. Nate had been set up.

"I think we've heard enough," Quinn said.

He held out a hand to Daeng, who gave him the suppressor-enhanced pistol he'd brought from the house. Armed, Quinn walked behind Burke.

"It's better if you look at the ground," he said.

"Wait, wait, wait, wait, wait," Burke said, rapid fire. "I cooperated. I told you what you wanted to know."

"And you sold our friend out, too."

"But he might have gotten away!"

"That doesn't change what you did."

Quinn put the end of the suppressor against the back of Burke's skull.

"Wait! Please! I'm sorry! I shouldn't have done it! I know that. I'll never do anything like it again. I promise!"

"You're right," Quinn said. "You *will* never do it again."

A half second before he pulled the trigger, he moved the gun to the side of Burke's head, pressing the barrel of suppressor hard against the man's ear and cheek.

Thup.

The bullet slammed into the ground, inches from the man's knee. A split second later, Burke yelled and fell on his side, his hand clutching his face. Quinn leaned down and moved the man's hand away for a moment to make sure he'd done a proper job.

He had.

An inch-wide strip of deformed red flesh ran across Burke's ear and down his cheek, almost all the way to the top of his mouth. It would create a scar that would grace the man's face for the rest of his life. It was a symbol within their world, a brand, of a person not to be trusted. Though Quinn had come close to simply killing him, he knew he might need the man again later. So he settled for the fact that Burke would never work in their business again.

But if it turned out Nate *was* dead, he'd find Burke again and finish the job. And if his former apprentice was still alive, it would be up to Nate how to handle the double-crosser.

THEY LEFT BURKE in the hills, and tossed his carry-on bag into a Dumpster in Calabasas as soon as they reached the San Fernando Valley.

"So who the hell is this bald guy?" Quinn asked as he drove them down the 101 Freeway back toward his house in the hills.

"We know one thing," Orlando said. "He has a fondness for British prime ministers."

Quinn had picked up the connection, too. Thatcher, Blair, Brown—all names of people who had led the British government. "Yeah, but that doesn't answer the question."

They fell silent.

Finally, Quinn said, "Let's put some feelers out. Someone's got to know him. Check with Albina and Roselyn." They were both well-connected job fixers. "And Peter, too. Maybe he can get Helen Cho to run this guy's picture through the CIA's system." Peter used to run an organization called the Office, and at one time had been one of Quinn's primary employers. Helen Cho was now the head of a group that basically filled the void left by the Office's dissolution.

Orlando pulled her laptop out of her bag. "On it."

By the time they reached Quinn's house, she had received replies from both Albina and Roselyn. Neither had ever seen the man before. Peter hadn't replied yet. Which was a bit odd. Thought it was much later back east where Peter lived, he was typically a night owl, and usually responded to inquiries such as this quickly.

Once they were inside, Quinn decided to give him a call.

The direct number to Peter's cell phone rang five times before clicking over to voice mail.

"Peter, it's Quinn. Need to talk to you right away. Call me as soon as you get this."

He hung up and joined the others in the living room.

"You know, it might not have been Nate they were after," Orlando suggested.

"Yeah," Quinn said. "I was thinking about that."

"You mean you?" Daeng said.

Quinn shrugged. "He's been using my name."

"If that's the case," Orlando said, "shouldn't you know who this guy is?"

Quinn pulled the man's picture up on his phone again and gave it another look. "You would think so, but I've never seen him before."

"What if he had hair?"

Quinn placed his thumbs over the top and side of the man's head, and focused on the guy's face. After a moment, he shook his head. "Nope. I'm sure I've never met him."

Quinn looked across the room, lost in thought. After a moment, his gaze fell on a piece of paper sitting on the dining table. He pushed up and walked over to it. Liz's handwritten note stared back at him.

Damn.

He'd momentarily forgotten about it.

"Can you do a location check on Liz's phone?" he asked Orlando.

"Sure." She opened her laptop, and a minute later said, "San Diego. Her GPS coordinates match up to a motel in Pacific Beach. The Otter House. Small place. Eighteen rooms." She looked up. "I could call her if you want. She'll talk to me."

He considered it for a moment, then shook his head. "No. She needs time to think."

Orlando frowned.

"What?" he asked.

"I know what you're doing. You're hoping this might break them up. You think it's better if she's not involved with someone in the business."

"Don't you think that, too?" he asked, surprised.

"I *am* involved with someone in the business."

"Yeah, but you're in it also."

"You can't decide her life for her."

"Who says I am? I'm not telling her to leave him. I haven't told her their relationship is a bad idea. All I'm saying now is that we give her some time for herself."

"And if she comes back and still wants to be in a relationship with him?"

"That's her choice."

"You'll support it?"

He paused for a moment. "Yes."

"If you honestly mean that, fine."

"I do."

"Then fine," she said, though the look she gave him was less than certain.

CHAPTER
TWENTY ONE

QUINN ROSE AT five a.m.

Careful not to wake Orlando, he put on a clean T-shirt and pair of gym shorts, checked his phone and was surprised to see there was still no return call from Peter. It was already eight back in DC, and Peter—who not only stayed up late, but woke early—would have certainly listened to Quinn's message by now.

He headed upstairs, and tried calling his old employer again, but was once more sent to voice mail.

"Peter, this is an emergency. I need to talk to you right away."

He hung up and thought for a moment. Peter *had* given him a number once for use only in an emergency and Peter could not otherwise be reached, but that had been before the Office had disbanded. Quinn wasn't even sure the number worked anymore.

He found it on Peter's phone in the notes section of contact page. He punched in the number and listened, fully expecting to receive a "this number has been disconnected" message.

One ring. "Hello?" A woman's voice.

"I think I might have the wrong number," Quinn said, almost sure of it. "I'm looking for Peter."

"Who is this?" There was a surprised tone to the voice, a voice Quinn realized he recognized.

"Misty?"

"Tell me who this is or I'm hanging up."

"It's Quinn."

Dead air for a second. "Quinn? How did you...how did you get my number?"

"I didn't know it *was* your number. Peter gave it to me a few years ago in case of an emergency."

"Typical. That man..." He could almost hear her shaking her head.

"I've been trying to get ahold of him, but he hasn't responded. I thought I'd give this number a try, but I don't suppose you've seen him lately."

"Not for a month or so." Misty had been Peter's assistant back in the Office days, and one of the few people Peter fully trusted. Since the end of their organization, she had been shuffled off to a far less interesting government job, while Peter had been labeled a consultant and stuck behind a desk. "When did you call him?"

"Last night, probably around midnight your time, and again just before I called you."

"And you left messages?"

"Yeah."

"That's not like him. He should have called you back by now. Are you sure you have the right number?"

Quinn read off the number he had for Peter.

"That's it," she said, sounding concerned. "Let me check and get back to you."

"You don't have to do that."

"No. I do."

Quinn knew it didn't matter who was officially paying her salary, Peter would always be her boss.

"I appreciate it."

"I'll call you right back."

Quinn put on the coffee, and made a bowl of instant oatmeal. He'd only taken two bites when his phone rang.

"I can't get through to him, either," Misty told him. "I'm about to head into work, so I'll swing by his place first and see if he's even home."

"If you don't mind, that would be great."

It was forty minutes before she called again.

"Quinn, something's wrong."

"What do you mean?" he asked.

Her words came out in a rush. "He didn't answer his door. I know the code to his place, so I let myself in."

"Slow down."

He could hear her take a few deep breaths.

"He's not here. But his bed's not made, and his glasses are still on his nightstand. He needs those these days."

"Maybe he has a second pair."

"His alarm clock is hanging by the cord over the edge of the stand, and the picture of his wife is on the floor, the glass broken."

Wife? Quinn didn't even know Peter was married. "What about her? She's not there, either?"

"Who?"

"His wife?"

"She's been dead for ten years."

"Oh. I didn't know."

A pause. "There's more."

"What?"

Another moment passed before she spoke again. "Some of the things on his dresser are knocked over." She hesitated. "It looks like there was a struggle. Quinn, what could have happened?"

Quinn made her go through the entire apartment, looking for anything unusual. Other than the disorder in the bedroom, though, nothing else stood out.

"Can you take the day off?" he asked.

"Of course."

"Good. I want you to stay there. I'm going to send someone to you who will give the apartment a thorough going over. Don't touch anything else, just sit down and wait."

"No problem."

"Give me the address."

Once he finished with Misty, he called Steven Howard.

"It's Quinn."

"Hey, what's up?"

"Where are you now?"

"Home." Home for Howard was Virginia, not far from DC.

"What's your day look like?"

"I'm open for the next seventy-two hours."

"Good. I need you to get to DC right away." He gave Howard Peter's address and filled him in on what he needed him to do. "Call me the second you're done."

"You got it."

"Thanks."

As he hung up, Orlando entered the kitchen, rubbing the sleep from her eyes.

"Was that Peter?" she asked.

He shook his head. "This might be an even bigger situation than we thought."

HOWARD CALLED JUST over an hour later. Using the camera on his phone, he gave Quinn, Orlando, and Daeng—who had joined them fifteen minutes earlier—a tour of Peter's apartment.

As Misty described earlier, the bedroom definitely showed signs of a struggle. In addition to the items she'd pointed out, Howard discovered spots of blood on the bed frame and in the hallway leading out to the living room.

"It's not a lot," he said. "So whatever it's from, the wound can't be that big."

"How long has it been there?"

"Hard to tell. It's all dry." The picture moved down toward the carpet, and Howard's rubber-gloved hand entered the frame. He touched a dark spot about four inches from the wall. The normally loose carpet fibers were stiff. "See? That's got to be a few days at least. Could be a lot longer, though. A lab might be able to figure it out."

The picture rose again as Howard stood.

"Something I want to show you in here," he told them.

He moved down the hall and into the living room. Almost every inch of wall space was covered with overflowing bookshelves. There were even more books stacked on the floor here and there. The furniture consisted of two easy chairs, a love seat, and coffee table. There was no TV.

For a moment, the camera caught Misty standing by the door, looking concerned, then it swung to the right and pointed once more toward the floor.

"See the books?" Howard asked.

While most of the image area was empty, there were four columns of books along one side. The two columns at either end were stacked neatly, but the two in the middle had been shoved back a few inches.

"I think they put him on the floor here," Howard said. "Look at this."

The image moved down again until it was just a couple inches above the carpet. Howard's finger moved back into the frame and rubbed across the surface. As it did, several tiny white spears, no more than an eighth of an inch long, jumped up and down. Howard pressed his finger against one of them, adhering it to the glove, and turned his hand so the spear was visible on the camera.

"Plastic," he said.

Both Quinn and Orlando had seen similar fragments before. Sometimes when plastic ties where used for handcuffs, the tips of the ridges could shear off, leaving behind spears just like the one Howard was holding.

Howard rose back to his feet, this time turning the camera around so he was looking into the lens. "I figure they surprised him in his bed, hauled him out here, and cuffed him. If it was me, I would have drugged him, too, so he didn't cause any problems on the way out."

The fact that they'd even found Peter, let alone broken into his place, was shocking. Peter was secretive even in the least threatening of situations. Quinn knew he had security in place that was at least on par with what Quinn himself employed, probably even better. Of course, even the best systems weren't perfect, and Quinn's methods hadn't always kept people out, either.

"Fingerprints?" Orlando asked.

"Checked the door when I first came in," Howard said. "It was clean. Spot-checked a few other places, too. Same thing. Could make another pass if you want, but I have a feeling I'm not going to find any."

Both Quinn and Orlando knew he was right.

"No. Not necessary," Quinn said. "Is that it?"

"So far. I want to do another look around, then check the building's common area and out front."

"Okay. Report back when you're done. Let me talk to Misty."

The image whipped around the room as Howard carried the phone over to Peter's former assistant and handed it to her. Though Quinn had talked to her hundreds of times on the phone, he'd met her in person only twice. The last time had been several years earlier. But it wasn't those intervening years that made her otherwise youthful face look aged this morning.

"Are you okay?" Quinn said.

"What do you think happened?" she asked as if she hadn't heard him.

"No way to know yet."

"You'll find out, though, right?"

"Yes."

"You promise?"

"I promise."

His words seemed to relax her, if only a bit. "If you need me to do anything, you just say the word. I can take some emergency leave. I have plenty of vacation time."

"Actually, there is something you can help with."

"What is it?"

"I need you to figure out the last time anyone saw him. Steve can help you. You can ask around there at his building, maybe talk to some of his friends."

"He doesn't really have a lot of friends."

"There's got to be some people he talks to now and then. Wherever they had him working, maybe."

She nodded.

"Whatever you do, though, be very careful. We don't

know what this is, and I don't want you walking into anything that'll get you in trouble."

"Don't worry about me. Just find Peter."

He gave her a reassuring smile. "Check in with me later."

"I will."

Quinn hung up.

"What the hell is going on?" Orlando said. "Nate *and* Peter?"

"Maybe what's happening to them isn't related," Daeng suggested.

Quinn and Orlando looked at him, their skepticism etched on their faces.

Daeng held up his hands defensively. "Or maybe it is."

Quinn knew Daeng had a point. They couldn't just assume the two disappearances were connected. The incidents had occurred sixteen hundred miles apart, in different countries, and Nate's main association with Peter was through Quinn. He'd seldom ever talked to Peter directly.

Then again, if those who'd done the taking thought Nate *was* Quinn...

"Maybe we should see if anyone else is missing," he said.

THEIR SEARCH WAS handicapped right from the start.

While Quinn and Orlando knew a fairly substantial number of people in the business, there were still plenty of others they'd never met. And pinpointing the current whereabouts of the ones they did know was not the easiest thing to do. It wasn't like there was some central switchboard operatives reported to, giving updates of their status. Usually if someone was suddenly unreachable, it was assumed they were on a gig.

When they finally took a break at noon, the list of potential missing contained over twenty people.

"We're not getting anywhere," Quinn said. "Most of them have got to be out on jobs." He frowned. "I think we might be wasting our time."

"No," Orlando said. "We're not." She glanced down the list of names. "Look, you're right. Most of these people probably are working. But this one..." Her finger stopped two thirds of the way down the list. "Alex Berkeley."

"What about him?"

"He works with a partner most of the time. Tom Benson. You know him, right?"

"Sure. I've worked with both of them."

"I talked to Tom. He said Alex had been hired on something that was supposed to last a week, tops, a surveillance thing that apparently didn't need both of them. He was supposed to be back a few days ago, but Tom hasn't heard from him. He's getting a bit annoyed because they have something scheduled for early next week."

"His project probably got extended."

"Probably," she admitted. "But you'd think Alex would have let Tom know."

"Maybe," Quinn said, unwilling to make the full leap just yet.

Orlando circled Berkeley's name and studied the list again.

"Hold on," she said. "I have an idea."

She pushed back from the dining table and went into the kitchen. Drawers and cabinets began opening and closing.

"Where do you keep your Post-its?" she called out a moment later.

"Used to be some in the drawer by the sink," he told her.

"Well, they're not here now."

"Try the pantry."

As her steps crossed the kitchen, the front door opened and Daeng walked in, carrying several bags.

"Who's hungry?" he said.

Quinn hadn't even thought about eating, but the intensifying aroma that preceded Daeng into the dining room was hard to resist.

"I've got two spicy chicken *banh mi*, two barbecue pork, some spring rolls, and a couple containers of *pho* we can split."

141

"I thought you were getting Thai?" Quinn said.

"I was, but I passed by a couple of those food trucks and wanted to check them out. One of them was Vietnamese food and looked too good to pass up."

"I'll take a spicy chicken," Orlando said as she walked back into the dining area, carrying three different-colored pads of Post-its and a bottle of Sriracha hot sauce.

While Daeng handed out the lunch, she set the hot sauce on the table, wrote NATE on a light blue Post-it, and stuck it to the window. Next, she wrote PETER on one of the same color, and put his name right below Nate's. On a yellow note, she wrote Berkeley, and started a new column on the window. Finally, she wrote out individual green ones for the other twenty-two names and gave them a third column.

She touched the glass above Nate's name. "Assuming Nate and Peter are connected, these are our known missing," she said. She moved her fingers to the yellow column. "Our possibles." To the green. "And our pool of potentials. When we can rule someone out, we'll start a fourth column."

"And what color will that be?" Quinn asked, an eyebrow raised. "I don't want to get confused."

"You only have the three colors, so it'll also be green, jerk."

He took a bite of his pork sandwich, and nodded at her makeshift bulletin board. "You're missing a name."

She looked at the glass. "Whose name?"

"Mine."

"Right." She wrote Quinn on a blue piece, put parentheses around it, and butted the square against Nate's. She then repositioned Peter's Post-it so that it was centered beneath them. "Okay, now look at the names. Anything stand out?"

Quinn set his sandwich down and examined the Post-its. "Well, the obvious connection is that I've worked with everyone up there, but that doesn't really get us anywhere."

"Just concentrate on you and Nate and Peter and Berkeley. Anything you all have in common? Any jobs you may have worked on together? Anything."

He frowned. "We've all worked together over the years. Nate not so much, of course, but sometimes." He looked at Orlando. "I could come up with a dozen or more connections that might or might not mean anything."

She turned back to the names and stared at them for several seconds. "We need to narrow down the pool."

As much as he thought they might be going down the wrong road, he didn't see what else they could do at this point.

After they quickly finished lunch, Quinn called the next name on his contact list. As he was in the middle of what he realized would be another fruitless call, Orlando yelled, "Quinn!"

He put a hand over his phone and whispered, "What is it?"

"I just got a ping."

"Sally, I'm sorry," he said into his cell. "I need to get off the phone. I might call you back later. Is that okay?"

"That's fine," the woman told him.

"Thanks."

He hung up and moved behind Orlando. On the screen of her computer was the program she'd set up to automatically ping Nate's emergency beacon until it made a connection. Which, according to the display, had finally happened.

"Can you get a location?" he asked.

"I'm trying. The signal's weak. I just need a little more—dammit!"

The readout in the program window switched from CONNECTED to SIGNAL LOST.

She tried to reestablish the link, but after a few minutes, it was clear it wasn't happening. She set the software on automatic, and opened a new window that was filled end to end and top to bottom with what looked to Quinn like a single string of numbers and letters. She scrolled through it carefully, her head angling back and forth as she scanned each row.

When she reached the bottom, she grunted in frustration and leaned back. "Partial coordinates. I can get us a range based on which satellite picked up the signal, but that's it."

"A range is better than nothing," Quinn said.

Not looking happy, she said, "Yeah, but I was hoping for more. Hold on." She ran the numbers through another program, and a map appeared on the screen. "Here's what we've got: St. Louis, Missouri, in the north; Trujillo, Honduras, in the south; Hermosillo, Mexico, in the west; and Roseau, Dominica, in the east."

The area included, among other things, pretty much the entire southern US, the Caribbean, and a good chunk of Mexico, with a little bit of Central America thrown in.

"Northern Mexico," he said, pointing at the map. He thought for a moment. "Can you bring up that news report about that manhunt?"

Before going to bed the previous night, Orlando had done a search of news sites serving northeastern Mexico to see if there was anything about the manhunt Pullman had mentioned. The only article she found was about a search police had conducted for someone they were calling "an important operator" in the drug trade. It had taken place in Reynosa, though, not Monterrey. And while witnesses said they saw someone taken into custody and flown away on a helicopter, the police had yet to confirm that. The timing was right, especially if Nate was making a run for the border, but it seemed iffy at best.

They had planned to make some follow-up calls once people woke up in the morning, but the disappearance of Peter and the possibility of even more missing had pushed the manhunt to a back burner.

Perhaps that had been a mistake.

Orlando opened a web browser, and brought up the bookmarked article. It was in Spanish, but that wasn't a problem. Both Quinn and Orlando spoke it fluently.

Quinn leaned in as he skimmed through the piece, stopping a third of the way down. There was a quote from a captain in the Federal Police, and a photograph that must have been his official police portrait.

"This guy," he said. "Captain Eduardo Moreno. Can you

find a number where we can contact him?"

"Give me a second."

It took more than a second, but not much. "This is interesting," she said. "He's not based in Reynosa."

"Where, then?'

She glanced at him. "Monterrey."

Quinn felt the tingling he got when he started making connections. Monterrey, where the job Nate had been working on was located. Where, if Burke was to be believed, several police cars had been waiting to intercept them. If they were actual officers and not just men dressed up in uniforms, someone would have had to organize them. Someone in a position of authority.

There are no coincidences.

"Maybe it would be better if we talked to the captain in person," he said. If Moreno was involved, he was the best lead they had so far, and the last thing Quinn wanted to do was scare him off with a phone call.

As Orlando returned her attention to her computer, Quinn looked over at Daeng. "US passport?"

"I have two."

"Break one out. We're going to Mexico."

CHAPTER
TWENTY TWO

AT WHAT HE guessed was around eleven a.m., Nate heard a door open somewhere outside his cell. It was too far away to belong to one of the rooms his neighbors were being held in, and seemed to be coming from a different direction than that of the courtyard he'd had dinner in the previous evening.

Several seconds passed, then he heard footsteps. Three...no, four pairs. As they neared, he moved over to the vent and scrunched down so he could look through the thin slats.

The light in the corridor was dim, but more than enough for him to see the feet as they walked by. There were three pairs of dark work boots, and one of men's black sneakers. The person in sneakers was between two of the people in boots, and it was clear they were assisting him.

The steps went on for another couple of seconds, then stopped. A door opened, this one much nearer than before. Intermixed with the shuffling of feet was a firm "In," then the door slammed shut, the locking rods shifted up and down, and the three booted pairs of feet walked away.

Apparently the new member of their party had arrived.

Things remained quiet for twenty minutes, then Lanier called out like he had with Nate. The new guy, though, didn't respond. Nate was willing to bet he'd been nearly unconscious when he was dumped off and completely knocked out now.

Back on his mattress, Nate pulled the threadbare blanket

over his legs and leaned against the wall. It wasn't that he was cold. He wanted to access the storage compartment in his prosthetic leg. Though he hadn't spotted a camera, it was safer to assume one was tucked away somewhere, keeping tabs on him.

Acting like his leg itched, he reached under the blanket and pulled his pant leg up over his fake calf. He separated the seam just enough so he could open the storage container and remove the bolt he'd hidden away. It was doing him no good just hitching a ride. If he was going to use it—as a weapon or whatever—it needed to be accessible.

He pulled at the shaft, but the bolt didn't move. Confused, he tried to get the tip of his finger all the way around it so he could give it a tug. The bottom end seemed to be jammed into the crevasse where the back panel and the side one met. The head of the bolt had been shoved up into the top of the container.

It took him a moment, but finally he got it to pop free. It wasn't the only thing he suddenly felt in his hand. He pulled it up so he could take a look. In addition to the bolt was a black piece of plastic that looked very much like part of the button that activated his emergency beacon.

He slipped his finger back into the container. It was part of the button, all right. He could feel where the bolt had pressed against it and broken it off. He wiggled his finger around and found that the entire button felt loose.

Was the beacon still on?

He cursed under his breath. He knew the container had been a tight fit for the bolt, but he hadn't had a choice. He played with the button for a moment, hoped the beacon was still active, and closed his leg again.

Clenching the bolt in his fingers, he lay back down and closed his eyes.

It's fine, he told himself. *It still works.*

Whether that was true or not, there wasn't a thing he could do about it, so he focused on trying to figure out why he was here. Once more, he was unable to come up with a satisfying answer.

At some point he drifted off, and found himself standing on the beach in Santa Monica, Liz beside him.

"Don't leave," she told him.

"I'm just going for a swim."

"Stay here."

"Liz, I'll be right there," he said, pointing at the water. "You can watch me the whole time."

He swam out through the waves and stopped just past where the swells began. He treaded water in a circle, turning back to the shore, intending to give Liz a wave.

Only the shore wasn't there. Just more ocean.

"Liz?" he called out. "Liz?"

There was no answer.

"HEY, NEW GUY. You awake yet?"

Nate shook off his sleep and rose on an elbow.

"New guy. Can you hear me? Hey!"

For a few seconds, Nate thought Lanier was talking to him. Then he remembered the person who'd been escorted in that morning.

He moved over to the door and leaned down by the vent.

"I think it's a trick," Berkeley said. "No one's down there."

"There *is* someone," Lanier said. "I heard the door."

"You're right," Nate said. "They put him in a room down here by me."

"Have you heard him?" Lanier asked.

"No. Nothing since he arrived."

"I still think it's a trick," Berkeley said.

"New guy," Lanier whispered loudly. "Can you hear us?"

No answer.

"New guy."

Silence.

CHAPTER
TWENTY THREE

HARRIS ENTERED THE suite and found Romero sitting in his wheelchair behind his desk, writing.

"Well?" his employer asked, without looking up.

"The shooter has arrived. He's a little banged up."

Romero's head shot up. "Why?"

"He apparently wasn't in a cooperative mood when he was taken."

Romero thought for a moment, then waved a hand in the air. "As long as he's alive, that's all that matters. So, they're all here now."

"Yes, sir," Harris said.

"And the schedule?"

"Set. Tonight I'll have dinner with Curson, and first thing tomorrow morning we begin."

"The camera? You haven't forgotten?"

"It will all be recorded as you requested."

"Good." A smile appeared on Romero's face. "I want to see everything immediately after the session."

"Of course. That won't be a problem."

CHAPTER
TWENTY FOUR

THE DAY BEFORE, as Liz listened to her brother's message telling her he and Orlando would be heading back to L.A. that evening, an idea began to form in her mind. She'd been feeling frustrated just sitting there alone, waiting for others to find Nate. That wasn't the way she operated. She was far from helpless and was used to tackling problems head on. Not that this was the normal kind of complication that usually came up in her life, but if she and Nate were going to have a future together, she needed to learn how to deal with it.

The problem was that when Jake and Orlando returned, she knew her brother would tell her as little as he could afford to. He may have seen it as a way to protect her, but to Liz it was unacceptable.

She needed to be looking for Nate, too. To do that, she needed to know the same things her brother did. Then the idea hit her—a way of putting herself firmly in the loop. She thought it through as thoroughly as she could, and when she was ready, she wrote her brother a note and left the house.

The first part of the plan was deception. She had to make sure Jake thought she was out of the way. Nate had once shown her how easy it was to lock on a cell phone signal and track its location. She had no doubt her brother would do just that when he realized she was gone. So to convince him that she had left, she drove all the way to San Diego, and spent the night in a small motel called The Otter House.

Early the next morning, she spotted a delivery truck

behind the building. While the driver was filling a vending machine, she put her phone on silent mode, and tucked it into the truck's glove compartment. Though she didn't have the training her brother and her boyfriend had, she was the smartest of the three, and remembered everything she'd heard them talk about. Putting the phone in the truck meant that during the day, her location would seem to be moving around, like she was driving aimlessly through the city, thinking.

Her location deception set, she headed back north, arriving in Jake's neighborhood at a quarter after two. Since she was driving his car, she parked on a side street not too far away, then snuck back and input her code into the gate security pad. She eased the gate open and peeked inside.

No cars in the driveway.

She walked quietly over to the house and looked through the windows as best she could, but the ones along the front were not designed to provide much of a view inside.

I'm sure it worked, she told herself. *It had to.*

She thought for a moment. If they were already gone, she was wasting valuable time. But if they were still here?

Just say you forgot something, and keep the conversation to a minimum.

She took a deep breath, put on her best distressed face, and let herself in the front door.

The house was as quiet as it had been the day she'd first arrived.

"Hello?" she called out. "Anyone here? It's Liz."

Dead silence.

As she walked through the living room, she began to worry that maybe Jake and Orlando *hadn't* come back yet. If that were true, she wasn't any better off than she'd been the day before. She scanned the living room. Everything looked exactly like it had been when she'd walked out the door. She glanced over at the dining room table. Even the note was still there.

Hold on.

She walked over to take a closer look. She had left the note facing up, and near the center of the table. Now it was flipped down, and a bit off to the side.

Someone *had* been here.

Moving into the kitchen, she checked the trash can. There were food wrappers and a couple of takeout boxes.

So not just one person. At least two.

Jake and Orlando.

Her hopes began to rise.

She all but ran through the living room, and down the hall to the linen closet on the other side of the bathroom.

Please, please...

Inside on the left was a hidden moveable panel. She had seen Nate open it only once. It had been on her first visit as he'd shown off the house to her. He'd let her in on quite a few secrets that day, probably more than he realized.

She opened the panel, activated the touch screen, and navigated to the sound recording control window. The presets she'd checked off were still in place: VOICE ACTIVATED, COMPLETE HOUSE. She opened the log of recordings. There were dozens, some brief, some considerably longer.

Nate had said Jake had installed it in case of emergencies, but hardly ever put it to use. There were cameras, too, both still and motion, but she hadn't bothered with them.

The only question now was, had they discovered where Nate was? Listening at double speed and working backward from the last recording, she had her answer seven and a half minutes later.

"This is interesting." Orlando's voice. *"He's not based in Reynosa."*

"Where, then?" Jake asked.

"Monterrey."

"Maybe it would be better if we talked to the captain in person." A pause. *"US passport?"*

"I have two." A new voice. Male, but not one Liz recognized.

"Break one out. We're going to Mexico."

She listened for another ten minutes to see if there was anything else important, then erased the recordings, closed the panel, and bought a ticket online to Monterrey.

CHAPTER
TWENTY FIVE

THOUGHT STILL HOT, the temperature had begun to dip.

Sun's down, Nate thought.

As if heralding the passing of day to night, he heard a door open. Three sets of heavy footsteps pounded down the hallway, and didn't stop until they reached the door of the newest prisoner.

Nate moved into position by the vent again, and was there in plenty of time to see them walk back by, this time accompanied by the man in the sneakers.

Seconds later, the door opened and shut again, and quiet returned.

Nate waited a few minutes, then said, "Did you see him?"

"See him?" Lanier asked. "Do you have a window?"

"No. Through the vent."

"Mine's angled down. Can't see a damn thing."

"Same here," Berkeley said.

"I saw him." The voice was a croak from farther away.

"Who the hell is that?" Lanier asked.

"It's the guy across from me," Berkeley said.

The one who'd been there a while, but hadn't responded in the past.

"Hey, buddy," Lanier said. "You all right?"

There was a grunt. It could have been a yes, or it could have been a none-of-your-business.

"What's your name?"

"Not important," the man said, his croak replaced by a gravelly bass.

"However you want to play it. Me, I'm Lanier. The guy across from you is Berkeley. And down there at the other end is Quinn."

It was quiet for a second before the man said, "Quinn, huh?"

Feeling the need to reply, Nate said, "Yeah. That's me."

The man let out a low laugh. "Okay. Call me Jonathan, then."

Both Lanier and Berkeley said hello, but Nate kept quiet. He had no doubt the man in the far cell had chosen the name Jonathan just to send the message he knew Nate wasn't Quinn.

"What's your specialty, Jonathan?" Lanier asked. "I assume you're in the biz."

"Whatever needs doing."

"A jack?"

"Sure."

The more the man talked, the more Nate couldn't help thinking he knew the voice, but he couldn't put a name to it.

"So Jonathan, why haven't you answered us before?" Lanier asked.

"I didn't hear you."

"We've been trying to talk to you for days."

Silence.

"How long have I been here?" the man asked.

"You came here right after I did."

"And how long is that?"

"I've been here eight days."

More silence.

"You okay in there?" Lanier asked.

Quiet.

"Hey, Jonathan. You still with us?"

A few more seconds of nothing, then a grunt like before, followed by, "I'm going to get some sleep."

"All right," Lanier said, sounding disappointed. "We'll be here when you wake up." His next words were directed at

Nate and Berkeley. "Either of you come up with any fresh ideas on how we get out of here?"

They talked for another few minutes, but no one had anything concrete.

Finally, Nate said, "I'm going to get some rest, too."

Putting a hand on the door, he started to push himself up, but his palm slipped, hitting the frame of the vent.

Unexpectedly, it moved.

He stared at it. Even if he could get the grill off, the hole would be too narrow for him to crawl through. That didn't mean it couldn't be useful, though.

Making sure his body shielded the vent from any potential camera in the room, he tugged on the frame. It moved again, creating a thin gap between it and the door. He tried again, but apparently it had gone as far as it could. If he had a hammer or a crowbar, he could have worked the tip into the gap and lever the grill out in seconds. But his holding cell had come equipped with neither.

He studied the gap, and wondered for a moment.

Maybe...

He worked the bolt out of his pocket, flipped it around, and lowered the cap end into the gap. Sure enough, his instinct had been right. Almost a perfect fit.

Working his way from one end to the other, he levered the bolt back and forth, expanding the length of the gap all the way across. Then he did the same on the ends. The bottom was the hardest part because he couldn't see what he was doing, but by the time he finished his first full pass, the frame had pulled away from the door a full quarter inch.

The second go-around was easier, and he was able to increase the gap half an inch more.

Before proceeding any further, he leaned as far down as he could and looked through the slats. He was worried that the front part of the frame might fall out into the hallway if it lost the support of the back half. If that happened, the bang would surely bring guards running. But the positioning of the front portion looked unchanged. In fact, now that the back had separated some from the front, he could see that the vent slats were actually attached to the front half.

That was good. He could actually do something to ensure the front didn't fall out.

He hurried over to the mattress and spent several minutes pulling loose four long pieces of thread. Back at the vent, he carefully worked an end of one of the strings over a slat, and used the barrel of the bolt to snag it and bring it back in. He tied it off, and repeated the procedure with the remaining strings.

Once more, he began working the back half of the frame out of the opening. It was slower going now, as he had to use one hand to hold the strings so that the front half wouldn't fall out.

It took twenty minutes for it to finally pop free. When it did, he tried to grab it to keep it from falling, but success only came at the expense of losing control of the bolt. It slipped from his hand and clattered onto the floor. As quickly as he could, he smothered it with his leg.

"What was that?" Lanier asked. "Did you guys hear that?"

"I didn't hear anything," Berkeley said.

"Quinn, you awake? You hear that sound?"

Nate held still.

"Quinn?" Lanier paused. "Hey, Quinn."

"He's asleep," Berkeley said. "Just let him be."

"You didn't hear that noise?"

"I didn't hear anything."

"It sounded like metal or something."

"Nope. Sorry."

"Jonathan, how about you?" Lanier asked.

There was no response from the man with the gravelly voice.

Soon, quiet returned to the hallway. Nate remained motionless, sure that Lanier was listening at his own vent for any new noise.

If they had all been in the same cell, he would have been happy to show them what he was doing, but blind to each other like they were, he couldn't take the chance. There was no way to know what kind of surveillance there might be in the hallway. Hell, for all he knew, Lanier or even Berkeley might not even be in a cell at all, and could be guards trying to get him talking.

It was best to keep what he was doing to himself.

He waited ten minutes before deciding it was okay to work again. With exceeding care, he did a hand dance between extracting the rear frame and holding the strings that ran through the middle of it as he lowered the frame to the floor.

All right, so will the front pop out as easily as the back did?

He eased the strings forward a little, giving them some play. The slats and front frame didn't move. With his other hand, he gently pushed the back of the top slat. No movement. Pushing on the bottom had the same response. It wasn't until he alternated back and forth rapidly that he got it to walk itself out.

He continued to push top, bottom, top, bottom until the frame neared the edge. There, he paused, examined his progress, then pushed harder on the top than the bottom. As he'd hoped, the upper part moved out of the opening first. The moment the bottom slipped free, the whole frame dropped toward the corridor floor, but the strings saved it from crashing to the ground.

Gripping the strings in his left hand, Nate turned his body so that his right shoulder was aligned with the opening. He stuck his arm out, testing how far he could reach. The narrowness of the vent stopped him about midway on his bicep, but it was enough to get his elbow outside, so he could bend it in different directions. It was enough to grab a leg, or maybe even a gun if the opportunity presented itself.

Satisfied, he moved his arm back into the cell, and pulled up on the strings so that he could set the frame back into the opening. It was only partway up, though, when the door at the far end started to open.

Too well trained to panic, Nate focused on raising it the remaining distance. Just before footsteps started down the hall, the frame reached the hole and he pulled it in as much as he dared, hoping it was far enough in the hole not to be noticed.

The strings, though, could still be a problem. He couldn't slip them off now without the risk of being noticed. He kept them taut so that they were as flush to the slats as possible, and watched through the vent as the footsteps neared. He half expected the men to stop right outside, but the booted feet continued by, the man in the sneakers once again being escorted between them.

As soon as they'd dropped off their prisoner and left, Nate seated the frame the rest of the way in the hole, removed the strings, and put the rear portion back in place.

CHAPTER
TWENTY SIX

NORTHEASTERN MEXICO

QUINN SPENT THE flight to Mexico thinking once more about the names on the Post-its.

Nate, Peter, and potentially Berkeley? Quinn, Peter, and potentially Berkeley?

Whatever the combination, he couldn't see the through-line yet, the connection.

Breaking it down to smaller groups made it even worse. He and Peter had interacted so much over the years, it would be nearly impossible to pinpoint anything specific the disappearances might be related to.

To a lesser extent, the same was true of Nate and Peter's relationship, the difference being only the number of jobs Nate had worked on since he'd entered the business versus those Quinn had done for the Office.

The wild card was Berkeley.

As far as Quinn knew, there were only six missions they had worked on together. He'd also never had a lot of interaction with the guy, more just "hello"s and "how you doing?"s during briefings.

The image he had of Berkeley was of a quiet man, efficient, a guy who stuck to whatever guidelines he'd been given until told to do otherwise. A team player, not a mission leader.

Quinn spent an hour thinking through each job they'd shared. The gigs had been spread out over a five-year period. None, as far as he knew, were tied to each other. Each mission had gone smoothly—the target taken down, the body disposed of.

Think wider, he told himself. *What about the others on each job?* He created a list in his head of names, and checked them off against his mental picture of the twenty-two green Post-its Orlando had created of the potential missing.

On three of the jobs, there were no matches at all. Two jobs, though, had single matches, and the final job actually had two. But none of the missions were filled completely by the names that had been on his window.

He focused on the three with matches, but still nothing stood out.

Frustrated, he looked past the sleeping Orlando and out the window at the night sky.

Maybe it had nothing to do with the jobs at all. Maybe it was random. Maybe the disappearances were not even connected.

Words echoed through his head. *Maybe Nate's already dead.*

No. Not possible. And not even something he wanted to consider.

But try as he might, he could only dampen the voice, not silence it.

THE RED EYE got them into Monterrey at just after five a.m. As soon as they cleared Customs and Immigration, Orlando pulled out her computer and pinged Nate's emergency beacon.

"Nothing," she said, annoyed.

"Maybe his battery died," Daeng suggested.

"Impossible," Orlando said. "The signal's passive, so it draws very little power. The battery that feeds it could last months."

"We'll try again later," Quinn said. "Let's go."

Much to Orlando's displeasure, she had been unable to

locate Captain Moreno's residence, so they would have to talk to him once he was at work. Given the time, that wouldn't happen for several hours. There was something else, though, that Quinn wanted to do in the meantime.

They picked up a rental car, and skirted around the edge of the still-sleeping city. Their destination was the set of coordinates Orlando had been able to dig out of Pullman's computer for the warehouse where Senator Lopez had been terminated. Quinn didn't expect to find anything there that might tell them where Nate was, but he wanted to take a look at it and get a feel for the mission his former apprentice had been on.

They found the large gray building just after the sun came up. It had multiple loading bays lining one side, and two cars parked at the end. The gate of the chain-link fence that surrounded the property was closed, but there was an intercom box mounted to a standalone pipe off to the side.

"I got this," Orlando said. She jumped out of the car.

She was at the intercom for half a minute, then jogged back and climbed in.

Quinn looked over. "Well?"

"Patience," she told him.

Several seconds later, a door at the near end of the building opened. A lean man with black hair and sun-darkened skin, wearing a security guard uniform, exited. As he walked across the dirt lot, Orlando climbed out again and met him at the fence.

After a quick conversation, the man unlocked a chain and rolled the gate out of the way. Orlando motioned for Quinn to drive through, and she and the guard followed on foot.

"This is Hector," she told Quinn and Daeng once they'd climbed out of the sedan.

"*Buenos días*," Quinn said.

"*Buenos días, señor*," Hector replied. He exchanged similar greetings with Daeng.

"Hector, *necesito un momento para hablar con mis colegas*," Orlando said.

162

"*Por supuesto.*" Hector smiled and walked several feet away.

Orlando, Quinn, and Daeng circled together.

"I told him we're from an American company looking for new warehouse space," she said. "I think he doesn't much care who we are, but I promised him a hundred dollars if he lets us look around."

"I'm assuming he's not alone here."

"Just him and another guy."

"Either of them speak English?"

"Hector doesn't. I don't know about the other one."

"Okay," Quinn said. He pulled out a small stack of folded bills, peeled off five twenties, then added three more. "Tell him the extra's for his friend."

While Quinn could have easily told the man himself, it was always better in situations like this for one person to act as translator.

Orlando gave the money to Hector, and he led them inside. The warehouse space was like most warehouse spaces—big, wide, and full of boxes.

"Ask him how long this stuff has been here," Quinn said.

"*¿Normalmente, cuanto tiempo se quedan aquí los envíos antes de salir otra vez?*" Orlando asked Hector.

The man shrugged. "*Tres o cuatro días. A veces una semana.*"

She nodded as if she'd learned something interesting. "*¿Y este inventario? ¿Cuanto tiempo lleva aquí?*"

"*Cinco días. La mayoría sale esta tarde y en la noche llegan más.*"

"Ah. Okay, *gracias*," she said. She turned to Quinn and Daeng, and played the part of interpreter. "Their turnover's a little slow. He says sometimes up to a week. The stuff here's been waiting for five days. Says it'll be gone this afternoon, though."

"Thank you," Quinn said, looking over at Hector. Then, with an intentionally imperfect accent, added, "*Gracias.*"

"*De nada*," Hector said.

"Can we wander around?"

Orlando translated the question, and Hector nodded, telling them they could go wherever they wanted, and that he'd be in the small office near the front when they were done.

"*Gracias* again," Quinn said.

Once Hector was gone, they headed down the middle of the aisle, and turned down the row Burke had told them had been used for the Lopez hit. Nate had done an excellent job of cleaning up. There were no bloodstains and no signs of any struggle. In fact, the only thing unusual was that about a dozen of the boxes were empty.

"All right," Quinn said. "So this is where it started." He crouched down in front of the empty boxes. "Wrap up the body, clean up any loose ends." He looked back down the aisle. "And get the hell out of here."

"Same as always," Daeng said.

"This part," Quinn agreed. "But not the rest." He stood back up and looked over at Orlando. "Find out from our friend if anyone else has been out for a visit in the last couple of days."

Orlando nodded, and headed off toward the office. Quinn gave the vanished crime scene one final look-over before he and Daeng headed out.

They found Orlando standing in the doorway to Hector's office.

"No one unusual," she said.

"Not even the police?"

"Nope."

Hector accompanied them back outside.

"*Gracias*," Quinn said as he shook the man's hand. "*Muchas gracias*."

Back on the road, they followed the route Burke had told them Nate had taken, stopping briefly near the point they guessed Nate had done his lights-off-turn-around maneuver, but instead of going back toward Monterrey, they continued on to where the cops had been waiting. There they stopped and climbed out. Dozens of tire tracks covered the ground, some less eroded than others, but they could have belonged to anyone. Down the canyon, they found the hole Nate had dug in the ground, untouched and waiting for its body.

Back on the highway, they drove toward Monterrey, looking for where Nate had dumped his van. Burke had said they'd driven behind a row of buildings near a gas station. It wasn't the most exact description ever, but when Quinn spotted the Pemex sign, he had a feeling it was the one Burke meant. He turned down the road between the station and a row of shops that faced the highway, and again down the road behind the buildings.

Two thirds of the way down, he knew for sure they had found the right place. Though Nate's van was no longer there, there were scorch marks and soot on the cinderblock wall. Not a lot, but enough to indicate a fire that was started but not allowed to reach its full potential.

"And from here, he ran," Orlando said as they stood in front of the wall.

"Apparently not far enough," Quinn said.

He stared at the black marks, his frustration returning. He glanced at his watch. "All right. We've seen it all. It's time to talk to the cop."

CHAPTER
TWENTY SEVEN

WHEN LIZ SAW her brother and Orlando waiting at the departure gate at LAX for the flight to Monterrey, she had not been surprised in the slightest. Though they hadn't mentioned on the recordings she'd listened to what airline they would be taking, Orlando had mentioned the time of their flight. Liz would have preferred to take another flight, but she knew her only chance was if she arrived before or at the same time they did. Before wasn't an option.

She noticed a man standing with them, and realized he had to be the third voice she'd heard. There was no mistaking Daeng. He looked just like the picture Nate had shown her once.

Hanging back, she waited until boarding was all but completed, then presented her ticket and walked onto the plane as the last passenger. Her hope was that if she got on board right before the doors closed, even if her brother did see her, it would be too late to leave her behind without causing a scene—something she was sure he would not want to do.

But she needn't have worried. He didn't see her. Upon entering the aircraft, she had turned right and headed to her seat two rows from the back, not seeing either her brother, Orlando, or Daeng anywhere in the economy section. Apparently, they had booked themselves business-class seats, and instead of going right had gone left when they entered.

At passport control in Monterrey, she'd pressed her luck and followed as closely as she could, afraid that if she gave them too much room, she'd lose them. She positioned herself so that she would be helped by a different passport officer a few stations down, and was fortunate enough to actually finish before them. She walked quickly through Customs and lost herself in the crowd on the other side, keeping an eye on the exit.

When the three others emerged, they paused for a moment to talk before heading through the terminal to one of the booths along the wall. Though her Spanish wasn't perfect, the sign above the booth clearly indicated it was a car rental agency.

She tensed, knowing that if she tried to rent a car herself, she'd never be able to keep up with them. Her only option would be to grab a taxi.

Once Jake and the others finished up, one of the clerks led them over to the door and outside. Liz took the exit fifty feet away, and watched as they climbed into a van with the name of the agency on the side.

She looked around until she spotted the line of taxis. She sprinted over to the one in front and jumped in.

"*¿A donde?* " the driver asked.

"That van," she said in English, pointing out the window. "Follow it."

CHAPTER
TWENTY EIGHT

"**UP!**" **THE SHOUT** came from down the hall. "Up, up, up!"

Every word was emphasized by a loud bang of something knocking against the wall.

Nate opened his eyes, suddenly alert. The lights in the hallway had come on, and seeped through his door vent, creating a rectangle of illumination on his floor.

"Up! Everyone. Wake now!"

As Nate pushed himself to his feet, the overhead bulb came on. He blinked several times, shuffled over to the toilet, and relieved himself. As he was zipping up his pants, the door behind him opened.

Janus took a step into the room, with one of the fatigues-clad soldiers following.

"I said up. I not say play with self," Janus said.

A thousand comebacks played through Nate's head, but he kept his mouth shut.

"Put this on."

Janus tossed something at him. As Nate caught it, he realized it was a black bag similar to the one put over his head when he'd been captured.

"Put it on," Janus repeated.

As much as Nate wanted to just throw it right back, doing so would only result in him being used as a punching bag. He pulled it over his head.

"Tie string," Janus said.

Nate started to tie off the cord that encircled the opening.

"Pull tighter first, so cannot take off your head."

Nate decreased the size of the opening and then tied it off.

"Good. Now hands out front."

Nate held his hands out. Instead of the plastic ties that had been used to this point, his hands were locked together in a much heavier set of cuffs that were wide, almost like wristbands.

"Bring him." This time the words weren't for Nate.

A hand he assumed belonged to the soldier grabbed his arm and yanked him into the hallway.

"No move." A different voice, the soldier's.

Nate stood in the middle of the hall and listened as Janus repeated the bag-and-cuffs routine from room to room. Soon, though he couldn't see them, he knew his four fellow prisoners were standing in the corridor with him.

"Everyone. Turn to my voice," Janus ordered.

As soon as Nate turned, the soldier grabbed him again and started pushing him forward.

It must have been an odd sight, the five black-bagged men walking down the stone hallway with at least one fatigue-wearing escort and probably more And Janus—*can't forget him*, Nate thought—the big dumb blond man leading the way.

If Lanier was right, and he and the others had been pretty much left alone since they'd arrived, then this little exercise was something new. Of course, the bald guy—Harris—had intimated they were waiting for only one more person to arrive. That had happened the day before, meaning the period of just sitting around was apparently over.

They were moved through several doors, and the echo of the hallway disappeared. A breeze pushed the side of the bag against Nate's cheek. They were outside. The courtyard again, Nate suspected, given the stone beneath his feet.

"Stop!"

The soldier clamped down on Nate's arm, halting him.

"Put them in their places." Harris's voice.

The soldier turned Nate forty-five degrees, then pulled

him backward until Nate's heel bumped into a solid surface.

"Step up," the soldier said.

Reluctantly, Nate raised his foot, sliding his heel against the surface until he passed above it. He moved his foot back, set it down, and pulled up his other foot.

"Back again," the soldier said.

Nate moved his foot backward and hit another rising surface. Stairs?

"Up!" the soldier said impatiently.

Nate did as he was told.

"Stay," the soldier said.

Okay, maybe not stairs. Whatever it was, he was now a good two and a half feet above the level of the courtyard. He tried to remember if he'd seen anything the night he had dinner with Harris that might match what he was standing on, but he couldn't recall anything.

He stood where he was for what seemed like forever, with only the sound of the breeze blowing against his hood as company. The others must be nearby, but no one was talking. After a while, he could feel the air warming, and knew the sun had risen.

"Hey!" It was Lanier. "Hey, what's going on? You can't just let us—" His words were capped by a *thud*, followed by a grunt of pain.

Then silence again.

More heat as the sun continued to climb into the sky.

Finally, there was a noise, at first nearly unnoticeable, a distant whine that could have easily been just a trick of his mind. But as it grew louder, it became impossible to ignore.

A motor. Electric, if Nate wasn't mistaken.

It entered the area they were in, moved along behind them, then circled in front and stopped.

The quiet returned, only this time it was short-lived.

"Good morning, gentlemen," Harris said.

From the sound of his voice, he was standing very near where the motor had stopped. Nate also got the sense he was lower, still at ground level.

"I trust you've enjoyed your stay so far," the man said.

No one replied.

"I'll take that for a yes. To start off this morning, my employer—your host—would like to have a word."

The sound of a throat clearing, then, "It pleases me to no end to see you all here." Though there was no denying the strength underlining this new voice, it also had a tremor that belied an older man. And an accent, Nate noted, like the soldier who'd grabbed him. Latin American, but Nate wasn't well versed enough to pin it down further than that. "This moment is one I have been anticipating for a long, long time. Just identifying you all was...an effort. But you're here now, and I no longer have to wait. Neither will you. So welcome, and we'll speak more later."

"Thank you, sir," Harris said. "Gentlemen, raise your arms."

"Why?" Berkeley blurted out.

There was a smack, and the man yelled in pain.

"Raise your arms," Harris said. "I won't repeat the order again."

Nate raised his arms until his cuffed hands hovered as high above his head as he could get them. If they were about to kill him, there was nothing he could do about it. But if they weren't, he needed to bide his time until there was an opportunity to do something.

He heard a metallic noise, like a ratchet. Three clicks. Someone unexpectedly grabbed his left forearm from above.

A moment later, metal slipped between his wrists and moved up until it was hooked through the cross section of his cuffs. The hand let go of him. For several seconds nothing happened. Then the ratcheting again, rapid fire, right above him, but whatever it was, it wasn't the only thing making the sound. There were more to his left and right. Five total, he guessed.

Click-click-click-click-click.

He felt the cuffs tug at his wrist as they were pulled upward.

Click-click-click-click-click.

Nate began rising off his pedestal, the cuffs digging into

171

the skin at the base of his palms. He pointed his toes downward, keeping them on whatever it was he was standing on as long as possible to help take on some of his weight.

Click-click-click-click-click.

Just before his toes would have lifted into the air, the noise stopped. Hands grabbed Nate's feet, tied a rope around his ankle, and secured him to the floor.

Beside him he could hear the same thing happening with his fellow prisoners.

"Do you feel helpless?" the older man asked. "Dangling there, unable to do anything? Do you?"

"Answer him," Harris said.

"Fuck off!" Lanier shot back.

The old man laughed.

"Answer him!"

No one else said a word.

"Even though you don't say it," the old man told them, "I *know* how helpless you are. I know what you are feeling. Consider this stage one of payback." Another laugh.

Payback? That was an unexpected choice of words.

A loud, chilling crack filled the air. The sound was impossible to mistake—the snap of a whip in the hand of someone who knew what they were doing.

"A bit old-fashioned, I admit," the old man said. "But I like it that way."

A pause, then the whip cracked again. Only this time it was followed by a cry of intense pain.

Nate counted twenty lashes. On the twenty-first, the next man in line began to scream.

Then the next, and the next.

Then it was Nate's turn.

CHAPTER
TWENTY NINE

QUINN LOOKED AT the picture on his phone, and back through his binoculars at the entrance to the police station. "That's him. The one on the left wearing the sunglasses." He watched the man for a moment, then said, "Daeng, you're on."

With a nod, Daeng handed his own binoculars to Orlando and took off. She stuffed it and the pair she'd been using into the bag she'd picked up at an outdoor market a couple blocks away. "All set."

Quinn lowered his binoculars and added them to the others. "Let's go."

They made their way through the streets to the abandoned building they'd found four blocks away from the station. Quinn checked the street to make sure no one was watching them, and then pushed the board that covered the window out of the way. Orlando entered first, and he followed right behind.

There were many ways they could have approached Captain Moreno—a discreet discussion at his office, buying him lunch and having a chat, or something a bit more direct. After Orlando finished digging into the man's life, it quickly became clear that option number three would be their best choice.

They checked the workroom they'd created, and found everything as it had been.

Quinn picked up the bottle of fake blood they'd whipped

up. "Are you ready?"

"Go ahead."

He squirted some of the sticky liquid into her hair, and let it drip down onto her forehead. He gave his work a critical eye. It wouldn't pass a close examination, but would be more than adequate for a quick look.

"You're good," he said.

She hopped onto her toes and kissed him.

He melted into her for a moment before he suddenly pulled back. "Hey, I don't want to get that stuff on me."

She pursed her lips. "Where's the trust?"

"Go," Quinn said. "They should be here any second."

She tapped the tip of her finger against the moist area in her hair, and wiped it off on Quinn's cheek. "Be right back." She headed quickly out of the room.

Quinn grabbed a discarded piece of paper off the ground and rid himself of the mark she'd given him. He followed after her, taking his position halfway between the boarded-up window, where Orlando was now waiting, and the workroom.

He heard a car drive by outside, and in the distance, a motorcycle in dire need of a tune-up. Then things quieted down. It was four minutes before he heard the footsteps—two pairs—hurrying along the street toward the building.

As they neared, he could make out Daeng's voice in the halting Spanish he'd picked up when he was a teenager in Los Angeles. It seemed their plan A had worked, and Daeng had been able to lure the man away on his own. If he hadn't been able to make it happen, they would have moved to plan B—isolation and forced relocation.

"*Ahí, ahí*," Daeng said. "*Más cerca.*" A pause. "*Aquí, aquí, aquí.*"

There was a bang on the board covering the window. Peeking around the pillar, Quinn could see Orlando standing next to the window, unmoving. The moment Daeng knocked again, she started panting as if she'd been running, and pushed the board to the side.

"Oh, thank God," she said, her voice panicked. "Back here. He's back here. We knocked him out and locked him in a storage room. Oh, oh, wait. You speak English, right?"

The cop, Eduardo Moreno, moved into the opening. "Tell me what happened."

Quinn leaned back out of sight as Orlando pushed the board further open so Moreno and Daeng could enter.

"It was horrible," she said, leading them through the room. "He seemed so nice, you know? Shared some beers. Said he knew a place we could spend the night that wouldn't cost us anything."

As they passed by Quinn's position, he circled around the pillar so that Moreno wouldn't see him.

"He brought us back here, and, you know, it seemed okay."

"You should have never come inside," Moreno said.

"I know, I know. It's just, well..."

Quinn stepped out from behind the pillar and followed, catching up to them just as they stopped a few feet shy of the workroom.

"He's in here," she said, sounding scared.

"It's okay. I'll take care of it," Moreno told her.

"Do...do you have a gun or something? I think he's dangerous."

"Don't worry. He won't hurt anyone."

Moreno moved his hand down toward his belt. At first Quinn thought the Federál was going for his gun, but instead, he pulled a cell phone out of his pocket.

"What are you doing?" Orlando asked.

"Don't worry. I am just calling for some of my men to come help me."

"Good idea," she said, sounding relieved. "Maybe...maybe you should check him first, though. I'm not sure how hard we hit him. You might, um, need to call an ambulance, too."

Moreno lowered the phone. "Show me."

Orlando opened the door and grabbed Moreno's arm, guiding him into the room. As soon as they passed inside, Quinn and Daeng followed, closing the door quietly behind them.

"Where is he?" Moreno asked. He froze as he noticed the chair sitting in the middle of the room. He turned back around, suspicion creeping onto his face. "What is—"

Quinn smiled as the man's gaze fell on him. "Captain Moreno, please have a seat."

Moreno's right hand shot toward the GLOCK 17 in the holster at his waist. Only it didn't get very far. The guiding hand Orlando had on his arm clamped down and yanked the man backward. Before Moreno could react, Daeng had a hold of his other arm, and Quinn took possession of the gun.

"What the hell's going on?" Moreno demanded. "Do you understand the trouble you're in? I'm a federal police officer. Let me go *right now!*"

"Sorry. No can do," Quinn said. "Have a seat."

"Let me go!"

Daeng and Orlando dragged the cop backward to the chair and shoved him down.

"I believe he said, have a seat," Orlando told him.

Daeng moved behind the chair so he could take hold of both the man's arms and free up Orlando. She, in turn, went over to the half-demolished cabinet they'd set their supplies on, and grabbed the rope they'd purchased on their supply run.

When Moreno saw what she was carrying, he tried to free his arms and jump up. That was a mistake. Daeng jerked the man's arms back and up, so the cop was forced to hunch his shoulders forward and remain in the chair.

Orlando looped a portion of the rope around one of the back chair legs and secured the man's wrists together. Once this was done, Daeng lowered the man's arms and Orlando removed the slack around the chair leg, pulling Moreno's hands tight against the back of the chair. After that, it was a quick job of securing his torso and tying his feet, one against each of the chair's front legs.

Finished, she stepped back and joined Quinn, while Daeng remained behind the cop.

"You all are in very deep trouble," Moreno said. "You will never get away with this."

Quinn, looking unimpressed, said, "Three days ago you were involved in a manhunt, correct?"

A flicker in the man's eyes. "You will let me go now."

"That's not going to happen. Answer the question."

"I'm not answering any questions."

"All right, that's a choice. Now let me give you another. Answer the question. If you don't, I'm going to blow out your joints one by one, starting with your right ankle." He pointed the captain's GLOCK at the man's foot. "So, were you or were you not part of the manhunt?"

His eyes smoldering with anger, the cop said, "Sure, yes. I was. Many people were."

"You're the one who organized and ran it, though."

"Someone had to. It was just my turn."

"Kind of out of your range, wasn't it? You're based down here, not Reynosa."

"I go where the investigation leads. Now let me go."

"Tell me, Captain Moreno. Do your Federál bosses know about your account in the Caymans? The one you just made a substantial deposit to?" He glanced at Orlando. "How much was it?"

"One hundred and fifty thousand dollars, US," she said, not missing a beat.

Moreno stared at them for a second, then forced out a laugh. "Is that what this is about? Money? You want my money?"

"Oh, we've already *taken* your money. The one hundred fifty thousand, plus the other one point seven million."

Now the captain was starting to look nervous. "You're lying."

Quinn shrugged. "Could be. I'm sure you'll check later. I mean, if there is a later. But you're wrong. This has nothing to do with your money."

"So you didn't take it?"

"Oh, we took it. We're just not going to keep it. That's dirty money. Bad karma. None of us wanted any part of that. We've already spread it around to a half dozen charities that will make your old cash feel better about itself. Your money's gone, and it's not coming back."

Moreno's jaw tensed. Through clenched teeth, he said, "If this isn't about money, then what is it about?"

"Are you dense? The manhunt. What happened to the man you apprehended in Reynosa?"

"We didn't catch anyone. The manhunt failed."

Quinn shook his head. "Try again."

"I'm telling you, we didn't catch anyone."

Quinn pulled the GLOCK's trigger. The cop screamed in pain as the bullet tore into his ankle.

"Go ahead. Yell as loud as you want," Quinn said. "No one can hear you."

"*¡Puta madre, hijo de la chingada!*"

"Now, about that man you captured," Quinn said, his voice calm.

Moreno grimaced with pain. "I...I don't know who he was."

"But there *was* a man?"

A hesitation. "Yes."

Quinn pulled out his phone and showed the man a picture of Nate. "Is this him?"

Moreno squinted at the image, then nodded. "Yes."

Not that Quinn expected any other answer, but actually hearing it made him pause for a second. "Where did you fly him to?"

"Outside...outside Tampico. Please, you have to get me to the hospital."

"Where outside Tampico?"

"Please!"

Quinn pointed the gun at the man's other ankle.

"Okay, okay," Moreno said. "There's...a facility there, north of the city...maybe twenty miles." A pause as a wave of pain rushed across the cop's face.

"That's where you took him?"

"Yes."

"Why there?"

"It has a private...runway."

That wasn't good news. "What happened when you got

there?"

"We took the prisoner into one of the buildings and locked him in a room. Then...then...oh, God." His eyes shut again and his face pulled taut. There was a hiss as he sucked in air through his teeth, and his head began to wobble.

Quinn, careful to avoid the growing puddle of blood on the floor, stepped closer and slapped Moreno's cheek. "Stay with us."

He glanced at Orlando and motioned down at the man's wounded foot.

Orlando nodded, cut off a piece of the cord, and tied it around Moreno's leg a few inches above the shattered ankle, stemming the flow of blood.

Quinn grabbed the cop's chin and gave it a little shake. "Hey, what happened after you put him in the room?"

A few seconds passed before Moreno's eyelids parted. "We...waited."

"For what?"

"A plane."

Exactly the possibility Quinn had been concerned about. "And then?"

"The man who...hired me was on it. He had us help his people load the prisoner...on board."

Again, Quinn held his phone up in front of the cop again, this time showing him the picture of the bald man.

"Yes, that's...that's Mr. Cameron."

"Then they left?"

"Yes."

"Where to?"

"I don't know. My job...was done."

"Which direction did the plane go when it flew off?"

Moreno looked at Quinn as if he didn't understand.

"Which direction *did it go*?"

"East. After it took off, it turned and...flew east."

The only thing east of Tampico was the Gulf of Mexico.

Moreno's head started to loll forward. Quinn put a palm on the cop's forehead and pushed back. "Tell me about the plane. Everything you remember."

THE COLLECTED

For the next few minutes, he extracted as much information out of Moreno as he could. The aircraft was a prop-driven cargo plane, not too large. When pressed, Moreno was able to recall part of the number on the tailfin, and the color scheme: white with two stripes—one blue, one black. There was also some kind of logo near the door. A black bird sitting on a blue branch. That was all Quinn could get before Moreno passed out.

They field-dressed the man's ankle, then pulled off his shirt and wrote with a black marker across his chest *CORRUPTO*—corrupt—and below that, the number of Moreno's Cayman account with the name of the bank. While they *had* removed a good portion of Moreno's money, they'd left enough in it so that there would be no mistaking that the cop had been on the take.

Fifteen minutes later, as they neared the airport to catch the first available flight to Tampico, Orlando called the personal cell phone number of a Federál she had previously identified as on the up and up.

"Who is this?" the man asked as he answered.

"Unimportant," she said. She gave him Moreno's name and the address of the building they'd left him in. "You should probably hurry. He's lost a lot of blood."

"What happened?"

"Nothing he didn't deserve."

"What?" the man asked, surprised.

"You'll figure it out."

She hung up.

CHAPTER
THIRTY

LIZ WAS SURE that at some point she would be discovered. If her brother had just stuck to the city, it probably would have been easier for her to stay hidden. But instead, he, Orlando, and Daeng had driven out into the countryside, stopping at some sort of industrial building before heading farther out on the highway, and turning off the road and driving into the wilderness.

Liz had motioned for her driver to follow them, but he refused.

"*No hay camino ahí. Yo no voy allá abajo*," he said.

She got the gist of what he meant, so she had him continue down the highway for a quarter mile then pull off to the side.

He'd been shooting her suspicious looks in his rearview mirror since not long after they'd left the airport. In an effort to placate him, she'd handed him a thousand pesos—about seventy-five dollars. It helped for a while, but now the look was back.

Liz tried to ignore it while she kept her attention focused on the place where her brother had left the road. When the other car finally showed up again, it turned back toward the city.

"Okay, go, go. Um, *vámonos*," Liz said.

Once more she and her driver took up pursuit.

It wasn't long before Jake turned off the road again, this time driving behind several cinderblock buildings. Liz had her driver turn down the road between the buildings and a gas station, and drive slowly past the road Jake had turned on.

She spotted her brother's car parked along the back of the buildings.

"Stop," she told her cabbie. She glanced back at the Pemex station. "*¿Necesitas gas?* I'll pay." She mimed giving him money.

"*Sí. Gracias.*"

He drove back to the gas station and pulled up to the pumps. While he filled the tank, she climbed out of the car and walked to the back of the lot so she could see behind the other buildings. The rental car was still parked at the side of the road, but unlike before, Jake and his friends were standing outside.

She wished she could hear what they were talking about, or, at the very least, knew the reasons for all these stops. They had to have something to do with Nate, but what?

After a few minutes, her brother, Orlando, and Daeng turned back to their car and climbed in. Liz ran back to the taxi. While the pump hose was no longer sticking into the gas tank, her driver was nowhere to be seen. She whipped around, looking everywhere for him, but she had no idea where he was.

She was going to lose her brother. She'd made it this far, but now she was going to lose him and that would be that.

Dammit!

Somewhere off to her right, a door swung open. She looked over and saw her driver exiting the toilet.

"Hurry," she said, waving at him. "Hurry, please. *¡Vámonos!*"

He began walking more quickly.

She pointed back at the highway. "Come on, come on. They're going." She climbed into the cab.

It was a full five minutes before they caught sight of Jake's rental again.

It's okay, she told herself, trying to relax. *It's all right.*

Deep in the city, Jake parked his car, then he and his friends got out and started walking away. Liz decided to chance that they wouldn't turn right back around and drive off, so she gave her driver another five hundred pesos, got out of the cab, and let him go, sure the man was happy to be rid of her.

Following on foot was nearly as tricky as it had been in the car, but she used her smarts and erred on the side of caution whenever necessary. Twice she lost them, but each time she caught sight of them again within a few blocks. They became very interested in an abandoned building, moving in and out several times alone or in pairs, sometimes bringing bags from stores back with them. Finally all three left so she followed again.

Several minutes later, they entered another building, this one not empty. As much as she wanted to follow inside, she didn't, and instead waited in front of a small grocery shop just down the street. They were there for nearly twenty minutes. When they came back out, Daeng split off on his own, while Jake and Orlando headed in her direction.

Liz stepped quickly into the store, moving down one of the aisles to avoid being seen from the doorway. Pretending to browse, she kept flicking her gaze toward the entrance. It wasn't long before she saw Jake and Orlando walk into view and then right back out again as they kept going.

Liz counted to ten, then headed out to the sidewalk. She was just in time to see her brother and his girlfriend turn down the next street. Judging by the direction they were going, she was almost positive they were headed back to the abandoned building.

Playing the hunch, she took a different route, running part of the way, and was able to get into the same hiding place she'd previously used half a minute before Jake and Orlando came into view.

They moved the loose board away from the window and entered. The street fell silent.

Liz figured Daeng would show up shortly, and she was right. What she hadn't expected was that he'd bring a police officer with him.

Daeng was acting strangely, too, like he was in a hurry.

When he reached the window, instead of moving the board to the side, he banged on it. When he hit it a second time, it slid out of the way. Orlando was standing just on the other side, something dark on part of her face and in her hair. Like Daeng, she seemed panicky. Soon she moved out of the way so the other two could enter, and the wood fell back into place.

What the hell is going on?

Liz hesitated for a moment, unsure what to do. Finally, she decided she had to take the chance, and moved quietly over to the board-covered window. She put her ear against the wood, heard distant footsteps, then nothing. Again, she hesitated. She could go back to where she'd been hiding and guess at what was going on, or actually find out.

Before she could talk herself out of it, she eased the board back just enough so she could peek inside.

At first she could see nothing, then her eyes adjusted to the lower light. Beyond the window was a large, gritty space littered with garbage. There was no one present.

You're doing this for Nate, she told herself. She took a deep breath and slipped inside the building.

As soon as she had the board back in place, she paused and listened. She had been hoping to hear something that would tell her which way they'd gone, but it was quiet. Thankfully, there was dust on the floor that recorded footprints leading back and to the left.

The prints stopped at a shut door. She put her ear against it, and heard faint, muffled voices on the other side, but could make nothing out.

She circled off to the right but came to an impassible wall. She went back in the other direction, passing the closed door, and continuing on until she came to an extension of the same wall from the other side. Frustrated, she started back for the point where she'd begun, but then noticed a bundle of cloth at the base of the wall that surrounded the room. The material seemed to be stuck *into* the wall.

She knelt down and tugged at it. The cloth was so weatherworn that it tore off in her hands. More gently this time, she worked at the bundle until it came all the way out, revealing a hole on her side of the wall.

She looked through it. There was no corresponding hole on the other side, so she turned her head, hoping to hear what was going on.

"...manhunt." Jake's voice, distant but understandable. "What happened to the man you apprehended in Reynosa?"

Someone else spoke up, an accented voice that she guessed belonged to the cop. "We didn't catch anyone. The manhunt failed."

"Try again."

"I'm telling you, we didn't catch anyone."

There was a loud bang. Liz jerked her head back, her ear ringing.

What in God's name was that?

She lowered her head again, but her ear was temporarily useless, so she turned and tried the other one.

Her brother again. "But there *was* a man?"

"Yes."

It was quiet for a moment. "Is this him?"

"Yes."

Nate? Are they talking about Nate? They must be.

"Where did you fly him to?" her brother asked.

"Outside...outside Tampico."

She continued to listen until the man stopped responding, then made her way quickly out of the building and all the way back to where her brother had parked his car.

Her mind was running a mile a minute. Not only had her worst fears been realized—*no, not worst, but damn close*—she'd also heard how ruthless her brother could be, the bang she'd heard undoubtedly a gunshot. She knew she should be horrified, but she didn't feel that way.

She felt a sense of...satisfaction.

She focused her thoughts back on Nate. What could she do? How could she help him get free? Could she do anything at all?

Though deep down she feared the answer was no, she wasn't willing to give up yet.

Her brother's next, logical stop would have to be Tampico, wouldn't it? Though Nate wasn't there anymore, maybe there'd be something that would point to where he'd been taken.

She spotted a cab turning onto the street a block away. She stepped out into the middle of the road and waved her hand.

"*Aeropuerto*," she said as she climbed in. "*Rápido*."

When she arrived at the airport, she was able to get onto a flight that was leaving forty minutes later. The next flight out wasn't for another two hours. She sat in her seat, her eyes glued to the door, expecting Jake and the others to come through it at any moment, but the doors closed without them boarding. She was going to beat them there.

For a moment, she felt relieved. But it didn't last long.

What if they're not going to Tampico at all?

CHAPTER
THIRTY ONE

NATE BARELY PARTED his eyelids as the door to his cell opened.

Janus entered, carrying something. "I bring water for you."

"Go away," Nate whispered.

A laugh, deep and scornful.

There was a clacking sound Nate couldn't place, followed by a moment of nothing, then pain, everywhere pain, as a bucketload of water splashed down on the exposed wounds across his back.

Arcing his whole body, Nate screamed. "You bastard!"

He wanted nothing more than to jump up and slam a fist into Janus's face, but his legs refused to move off the bed.

More laughter as the pain echoed in waves, each as strong as the last. Nate cringed as he tried to force the pain away. He could feel another scream of agony growing in his belly, but he refused to release it.

"Get. Out!" he managed.

"You want more water, you let me know," Janus said. "Oh, and even if you are tempted, I would not lie on my back if I were you."

There was a final bout of laughter as the man left and the door closed.

Sleep. I just need to sleep, Nate thought, desperately clawing at oblivion.

But as soon as his mind started to relax, there was

another scream from down the hall as Janus played his water trick on one of Nate's cellmates.

Nate slowly moved his hand into his pants pocket and gripped the bolt, as if it were a talisman that could give him the power he needed. Surprisingly, doing so seemed to relieve a bit of the pain, and he finally felt sleep begin to sweep over him.

As it did, he thought he heard Liz's voice again.

"Keep your head clear, and always be ready. It's the only way you'll make it."

"I love you," he mouthed soundlessly. "I love…"

CHAPTER
THIRTY TWO

EASTERN MEXICO

THE NAMES ON the Post-its were once more nagging at Quinn. Maybe it was just being on a plane again, but he was sure there was something there.

Peter. Berkeley. And either himself or Nate.

He tried slotting in each of the other names, looking for a combination that might ring a bell.

No.

No.

No.

Nothing. No set of players that made any sense.

He finally gave up and looked over at Orlando. She had her laptop open, and, against airline regulations, connected to the Internet via an unused channel she'd hacked into through the plane's own datalink system.

"Anything on the cargo plane?" he asked.

"Oh, yeah. Got that a while ago," she said.

"And you weren't going to tell me?"

"You were resting."

"I was *not* resting."

"Well, that's what it looked like."

He frowned. "So, the plane?"

"Byrd Cargo. Named after founder Norman Byrd. Established nineteen sixty-five. Based out of Tampa, Florida."

"Anything on the specific aircraft?"

"On a long-term charter."

"To who?"

"A company called Gene/Sea International. And before you ask, they don't exist."

"And Byrd Cargo knows this?"

"No. Gene/Sea's got a pretty good front. Websites, bank accounts, PR releases. They claim to be a biochem company focused on the ocean. Even have a few research papers you can download. All very legit-looking."

"But they're not real."

She looked over at him, her face blank. "Didn't I already say that?"

"Yes, you did," he conceded. "Who are they fronting for?"

She looked back at her screen. "That part, not so easy."

"That's what you're trying to figure out now?"

"No. A little difficult from here. I have a friend looking into it."

"So what's that you're working on?"

"I finally got some hits back on one of the bots I sent out." Her bots were programs that wormed their way through the Internet, looking for whatever they'd been instructed to find.

"Concerning?"

"Senator Lopez."

"And?"

"*And* what my bot dug up might not mean anything," she said. In a tone indicating Quinn should have already figured that out, she added, "Which is why I'm working on it."

"What did it turn up?"

She took a deep breath, and turned to him again. "Sweetheart, let me figure out if this means anything, and if it does, you'll be the first to know. Cool?"

Quinn held up his hands in surrender. "Cool."

She looked unimpressed. "Can I get back to work now?"

"Be my guest."

He leaned back in his chair, thinking he could get a

couple minutes of shut-eye before they began their descent.

Just as he was drifting off, Orlando shook his arm and said, "Hey!"

He opened his eyes, sleep retreating as fast as it had come.

"What? Now you're ready to talk?"

Her face scrunched up. "What are you talking about?"

"Lopez? I didn't just dream all that, did I?"

"Don't worry about Lopez right now." She nodded her chin at her screen. "Just got an email from Crissy Franklin."

Franklin was one of the people they'd contacted, trying to locate one of the ops on their potential-missing list.

"And?"

"She says Maurice Curson is unaccounted for."

Quinn thought for a moment. "Curson? He wasn't on our list."

"We didn't include him because he's been out of the business for a few years."

"Blackballed," he said, remembering. Something had happened on one of Curson's jobs that forced him out of the game.

"Apparently he's been working private security since then," Orlando said. "But Crissy says he recently got a gig, a *real* gig. He was supposed to be back a few days ago, but there's been no sign of him."

Quinn frowned. "The connection's kind of iffy, don't you think?"

"We should still put his name on our list."

"If you think so," Quinn said.

A bong sounded throughout the cabin. A flight attendant came on the intercom, telling them in Spanish that they were descending into Tampico, and that electrical devices needed to be turned off and stowed away.

As soon as they were on the ground, Quinn checked his phone. There was a message from Steve Howard asking him to call back via vid-chat ASAP. Unfortunately, there wasn't any place private enough in the small terminal to see what he wanted, so they arranged for a car first, and made the call from inside the sedan.

Quinn held his phone out so that both Orlando and Daeng could see Howard's face when it appeared.

"Sorry for the delay," Quinn said. "What's up?"

"I was finally able to get a look at the security footage from Peter's building," Howard said. "Unfortunately, there's a chunk missing."

"From when?"

"Seven days ago. Eleven p.m. to one a.m. I've checked all the days between that and when Misty came to the apartment, and also five days on the other side, but found nothing unusual."

"So you think seven days ago is probably when he went missing?"

"It *is* when he went missing," Howard said.

Quinn's eyes narrowed. "Explain."

"Peter's building isn't the only one with security cameras. I checked the others in the area, and hit the jackpot on a building same side of the street and a few doors down. One of their cameras is aimed just wide enough to catch the front of Peter's building. Here, let me show you."

Howard's face disappeared as he pointed his camera phone at a laptop sitting on a table next to him. On the screen was a nighttime image of a street. The camera that had shot it obviously had a low-light setting, because despite the hour it was taken, it was easy to make out details.

"This was shot at 11:57 p.m. You see that station wagon?" A finger moved into view and pointed at a car parked along the left edge of the screen. "That's right in front of Peter's building. That's where you should pay attention."

The finger pulled out of the picture, and the image began to move, jerking for a moment as Howard played it at an increased speed, then slowing to normal as a van pulled up next to the station wagon. Four men exited, and the van drove away. The men walked purposefully toward Peter's building and were soon out of frame.

Quinn's jaw tightened as the picture paused.

"There's an eight-minute span when nothing happens,"

Howard said. "I've cut that out."

The security footage started playing again. The street remained quiet for a few more moments before the van returned, pulling to a stop in the same spot as last time. It sat idling for several seconds, then the men exited the building, only their number had increased by one. Peter was propped between two of the men, his head drooping forward.

As disturbing as that was, the thing that stuck out the most to Quinn was the image of one of the four men with Peter, the same man Quinn had keyed in on when the group originally climbed out of the van. A bald man, the same size and shape as the man who'd been in Bangkok, whom both Burke and Moreno had confirmed was their contact.

He glanced at Orlando and Daeng and saw they'd made the connection, too.

The image stopped again and Howard reappeared. "I ran the van's plates. Stolen, and so far not recovered. I could keep hunting around, but I think we've pretty much run out of leads here."

"No, it would be a waste of time," Quinn agreed. "Can you stand by in DC in case something else comes up?"

"Absolutely."

"Thanks. Is Misty there with you?"

"I'm at her place right now," Howard said. "But she's in the other room. She didn't want to see the footage again." He paused, and added in a low voice, "She's pretty upset."

"Can you get her for me?"

"Sure."

The image became a blur as Howard carried his phone through Misty's apartment. A moment later, they could hear him say, "Quinn wants to talk to you."

"Give me a moment," Misty told him, her voice distant. The wait lasted nearly a minute, then, "Okay."

The phone switched hands, and Misty, looking tired and scared, stared into the camera.

"I have a few more questions. Is that all right?" Quinn asked.

"Yes, of course."

"When the Office was closed, all the records were either taken over by another agency or destroyed, correct?"

"Mostly we were ordered to destroy them. A few select files were transferred, mainly ongoing operations."

"So, in effect, there's no way to access information about any job the Office undertook?"

She looked uncomfortable. "Um, right."

"Misty?"

She stared off for a moment, and then turned back to the camera. "Do you think there's something in one of the files that will bring Peter back?"

"That's what I was hoping."

"We…we kept a digital backup," she said. "Well, Peter did. I helped him collect it. When we were done, he told me never to mention it."

A backup was exactly what Quinn had been hoping for. He knew Peter would never permanently destroy everything. It would have gone against his always-prepared nature. "Do you know where it is?"

She hesitated before nodding.

"And you can access it?"

"If he didn't change the codes, yes."

That was a potential problem. "Okay, I need you to see if you can get in. If the codes are changed, let us know and we'll try to break them." By "we," he meant Orlando.

"What am I supposed to be looking for?"

"You have something you can write on?"

"Hold on." She set the phone down, giving them a view of the ceiling. She returned a few seconds later. "Okay, go ahead."

"I'd like you to pull any information on jobs that had the following personnel attached: Evan Berkeley, Maurice Curson, and myself."

"Am I supposed to pull jobs where there was just one of you? Because if I am, that's going to be a hell of a lot of—"

"No," Quinn said. "Any pair combinations, and with the three of us together only."

"Okay," she said. Now that she had a task to perform,

much of the stress had left her face. "I'll call you back as soon as I can. A few hours should be enough."

CHAPTER
THIRTY THREE

TAMPICO, MEXICO

LIZ ARRIVED IN Tampico planning to find another taxi like she'd done in Monterrey. Instead, before exiting the building, she spotted a booth advertising tours and local hotels, and learned that yes, she could hire a personal English-speaking guide, and yes, one who could start as soon as she wanted.

"In an hour would be perfect," she said, paying the fee.

Right on time, a young man named Oscar met her at the booth. He was all smiles and service as he guided her out to his car, rattling off a list of places his standard tourist route would take her.

"Actually, I'm looking for something a little more specialized," she said when he finished.

"Specialized?"

Her first instructions were for him to wait in the car outside the terminal while she went back in for a few minutes. "Circle around if you have to, but don't be gone long. As soon as I come back out, we'll leave."

Confused and a bit wary, Oscar had reluctantly agreed. He drove her from the parking lot back to the terminal.

Inside, she checked first on the status of the next flight from Monterrey, and learned that it would be landing in a matter of minutes. This being a small airport meant the time between touchdown and exiting the aircraft would be short, so she found a spot from where she could see the corridor that all arriving passengers would be funneled through.

As the people from the Monterrey flight began trickling out, her stomach started tying itself in knots, as she worried again that Jake and his friends had gone someplace other than Tampico. Then she spotted Daeng, and a moment later, Jake and Orlando.

Liz headed outside and spent a couple nervous minutes waiting for Oscar to return. The second he pulled to the curb, she jumped into the back.

"Wait," she said as he started to pull back into traffic.

He glanced back at her. "We can't wait here."

"We won't be long. Just hold on, okay?"

"What are we waiting for?"

She didn't answer his question until the other three stepped outside.

CHAPTER
THIRTY FOUR

WHILE MORENO HAD not told them the precise location of the abandoned facility, he had given them enough information that Orlando was able to pinpoint the most logical location, using satellite imagery.

They drove twenty-five minutes into the Mexican countryside, the only words spoken Orlando's as she doled out directions when needed. Finally she pointed at a narrow, blacktop road that branched off to the east, and said, "There, turn right."

As Quinn did as instructed, he checked his rearview mirror. There had been a car behind them all the way from the city, never falling too far back and never coming too close. A tail? Perhaps, but he couldn't be sure.

His gaze switched back and forth between the road ahead and the mirror, but the other car drove past the road and didn't make the turn behind them. Maybe it was just a local who'd happened to be going in the same direction. Maybe. His cautious mind wasn't willing to go one hundred percent there just yet.

"That's got to be it, right?" Daeng asked.

He was leaning forward between the two front seats, looking at a building about a quarter mile away on the left.

"Should be," Orlando said.

A ten-foot high chain-link fence surrounded the property. Here and there, signs hung on it, warning people to stay away.

Quinn parked in front of the gate and they all climbed

out. Standing near the fence, he examined the building. It was about the size of an average apartment building back in Los Angeles. Two stories, made of concrete. It looked like it had been built to last centuries. An old office building, perhaps, or manufacturing facility.

"Up and over or through?" Daeng asked.

The fence was topped by two strands of barbed wire. Not exactly inviting. As for the gate, it was held shut by a chain secured with a heavy padlock. It would have been easy enough to unlock if they'd had a set of picks.

"Up and over," he said.

They found a point where the top barbed-wire strand drooped, no longer taut. They climbed over one by one, all avoiding getting snagged, and headed toward the building.

It was set back a good hundred yards from the fence, with wild grass and weeds covering the wide expanse between the two. To the far side of the structure they could see part of a long, flat road to nowhere that could only be a runway.

As they neared, Daeng stopped and crouched down, looking at the ground. "Look," he said.

In the dirt was an imprint, several feet long but only a few inches wide.

"Helicopter," Orlando said.

Daeng nodded, and pointed at a less obvious, parallel imprint. "If Moreno was telling the truth, this must be where he landed."

"At least we're at the right place," Quinn said. "Let's have a look inside."

There were two doors along the side of the building facing them, each made of metal that had seen better days. Quinn was about to head toward the one on the right when the other one opened, and a man in a uniform stepped out, holding a gun.

"*Esta es propiedad privada. No pueden entrar aquí,*" he said, telling them they shouldn't be there. He motioned back toward the fence. "*Regrésense a su coche. No pueden estar aquí.*"

"*Buenos días,*" Quinn said, and continued in Spanish, "Captain Moreno told us we'd find you here."

"I don't care who sent you. You can't be here."

"Captain Moreno from Monterrey? I'm sure you remember him. He was here a few days ago."

Caution crept into the man's eyes. "Who are you?"

"Duncan. DEA." Quinn held his hand out. The man didn't take it, so Quinn shrugged and said, "These are my colleagues, Travers and Song. We've been running a joint investigation with the Federal Police in Monterrey."

The man's expression remained the same. "No drugs here."

"We realize that," Quinn said. "We're here about the prisoner transfer."

"Prisoner transfer?"

"Yes, the man who Moreno escorted here and handed over to the other agents. Were you not here? He said you were here. Are you...um...um..." Quinn turned back to Orlando, as if looking for help remembering.

"Diaz?" the man offered.

"Yes, Diaz."

"That's me."

"And weren't you here?"

Diaz looked at them one by one. "I need to see your IDs."

"Really?" Quinn huffed, exasperated. "Moreno was supposed to have set this up. I get the impression you didn't know we were coming."

"No."

"That's just great." He looked at Orlando. "Get him on the phone."

She pulled out her phone and pretended to dial.

"No," Quinn said. "Don't call Moreno. Call Grayson in DC. Have him get ahold of Director Arroyo at CISEN." *Centro de Investigación y Seguridad Nacional* was Mexico's chief intelligence agency. "Let him deal with his screwup."

Orlando nodded and walked several feet away, her phone to her ear.

Diaz eyed her nervously.

"Don't worry," Quinn said. "I'm sure you'll get a call in just a minute to straighten all this out. Wouldn't want to be in Moreno's shoes right now. Though I guess he might not be the only one who hears the wrath."

The man licked his lips, looked at Orlando again, and said, "It's okay. No problem. What is it I can do for you?"

"That's very cooperative of you. I appreciate that." Quinn glanced over at Orlando. "Never mind. We're good."

She said something into her phone, acted like she was disconnecting the call, and slipped it into her pocket.

Quinn looked back at the guard. "So, were you here during the prisoner exchange?"

"Yes. I was here," Diaz said. He quickly added, "But I stayed out of the way. Only unlocked the doors they wanted."

"Good. That'll make things easier. We need to take a look at the room where the prisoner was held. Can you please take us there?"

"Um, sure. Yes. This way."

Quinn turned to Orlando and Daeng. "Travers, you're with me. Song, wait out here. Have a look around."

Both Orlando and Daeng took a step toward Quinn, stopped, and looked at each other as if saying, "I thought I was Travers."

Quinn looked directly at Orlando. "Travers, let's go."

She gave Daeng a quick, smug smile as she joined Quinn.

As soon as they passed inside, Diaz flicked on a flashlight and led them down a long, dim corridor. Given the appearance of the building from the outside, the interior was surprisingly clean and in order. Doors lined both sides of the hallway. All were closed so there was no telling what was in the rooms.

After turning down another corridor, Diaz finally stopped.

"This is it," he said.

He pulled out a ring of keys, selected the proper one, unlocked, and opened the door. The room inside was dark.

THE COLLECTED

Diaz moved enough out of the way so that Quinn and Orlando could get a look while he shined his light through the space. It was small and had no windows or vents, just a drain in the corner and a threadbare cot along the side. The room was a temporary holding cell, plain and simple.

"You put the prisoner in here yourself?" Quinn asked.

"I only unlocked the door. Captain Moreno and his men put him inside."

"May I use your light, please?" Quinn said, holding out his hand.

Diaz reluctantly handed over his flashlight.

Quinn played the beam through the room, carefully examining the space in case Nate had been able to leave some kind of message. He spotted nothing.

When he was done, he stepped back and handed the light back to the guard. "How long was he held in here?"

"An hour, maybe two," Diaz said. "I don't remember exactly. I can check the log if you want."

"Yes, please."

Diaz led them back in the direction they'd come. Now that Quinn had seen the cell Nate had been in, he was sure most of the other doors along the corridor would open onto similar rooms. Low profile, out of the way, and with its own airstrip, it was the perfect transfer point for the problematic and unwanted.

Diaz's office was a room near the building's exit and about twice as large as Nate's cell. Crammed inside were a desk, a small couch, and a television that was currently playing a security feed from outside the building, the same feed on which the guard had no doubt spotted Quinn and the others.

Diaz stepped behind the desk and typed into his computer. "The prisoner arrived at 12:48 p.m., and left again at 3:06. So, over two hours."

Without looking at her, Quinn knew Orlando had taken special note of the departure time. It was a more exact number than the estimate Moreno had given them.

"And how was the prisoner when he left?" Quinn asked.

"Fine, I guess. Why? Has there been a problem?"

"What do you mean, you guess? Either he was or he wasn't."

"I don't know," Diaz said, flustered. "I couldn't see his face with that black bag over his head."

Quinn leaned back. Moreno had not mentioned that little detail. "Of course. Right."

Though in truth it changed nothing, the thought of Nate in a bag angered Quinn even more.

"The pickup team Moreno handed the prisoner off to—did you speak with them?" Orlando asked.

"No. Just like I said, I opened doors and stayed out of the way. That's my job."

"Good," Quinn said. "That's exactly what I wanted to hear. We'll note that in our report."

Worry once more crossed the guard's face. "Report?"

"Routine," Quinn said with a smile.

Diaz stood up as if he planned to escort them back to their car.

"No need," Quinn said. "We want to take a look outside, then we'll be on our way."

"But the gate's locked."

"We got in. We'll get out."

Outside, they found Daeng waiting near the door.

"Find anything?" Quinn asked.

"Some rubber marks on the runway over there," Daeng said, looking toward a spot just beyond the building. "No more than a week old."

"We're done out here, right?" Orlando said. "If I'm going to find where that plane went, I need a good Wi-Fi signal."

Quinn nodded. "Yeah. I don't want—"

"Hold on," Daeng said.

"What?" Quinn asked.

"We seem to have picked up some interest."

Quinn tensed.

"A car drove by a few times while you were inside," Daeng said.

Frowning, Quinn said, "It was a dark blue Ford sedan, wasn't it?"

"As a matter of fact, yes."

Son of a bitch.

CHAPTER
THIRTY FIVE

THIS TIME NATE didn't hear the door to his cell open.

He had passed out, his mind in survival mode, cutting him off from all external input. What it couldn't ignore, though, was the hand that grabbed his shoulder and shook.

Immediately, the pain that his unconsciousness had masked flooded back. Though it no longer felt like he was constantly being stabbed, the searing ache was almost worse.

"Get up," Janus ordered.

He pulled on Nate's arm as if he were going to roll him onto his back. Realizing this, Nate shoved the man's hand away, and twisted up into a sitting position to avoid his wounds coming in contact with anything but air.

"You feeling better, I see. On your feet."

"Why?" Nate croaked.

"You have appointment."

No bag was placed over his head this time as Janus led him from the room and down the now-familiar stone hallway. Instead of taking him to the courtyard, though, Janus escorted him up an old staircase and out onto a large stone deck. For the first time, Nate was able to see beyond the walls of the building, but the view didn't comfort him.

Water as far as he could see swept out from the building on three sides. The view of the fourth side was partially blocked by more of the stone building, allowing him to see only the hint of vegetation growing in that direction. At least it wasn't more water.

"Keep moving," Janus said with a nudge.

Janus half dragged him to a door at the edge of the terrace, pulled it open, and pushed Nate inside.

They went along a corridor, down a set of stairs, passed by several doorways, and into a room that was dimly lit despite the afternoon sun outside.

Harris was there, looking out at the ocean through a tinted window. There was an older, frail-looking man also present. He was sitting in a padded leather chair behind an ornate desk. In his hands was a tablet computer that he was watching intently while listening to whatever was playing through a set of earphones.

"Please have a seat, Mr. Quinn," Harris said without turning around.

Janus gave Nate a push toward the guest chair in front of the desk, then let go of his arm. Nate staggered forward and had to grab the back of the chair to keep from falling down.

"Sit," Janus said.

Exhausted, Nate did as ordered, sitting up as straight as he could so his wounds didn't touch the back of the chair. Behind him, he heard Janus step out of the room and shut the door.

The old man's gaze stayed fixed to the tablet, and he'd smile every few seconds. Behind him, Harris continued to stare out the window.

Nate used the silence to try to refocus his mind. He was in a hell of a lot of pain, and it wasn't going away, but he couldn't let it control him. If he did, he might as well give up. Which, of course, was not an option.

He steadied his breathing and channeled the pain to one part of his mind. He couldn't make it completely disappear, but he was able to box it up enough to manage it. With each passing second of silence, more focus returned, so that when the old man finally set the computer down and pulled the earphones out of his ears, Nate's mind was as sharp and ready as he could have hoped.

The man stared across his desk at Nate for a moment, then smacked his lips and closed the folder. "You are quite accomplished, Mr. Quinn," the man said. Though he had an accent, he spoke English like he'd known it all his life. "What you do is almost like an art form, wouldn't you say?"

He waited for Nate to respond, but Nate kept his mouth shut.

"Not like the others, I mean," the man went on. "They have their specialties, but what you do takes a whole different mindset. The removal of the dead. The erasing of all signs that something had happened. Not just anyone could do that. Of all of you, you're the one I come closest to regretting bringing here. Unfortunately, guilt by association is still guilt."

Again he paused as if he expected Nate to say something, and again Nate disappointed him.

"This morning's session was painful, I know. And I'm not going to lie to you. It's only going to get worse."

Nate almost kept silent again, but then decided, what the hell. "Thanks for the breaking news."

A momentary spike of anger flashed across the old man's eyes, but a second later he was smiling again. "I had you brought up here, as I did with all of your colleagues, to see if you understand why you are my guest."

"That's an easy answer. No."

"I thought as much. Perhaps this will clear things up." There was a pause that Nate was sure was meant to be dramatic. "Isla de Cervantes."

Nate had heard of the place. Isla de Cervantes was a small but strategic island nation in the Caribbean Sea. The few pictures Nate remembered seeing of the place were the typical gorgeous beach shots like all the other islands in the region, but he'd never had reason to go there.

He stared at the man, his expression unchanged. "And?"

Once more, the hint of anger, then quick containment. "You have an actor's face. I'm sure that comes in handy sometimes. But I'm told you have an excellent memory, which means there's no way you could have forgotten."

Nate ran the name through his mind, trying to recall if Quinn had ever mentioned it. He was pretty sure the answer was no. But that wasn't surprising. His mentor had a way of not mentioning a lot of things.

"Maybe I remember. Maybe I don't," he said. "What does it matter? It's not going to stop you from doing whatever it is you have planned."

That was not what the old man wanted to hear. His chair scraped backward. Harris turned quickly around, and rushed over to help as the old man stood up.

"That's right," the man said. "It *is* going to happen. You and all your *friends* will pay for what you tried to do. Do you understand me? This is where you will die!"

"Was that the big reveal? That we're all going to die? Shocking."

"You! You're not any better than the rest of them. You're no artist. You're a hack. A pretender." He shot a glance at Harris. "Put me down!"

Harris eased the man back into his chair.

"Bring me the next one," the man said.

"Janus!" Harris called out.

The big man reentered the room.

"Take him back and bring the next one," Harris sneered.

Janus yanked Nate to his feet.

"I can walk on my own," Nate said. He tried pulling from the man's grasp, but Janus held tight, and alternated between jerking and shoving him all the way back to the hallway where the cells were located.

As they passed the door of the cell farthest from Nate's, Janus reached over and pounded on it. "Wakie, wakie, Petey. You next."

Once Nate's door was open, Janus sent him into the room with a shove to his shredded back. Nate pressed his lips shut to prevent any sound of the pain he felt from escaping.

He stumbled over to his mattress and lay down. Two things stuck in his mind from his trip out of his cell. The first was Isla de Cervantes. It apparently had something to do with the reason he was here. And while *he* might not know why, one of his cellmates should. Unfortunately, he couldn't just come right out and ask them. One of the cards he still held was that he wasn't who everyone thought he was, and that was a secret he wanted to keep for now. Not knowing the significance of Isla de Cervantes could betray him to the others.

The second thing he'd noted happened right before he was locked back up. Janus had knocked on the door of the far cell, the one Nate was sure belonged to the prisoner who had called himself Jonathan.

Only Jonathan wasn't what Janus had called him.

Wakie, wakie, Petey.

Now Nate realized why the guy's voice had sounded so familiar.

CHAPTER
THIRTY SIX

WHOEVER WAS IN the Ford sedan would want to be in a position where they could see the car Quinn, Orlando, and Daeng had left at the gate, but not *be* seen by the three of them as they walked around the property.

Daeng figured that after the last time the car had driven by, it would have probably parked in the trees along the gentle rise in the road less than a quarter mile back toward the highway.

Quinn scanned the fence that ran parallel to the road. "They shouldn't be able to see us approach from the end of the runway, and that should put us on their far side."

It was agreed, with some resistance, that Orlando would wait until she received the signal from Quinn before proceeding to the car and driving it toward the highway. That settled, Quinn and Daeng skirted along the edge of the runway until they reached the end, then sprinted across the empty field up to the fence.

There was no conveniently loose barbed wire there. Quinn climbed up first, and draped his jacket over the wires for protection. Daeng followed. Once on the other side, they worked their way over to the road.

Sure enough, the Ford sedan was there, a man sitting in the driver's seat. A second person stood outside just beyond the vehicle, partially hidden in the brush and looking toward the gate where the rental was parked.

Quinn pulled out his phone and sent Orlando a text:

NOW

He and Daeng moved in as close as they could safely get without being detected. Since neither of them was armed, Quinn thought it best to avoid a confrontation. He simply wanted to get a look at whoever the people were and note the car's plate number. What he really wanted to do was turn the tables on them later and see where they went, because nine times out of ten, it was who the tail reported to that was important, not the followers themselves.

When the person standing in the brush suddenly tensed, Quinn guessed Orlando had been spotted. A moment passed, then the watcher headed quickly out of the bushes toward the car.

Quinn jerked his head back, sure his eyes were playing tricks on him.

The passenger door of the Ford opened, and the woman who'd been outside started to climb in.

"Is that—" Daeng began.

The words were enough to shake Quinn out of his shock. He popped out of their hiding place and grabbed the door just before it shut.

There was a shout of surprise from inside, and the engine roared.

"Shut it down," Quinn said, staring across at the driver.

The man, looking like he was about to have a heart attack, fumbled with the key and turned the engine off.

Quinn's attention refocused on the woman in the passenger seat, the woman who couldn't possibly be glaring back at him. "What the hell are you doing here?"

"What do you think?" Liz said. "Trying to find Nate."

ORLANDO STARTED THE rental and backed it into the street. Keeping her pace unhurried, she headed down the road toward the highway. The hill wasn't a large one, and as she crested it, she expected to see the car gone, and Quinn and Daeng farther down the road waiting for her. Instead she found Quinn leaning *into* the other car, and Daeng standing nearby.

She slammed on the brakes and jumped out, in case they needed help.

"What's going on?" she asked.

"A hundred dollars says you won't believe it," Daeng said. He poked his finger a few times toward the inside of the cab.

Orlando leaned down and looked in. "What the…" She stepped over to the driver's door and wrenched it open. The driver had been looking the other way and almost fell out, but Orlando paid him no attention. "Liz?"

Quinn's chest was moving up and down, anger swarming across his face. His sister was doing a pretty fair job of keeping pace with his mood.

"Hey! You two. Stop it," Orlando ordered. "Acting all upset isn't going to change anything. Just calm down and let's all have a nice little chat."

"Please, please, I've done nothing," the driver said. "You can have my wallet if you want. Please, just let me go."

Quinn's and Liz's eyes were locked on each other, neither wanting to be the first to look away.

"We're not going to hurt you," Orlando said to the driver. "We don't want your money or anything. Everything is going to be fine." She looked across the cab again. "Liz, why don't you get out so we can let this nice gentleman go?"

She didn't move.

"Quinn, step out of the way so she can get out."

He didn't move, either.

It was as if Orlando hadn't said anything at all. With a look of determination, she headed around the car and didn't stop until she was right next to Quinn.

"For God's sake, it's like you two are the same person!"

She ducked under the arm Quinn had braced against the car, and pushed him in the chest, forcing him to take a couple steps backward. Not stopping there, she turned, grabbed Liz's arms, and pulled her out of the car. As she did, she spotted a backpack in the rear seat.

"Is that yours?" she asked.

Liz blinked. "What?"

Orlando thrust her chin at the car. "The bag? Yours?"

A quick glance. "Yes."

Orlando opened the back door and pulled it out. "Any more?"

"No. That's it."

Orlando leaned into the open front passenger doorway. "Okay, my friend. Sorry for any problems." She pulled a hundred dollars from her pocket and tossed it on the seat. "You can take off."

The driver immediately cranked the key and dropped the car into Drive, as if worried she might change her mind. With a spin of tires, he was gone.

"What the hell are you doing here?" Quinn yelled.

"I already told you!" Liz volleyed back, matching his tone and volume.

"You're trying to get yourself killed. That's what you're doing!"

"And if you were me, you'd be doing the same—"

"Whoa! Stop it!" Orlando said, inserting herself between them. She looked at Quinn. "Do you really think barking at Liz is going to help?" She turned to Liz. "And you, showing up here like this? Do you really expect him not to be mad?"

"I don't care if he's mad! I'm not here for him. I'm here for Nate."

"Who the hell do you think *we're* here for?" Orlando said.

There was a snort of laughter from near the rear of the car. All three of them looked over.

Daeng held up his hands. "Sorry," he said, unable to keep the smile from his face.

Orlando gave him a "you are *not* helping" look before she turned back to the others.

"You two calm down. Now. Understand?" When no one replied, she raised her voice. "Understand?"

A pause, then Quinn nodded and Liz followed suit.

The looks on their faces were almost identical. If

Orlando hadn't known they were related, there'd be no missing it at that moment.

Now that she thought about it, it was actually kind of funny seeing Quinn up against himself, but she suppressed the smile that had almost made an appearance, knowing it would have only made things worse.

"See that rock?" she said to Quinn. The medicine ball-sized rock was near the edge of the brush. "Take a seat. And you." This time she directed her words at Liz. "Take that other one." Liz's rock was about five feet from her brother's and approximately the same size.

"Look, Liz," Quinn said. "You can't be here. It's too dangerous."

"I don't care if it's dangerous. I'm not leaving until—"

"I. Said. Sit," Orlando ordered.

With a glare, Quinn lowered himself onto his assigned rock. Liz, seeing her brother comply, did the same.

"Okay," Orlando said. "Liz, how did you find us?"

"I followed you."

"Yeah, but how did you know to find us in Tampico?"

"No," Liz said. "I followed you from L.A."

"You followed us from L.A.?"

"Yes."

"And how the hell did you do *that*?" Quinn asked, still unable to mask his anger.

Liz clammed up.

"Actually," Orlando said. "I'd like to know the answer to that, too."

Reluctant at first, Liz told them about how she had only pretended to be in San Diego, and described what she'd done to make them believe it. She told them how she'd recorded their conversations at the house.

While the admission surprised Orlando, she could see it had shocked Quinn. He would have never believed his own system could be used against him, especially by his sister.

When Liz told them about Monterrey, Daeng said to Quinn, "Maybe you should hire her sometime. She's almost as good as you."

The comment was not received in the humor with which it was meant. For a few seconds, Quinn's anger with his sister transferred to the former monk. But by the end of Liz's story, Orlando could see that even though Quinn was still mad, the edge had been dulled.

"I'm not leaving," Liz said. "I want to help find Nate. I *have* to."

Quinn, his voice much calmer than before, said, "Liz, I understand, okay? I really do. But it's too dangerous. Whoever's taken him has some pretty extensive resources, and know what they're doing."

"You know what you're doing, too," she pointed out. "And I followed you all the way here."

"And we caught you," he said. "Trust me. If they got ahold of you—and they would—they wouldn't be as nice as we're being."

"I don't care. Nate saved my life more than once. I can't just step out of the way when he's the one in danger."

"I get it. But you're not trained for this. You could get us all—"

"You're not listening to me. *I don't care.*"

"Liz, do you mind if Quinn, Daeng, and I talk for a moment?" Orlando asked.

Liz looked at her and shrugged. "Sure, go ahead. But I'm not changing my mind."

"I think you've made that clear."

Orlando motioned for Quinn and Daeng to follow her. They walked down the road far enough so Liz couldn't hear them.

"She's going back to L.A.," Quinn said. "There's no other choice."

"I don't think the choice is actually yours," Orlando said. "You can try sending her back, but unless you're going with her and sitting on her lap, she's not going to stay."

"I'll hire someone to watch her."

"You do realize how intelligent your sister is, right? What do you think the chances are that she figures out a way to get free from whoever that might be?"

"I know the answer," Daeng said. "One hundred percent, right?"

"Shut up," Quinn told him.

"Oh, hell, no. This is too much fun."

"You enjoy seeing me fight with my sister?"

"No, but I see the only path you can take," Daeng said. "You'll eventually find it yourself. It's just fun watching you get there."

"Oh, you can see the path, can you? What path would that be?"

"Best if you find it on your own."

"Go to hell."

"This isn't helping," Orlando said.

"She's going back to L.A.," Quinn said. "If I have to, I'll have her locked in a room."

"And she'll never talk to you again. Is that really what you want?"

He seethed for a moment. "Better that than she gets killed. Look, I don't care if she gets free of whoever's watching her. By then we'll be gone and she won't be able to catch up."

"Think about it," she said. "What if she comes back to Mexico and starts nosing around? Maybe the people who have Nate won't know or care, but there are people here who could become concerned and would have reason to shut her up. Moreno, for one."

"He's in no condition to do anything."

"You're letting your overprotectiveness cloud reality. Moreno will have friends, and if he even gets a hint she's associated with us, he'll be more than happy to take out his retribution on her. You *know* that. And there are so many other things she could stumble on, and you won't be there to help her."

"So, she stays with us? Is that what you're suggesting?"

"Do we really have a choice? This way we'll know where she is. I'm sure we can find some things for her to do."

"And when we find out where Nate is? What do we do with her then?"

"Hope that she's clear-minded enough to see that things will go smoother if she's out of our way."

"What if she doesn't?"

Orlando looked at him, her eyes softening. "I ask you again, what choice do we have?"

Quinn stared down at the ground and closed his eyes. "Dammit."

"So that's a yes?"

"It's *not* a yes."

"But it's not a no, either."

Quinn's eyelids parted, but he said nothing.

Daeng clapped him on the back. "See, I told you you'd find the path."

CHAPTER
THIRTY SEVEN

HARRIS TOOK HIS normal position by the window as the final prisoner was brought into his employer's office. Like him, the man was bald, but that's where the similarities ended. The prisoner was several inches shorter than Harris, and stocky. The prototypical human bulldog.

Janus shoved the man at the chair.

"I can walk," the prisoner growled.

Even though he was older than the others they had collected, he showed no signs of being more affected by the whipping.

The man took his seat.

As before, Harris's employer was watching a replay of the morning's whipping session on his tablet computer. A few minutes passed before he turned it off and looked at his guest.

"I think you know who I am," Romero said.

"Sure," the prisoner said. "A discarded piece of shit."

Harris could almost feel the temperature of the room increase.

"If there is anything discarded here, it's you! You see, *I* know who *you* are, too. *I* know what *you* did."

"Congratulations. Can I go back to my suite now? I have a massage scheduled in a few minutes."

Romero began to shake with anger. As he tried to speak, he suddenly began to cough.

Moving quickly to his side, Harris could see that Romero's face was turning red as he continued to hack. Harris ran over to the water pitcher on the credenza, filled one of the glasses, and hurried back. "Drink this," he said, holding it to the old man's lips. "Janus!"

The big Ukrainian threw open the door and rushed into the room.

Harris shot a glance at the prisoner. "Take him back to his—"

"No," Romero croaked. He coughed again, and took another drink. "No. I'm not finished."

Janus looked at Harris, unsure of what to do.

"Maybe you can continue this later," Harris suggested.

Romero shook his head, no longer coughing. "No. Now."

"At least allow me to get your nurse."

"No!"

Through it all, the prisoner had watched the old man, his only movement a growing wry smile. "How much longer do you have?" he asked.

"Longer than you," the old man shot back.

The prisoner snickered, his smile unwavering.

Harris studied Romero for a moment longer, then took a step back and nodded at Janus. With a shrug, Janus walked back into the hallway and shut the door.

The old man locked eyes with the prisoner.

"I assume you also know why you are here," Romero said.

"A petty act of revenge?"

Harris eyed his boss, worried the old man was going to lose it again, but Romero seemed to be in control now.

"Petty is a matter of perspective. If you wish to think of it that way, be my guest. As long as you know why you're here, that is all that is important to me."

Romero paused, as if expecting some kind of retort, but the prisoner merely stared at him.

"One more thing before you return to your cell, something I want you to know and live with in the short time you have left. Since you were the one in charge and organized the...what do they call it?"

That was Harris's cue. "Termination," he said.

"Right. The one who organized the *termination*, you will be the last to die. That way, you can watch each of the men from the team you put together take their last breath, and know that you are the one who brought this on. You are the one killing them."

If the smile faltered on the prisoner's face, Harris didn't see it.

The old man leaned back. "Okay. Now I'm done."

"Janus!" Harris said.

As Janus reentered the room, the prisoner stood up. He gave the old man a slight nod, and did the same with Harris. As he rounded his chair, Janus latched on to his arm and guided him forcefully toward the door.

Before they could exit, the prisoner stopped and looked back. "One thing you should probably know."

Both Harris and the old man looked at him.

"You're wrong about which one of us is going to die first."

"Get him out of here!" Harris yelled at Janus.

Janus all but threw the prisoner into the hallway. Once the door was shut, Harris looked at Romero. The old man's head was bowed, his hands tightly clutching the edge of the desk.

"He's just trying to—"

Romero cut him off. "I want you to move up the start time of the next round."

"Of course. When would you like to begin?"

"Right now."

"WHAT NOW?" ONE of Nate's fellow prisoners whispered.

They had once again been hooded and led from their cells into the courtyard, but instead of being guided onto pedestals, they had been lined up next to each other and told not to move.

The cooling breeze bespoke the onset of evening, and would have felt good if not for the fact it kept blowing the new shirt Nate had been given against the untreated wounds on his back. But that was more of an annoyance. The true pain that continued radiating through his body at a steady, unrelenting pace needed no wind to aid it.

Thirty minutes passed with no new instructions. Nate knew it was meant to weaken their minds, by allowing them to speculate what might be coming and letting their worst fears rise from their unconsciousness. But Nate—and the others, he was sure—had been too well trained for such a simple trick to work.

In the distance, he heard the whine of the same electric motor he'd heard that morning before the whippings occurred, and now knew it must be a wheelchair bearing the old man from the office.

This was obviously his show.

The noise grew until it was somewhere in front of them, and then stopped, silence filling the courtyard.

Nate expected either Harris or the man in the chair to lecture them on what was about to happen, but instead a sudden hum filled the air. Before he could even figure out what it might be, there was a loud, unmistakably electric crackle.

There was a pause, then another crackle, this time only a dozen feet in front of him, the air nearby tingling with the charge.

And yet another, a little farther away.

"Who would like to go first?" Harris asked.

No one said a word.

"No volunteers?"

Silence for several seconds, then the old man said, "Him."

The sound of bodies moving. Nate was jostled to the side, and the man who'd been standing next to him was grabbed and pulled forward.

"Hey!" the prisoner called out. It was Berkeley. "What are you doing?"

"On the table," Harris said. "Strap him down and remove his shoes."

Nate tensed. *Shoes*?

"What…what are you doing?" Berkeley asked again.

"Remove the hood."

A pause, then Berkeley said, "Oh, God. No! Please, no!"

"It's going to happen one way or another, so there's no use struggling," Harris told him.

For the next few minutes, there was only the sound of movement.

"We're ready," Harris finally announced.

"Proceed," the old man told him.

The hum started up again.

"Oh, God, oh, God, oh, God," Berkeley repeated.

Without warning, the volume of the hum increased, and Berkeley's pleading became a guttural, stuttering groan. This lasted several seconds before the hum decreased. Berkeley sounded like a balloon giving up its last bit of air.

Electroshock. There was no question. And from what Harris said earlier, at least one of the electrodes must have been attached to a foot. That was a big, *big* problem. While the synthetic material around Nate's faux foot was good, it wasn't skin. Even if they didn't notice it, which he was sure they would, the material would melt as the massive amount of electricity shot through it.

"Again," the old man said.

The hum increased, sending another shock through Berkeley's system.

Next up was Lanier. He made no struggle or pleas for divine intervention. The only thing he said after he was strapped in was, "What are you waiting for?"

"Next?" Harris asked.

"Him," the old man said.

This time the hands seized Nate. He let them maneuver him to a table.

"Here. Let me help," he said. He kicked off his left shoe before the hands moved to his feet.

What he didn't know was if they needed both or just one.

As the bag was removed from his head, he looked down to see a man remove his left sock and place an electrode against the sole of his foot. His right shoe, the one on his artificial leg, was left untouched.

He was so relieved that he barely noticed as they placed the secured electrodes to his body.

"Ready," Harris said.

"Proceed."

All thoughts vanished from Nate's mind as every nerve in his body caught fire. There was no time, no place, no nothing. Just a brilliant spike of white, searing pain.

He suddenly found himself lying on the table, panting. Throughout his body, muscles contracted and stretched on their own. He could still feel the electric current under his skin like it was a living thing, randomly jumping from one part of his body to another.

"Again," the old man said.

Before Nate could even register the word, oblivion descended again.

CHAPTER
THIRTY EIGHT

THEY TOOK A room in a hotel near the center of Tampico that Orlando deemed to have adequate Wi-Fi coverage.

While she buried herself in her laptop, Quinn tried calling Misty, but only got through to her voice mail. He left a message, then called Steve Howard.

"She wanted me to stay here at her place," Howard said. "Said she'd be back within a few hours."

"Where did she go?" Quinn asked.

"To get something for you, I gathered, but she wouldn't say where that was."

"You should have gone with her."

"Oh, I know. I actually did try to follow her, but damn if that woman didn't give me the slip. Are we sure she was only Peter's assistant?"

Quinn told him to call back as soon as she returned, and hung up.

Waiting was a prominent part of a cleaner's job. If you weren't good at it, you might as well find some other profession. But this wasn't waiting for someone to give him the signal to remove a body. This was waiting for information other people were gathering for him, and it made him feel restless.

"Anyone else hungry?" he asked, needing to do something. "I'll go out and see what I can find."

"I'll join you," Daeng said, pushing himself off one of the beds.

"No, I'll go." Liz jumped up.

Even Orlando looked up in surprise.

Quinn headed for the door. "All right. Come on."

There was no need to use the car. There were plenty of places within walking distance to pick up a meal.

For the first few minutes, neither of them spoke as they headed down the street.

As they neared a few restaurants, Quinn said, "Any preference?"

"Mexican?" she said.

"Very funny."

Quinn flipped a coin in his head, and the second restaurant won. They ordered four *tortas de la barda*, a half dozen *empanadas de camaron*, and some freshly made tortillas, then took the empty table near the window to wait.

Quinn stared outside, watching the cars and checking the people on the street out of habit.

Something touched his hand. He jerked it back before he realized it had been Liz.

"I know that you're upset I'm here," she told him. She put her hand on his again. "If I were you, I would be, too."

The corner of his mouth ticked up.

"But if you were me," she went on, "you would do what I've done also."

"But I have the experience," he countered.

"Even if you didn't."

There was no need for him to respond. She was right. They both knew it.

"I won't get in your way. But I need to be close."

"It's dangerous, Liz. We don't know what we're dealing with."

She squeezed his hand. "I know it's dangerous. Don't forget I've seen how crazy things can get in your world. But, Jake, I love him. I'll do anything for him, just like I know he'd do anything for me. Just like you'd do anything for Orlando."

"Or you."

She smiled. "Or me."

"So what am I supposed to say? 'Sure, you can tag along anytime you want, just duck if anyone shoots'?"

She laughed, natural and light, something he hadn't made her do in forever. Though he tried to suppress it, a smile cracked on his face.

"There are certain situations when you should probably tell me no," she said. "But you can't shut me out of everything. I'm not a little girl anymore. I'm not someone who needs her big brother to decide everything for her."

Quinn tensed, knowing he hadn't been there when she was that girl who needed him. But instead of going down that road, she said, "I know how much you care about me. I know the things you've done to help me. I may not always agree with your choices, but I do know your heart has always been in the right place. And…" She paused. "I love you for that. You're my big brother. I love you. Period."

It was something he hadn't allowed himself to hope to hear from her lips again. He turned his hand so they were palm in palm.

"Everything I've done is only because I love you," he whispered.

"I know."

She squeezed his hand.

He had told himself that his hope for Liz and Nate's relationship to eventually fade away was for her protection, to keep her from getting emotionally—and maybe even physically—hurt. And while that was true, he now saw that desire for what it really was—his own selfish need to control the world around his sister and keep her from harm.

"If I tell you that you can't do something or come with us somewhere, you have to listen to me," he said.

"I can't guarantee I'm always going to be happy about it."

"And I can't guarantee I'll always be nice about it."

She pulled her hand from his, turned it sideways, and held it across the table. "Deal."

He took her hand and they shook.

QUINN PUT AN arm around Liz as they walked back to the hotel. She returned the gesture, even resting her head on his shoulder for a moment.

The smell of the food they were carrying preceded them through the doorway as they reentered the hotel room. It'd been a while since their last meal, so Quinn was sure Orlando and Daeng would hurry over to grab what they wanted. But they both remained by Orlando's computer, looking at the screen.

"You'll want to see this," Orlando said.

Quinn immediately set the bags down and joined them, Liz only a step behind him.

"What've you got?" he asked.

"Nate's beacon went active again for a few seconds."

"What?" Liz said. "You know where he is?"

Orlando shook her head. "No. There seems to be some sort of interference. Only bits and pieces got through. There was enough, though, for me to narrow it down some more."

"How much more?" Quinn asked.

Orlando didn't look as hopeful as he would have liked. "Pretty much the whole Caribbean, with the tip of Florida and a bit of Colombia thrown in."

"You said you only had it for a few seconds?"

"Yeah."

"Like last time," Quinn said, disappointed.

"Actually, not quite like last time. Before, it kind of faded out. This time it was just there, then gone. No fade. Like he turned it off."

"Why would he do that?"

"Could be anything."

As Quinn straightened up, a whiff of the empanadas drifted by, but the hunger he'd been feeling moments before was gone.

"There's more," Orlando said. "Before Nate's signal went active again, I dug into the radar database for this area. Given the time our security guard friend told us the plane took off, I was able to isolate the cargo plane's flight path. The database only saves snapshot readings once a minute, and it's from only the first thirty minutes of the flight before the plane moved out of range, but it gives us direction."

She brought up a map showing Tampico and the rest of eastern Mexico. A line of unconnected blue circles started at approximately the location of the private airstrip, then headed almost due east over the Gulf of Mexico. After eleven circles—or minutes—the plane adjusted its path into a more southeasterly direction. After nineteen more, it was gone.

"I did a projection," she said, and hit a few more keys. The map zoomed out to include the entirety of the Gulf of Mexico and the Caribbean Sea. Where the blue circles stopped, a straight, red line took over. "If they didn't make any other course corrections, their flight path would have taken them over the northern tip of the Yucatan, between Cuba and Jamaica, over part of Haiti, south of the Dominican Republic and Puerto Rico, and finally over Dominica before moving out into the Atlantic."

"*If* they didn't change their flight path," Quinn said. "If they did, they could be on any of those islands."

"I didn't say the info was perfect, but I think there's better than an even chance that I'm right."

Even if she were right, the area Nate might be in was still huge.

"Anything else?" he asked.

She scowled at him. "You weren't gone *that* long. I was just finishing up programming a worm that I'll send out to search for radar data along that path. Hopefully, we'll pick up the plane again. It's a long shot, but it's automated so worth trying."

"I'll keep my fingers crossed."

Letting her get back to work, he helped Liz unpack the food. He then took a tentative bite of a *torta*, but set the sandwich back down.

Once more he was waiting, and once more he didn't like it.

He pulled out his phone, needing to do something, and moved toward the window. Misty's line rang five times, and he was kicked again into her voice mail.

"It's Quinn. Really hoping you found something. Call me back."

CHAPTER
THIRTY NINE

WASHINGTON DC

THE EVER-PARANOID Peter had chosen his hiding spot for the Office's archives well, storing them digitally in servers belonging to the Library of Congress. Each file was encrypted within an existing text, meaning that if anyone accessed the file, they would only see a book or collection of documents that had nothing to do with the world of secrets.

To actually view the Office's information, one had to know where in the document to click. This would take the user to a command program that looked like a computer error. But if the correct twelve-character password were input, the hidden information would appear.

For extra security, there were two additional steps needed if one were trying to access the files remotely. Unfortunately, Peter had kept those steps to himself, so Misty was forced to visit the John Adams Building of the library in person.

There, she had to wait until one of the public workstations freed up. When one finally did, she located the manuscript that hid the Office's main index and began her search. Cross-referencing and matching up the names Quinn had given her with particular assignments was slow going. If the Office had still been in business, with all its data living on its own servers, she could have finished the search in no time.

The method she had to use now meant going back and forth between dozens of documents, opening the secret information, and, more times than not, closing the file again when she realized the job she was looking at was unrelated to what Quinn requested.

So far she had amassed a list of twenty-three projects that met at least part of his criteria. None, however, was a homerun. She returned to the index, found the next potential match, and opened the appropriate file.

As she read through it, she unconsciously leaned closer to the monitor, the skin on her arms beginning to tingle. The ops crew was nearly a complete match. It wasn't until she read the second page, where the cleaner was mentioned, that she leaned back, disappointed.

Close, but not close enough.

Still, she jotted down the project number and list of participants, then read through the summary in case Quinn asked her any questions about it.

That's when the tingle returned.

She remembered this job. How could she forget? Jobs that went well were soon distant memories, but the ones that went badly stuck in her mind for a long, long time. This was one of those jobs.

There was something else about it, she remembered. Something unusual. *What was it?*

She looked beyond the summary pages to the meat of the report, and found her answer on page seventeen.

After first making sure no one was watching her, she used her phone's camera to photograph each page of the report. She then closed out of all the Office-related documents, packed away her things, and left.

There was no reason to look for anything else.

She had Quinn's answer.

CHAPTER
FORTY

SLUNG BETWEEN THE guards' arms, the prisoners were returned to their cells one by one and dumped on their mattresses.

As the third one shocked, Nate was the third to be brought back. His body didn't know if it should scream from the welts on his back, or the near electrocution the rest of his system had just received.

He lay on his side, wanting nothing more than for sleep to overtake him, but there was something he had to check first, something he was afraid he already knew the answer to.

He worked the pant leg over his right calf, and opened the seam so he could get into his prosthetic. He slipped his finger into the empty storage space, and immediately knew he'd been right to be concerned. The walls of the container, usually smooth, felt gritty. He pulled his hand out and examined his fingertip.

Black.

Dammit.

He stuck his finger into the compartment again, and hooked it up toward the previously damaged emergency beacon button. Not only was there more grit, but what was left of the button was now deformed, melted. He tried pushing it, but the button was frozen in place.

No! Dammit!

Though most of his carbon-fiber prosthetic was purely mechanical and undamaged by the electroshock, the excess electricity had gotten to the emergency beacon and destroyed it.

For the first time, Nate began to despair. Though he'd known there was a chance the beacon had already stopped working because of the bolt, he'd still been hopeful. Now he knew whatever help it might have brought wasn't coming, and if he was going to get out of his situation alive, it would be up to him alone.

Given his current physical condition, he wasn't a big fan of his odds.

CHAPTER
FORTY ONE

QUINN STOOD ON the balcony at the back of their room and looked out at the city. While the sun was still hovering above the western horizon, lights had begun to flicker on here and there. He heard the sound of a jet engine not far away as a plane roared down the airport runway, and from below the sound of cars moving toward home or work or who knew where.

The sliding door opened behind him, and Orlando stepped out.

"Anything?" he asked her.

She shook her head. "Some of the storage systems the radar data's on leave a lot to be desired, so that's slowed things down."

He nodded, returning his gaze to the city.

"What did you say to Liz?" Orlando asked, coming up beside him.

He looked at her, concerned. "Why?"

"It's just, well, she said something nice about you."

"Oh, she did, did she? And what was that?"

Before Orlando could answer, Quinn's phone vibrated. He pulled it out of his pocket and looked at the display. It was a video call.

"It's Misty," he said.

As they headed back inside, he pushed ACCEPT. Misty appeared on the screen.

"Hi," he said. "Was beginning to worry about you."

"Sorry. It, uh, took me a bit longer than I'd thought it would," she said.

"Did you find anything?"

"Yes."

Not *maybe*. Not even *I think so*. But *yes*.

The others crowded around him as he said, "Tell me."

"First I checked on jobs you and Berkeley shared. There were six."

Exactly the number Quinn remembered.

"You and Curson were on seven," she went on. "And Curson and Berkeley had ten in common."

Twenty-three jobs. That was a lot to sift through, but better than it could have been. "Maybe if we go through them one at a time, something will stand out."

"Wait. I'm not through. At first there didn't seem to be any jobs the three of you were on together."

"That's because there weren't any jobs the three of us worked on together."

"You wouldn't have known."

He hesitated a moment. "A blind job?" Blind jobs were the kind where most of the players didn't come in contact with each other. Quinn had tried to avoid those as much as possible.

"Not a blind job."

"Then I'm not following you, because we were never on the same job. I would remember that."

"You don't remember because *you* didn't actually work the job."

He frowned. "Now you've lost me completely."

"This particular job, you were originally assigned to it, but the date was pushed and ended up conflicting with something else Peter needed you for."

That made more sense. Though it didn't happen often, Peter had moved his schedule around sometimes. "So what job are we talking about?"

"Does Isla de Cervantes ring a bell?"

He thought for a moment, then nodded.

Four years earlier, Peter had called him with an

assignment. The only thing he told Quinn at the time was the location: Isla de Cervantes. "Straightforward," Peter had said. "You'll get the details next week." Only the details never came. A few days later, Peter called back, reassigning him to a job in Oslo.

But the memory wasn't why the nape of Quinn's neck was tingling. It was because Isla de Cervantes was in the same zone Nate's beacon was in.

"I remember," he said. "So if I hadn't been removed, all three of us would have been on this job?"

"Yes. It's the only time your names overlap on anything Peter was running."

"Who else was on it?"

"Three others. Four, if you count the man who replaced you. Geoffrey Saban was team leader, and Oren Karper and Zach Lanier were ops."

"And the new me?"

"Michael Stallard."

A competent cleaner, not quite Quinn's level, but...

He looked over at Orlando. While Stallard and the first two names Misty had mentioned weren't on their potential-missing list, Lanier's was.

Orlando immediately understood what he wanted her to do. She walked several feet away, pulling out her phone.

"What was the job?" Quinn asked Misty.

"Termination of a man named Javier Romero."

Romero? Quinn ran the name through his mind a few times, but came up blank.

"Any mention of why he was important?"

"No. The file only contains what was necessary for the job. There *are* a few notes at the end in Peter's personal code. They indicate that there was some kind of problem. No mention of what that might have been, though."

"Do you think it's somewhere else in the files? Was there a photo of this Romero?"

"I, um, took pictures of the entire file."

"You did? Can you send them to me?"

Her face tensed. "I probably shouldn't."

236

"Misty, all I care about is finding out what's going on, and bringing our friends home. Once I'm done with the file, I'll trash it. No one will ever see it."

Looking unsure, she said, "You promise?"

"Of course I do. You know me. You know you can trust me."

She turned to the side in thought, then looked back and nodded. "Okay, but you *have* to destroy it later. And don't say anything to Peter. *I'll* tell him I gave it to you."

"Whatever you want to do," he said. "Thanks. I'll call you if we need anything else."

"And when you find him, too."

"Yeah. When we find him, too."

As soon as he hung up, he looked over at Orlando. She had moved into the bathroom entrance and was talking into her phone in a low tone.

"Could that be where Nate is?" Liz asked.

He turned to her. "I'm sorry. What?"

"Isla de Cervantes. Could that be where he is?"

"No way to know yet."

"But…but…" She stepped over to the desk and turned the screen on Orlando's laptop so Quinn could see it. "Look. Isla de Cervantes is right along this track." She pointed at a spot between Cuba and Puerto Rico, a bit south of the red line representing the possible flight path of the cargo plane. "It's right here."

"I know. But—" He stopped as his phone vibrated multiple times. Not a call, but messages. He watched them come in. There were twenty-nine when they finally stopped, all from Misty, the images of pages from the report.

Across the room, Orlando ended her call and made another. Quinn held up his hands, silently asking her what was going on.

She covered her phone and mouthed, "One minute."

While he waited, Quinn brought up the first image from the report, scanned quickly through it, and opened the second. When he neared the bottom of the page, he stopped on a photograph and enlarged it. The picture was of a vigorous man who looked to be in his early sixties, speaking to an unseen crowd. His body language oozed determination and conviction. Someone had written in pen just above the man: ROMERO.

So this was the target.

Though Romero was the main focus, there were others in the picture, gathered in a group behind the man, watching him. Some had names written above their heads, too. He scanned each face, stopped suddenly, and used his fingers to zoom in.

Well, well, well.

Not wanting to completely believe his eyes just yet, Quinn went to his saved photos and retrieved the one of the bald man in Bangkok. He switched back and forth between it and the group shot.

Neither image was perfect, but they didn't need to be. There was no doubt that the bald guy was also the man in the other shot, with the name HARRIS written over his head.

"I appreciate it," Orlando said.

Quinn turned around in time to see her hang up her phone.

"The reason Saban and Karper weren't on our list is because they're both dead," she said. Quinn raised an eyebrow, but before he could ask the obvious question, she added, "Job-related. Eighteen months apart. No apparent connection."

"Lanier?" he asked.

"While no one's reported him missing, he hasn't been seen in a couple weeks."

"That sounds like missing to me," Daeng said.

"Me, too," Quinn agreed. "What about Stallard?"

"He's sitting at home. Has an assignment starting next Tuesday, but says if we need him for anything before then, he's available."

"Replace Stallard's name with yours," Daeng said, "and that accounts for everyone."

Yes. It did. Nice and neat.

"Here's something else you're going to like," Quinn

said. He showed them the photo he found.

"That cinches it," Orlando said. "No question."

"None at all."

"So does that mean Nate is on this Isla de Cervantes?" Daeng asked.

With a quick look to his sister, acknowledging she'd been right, Quinn said, "He's in that direction somewhere, so that's where we need to go."

"I'll get us some tickets out of here," Orlando said.

She took a step toward her computer, but Quinn stopped her.

"Liz can do that." He looked over at his sister. "You can, right?"

"Sure," she said, surprised. "Of course."

His eyes back on Orlando, he said, "You and I need to find out what we can about this Harris guy."

They sent out copies of the new picture of the man to several of their trusted contacts, this time with the name David Harris attached.

"There's a flight to Mexico City leaving in an hour and a half," Liz announced after a few minutes. "It'll arrive in time to connect with a flight to Puerto Rico. There are dozens of ways from there to get to Isla de Cervantes."

"Book it," Quinn told her.

She glanced nervously at him. "Three tickets? Or four?"

A pause. "Four."

CHAPTER
FORTY TWO

NATE WOKE WITH a start.

At first, he thought someone had come for him again, and he was about to be dragged away to some other round of torture. Waterboarding this time, or maybe something even more medieval, like the rack.

But it had only been the nightmares playing in his head. His cell was empty, the door firmly shut.

He lay on his stomach, letting the adrenaline coursing though his body dissipate. Once his heart rate had come back to normal, he sat up. The roar of the pain along his back had dropped a notch from cataclysmic supernova to titanic molten lava eruption. The spasms caused by the electricity, though, seemed to have stopped altogether.

Gingerly, he rose to his feet, felt his way across the dark room to the toilet, and relieved himself.

Time was a problem. His internal clock was misfiring, one moment telling him it was ten p.m., and the next, time for breakfast. He knew, though, that it was late, or, rather, early, because no light seeped in through the vent. The corridor lights so far had only been off at night.

The vent. There was something about the vent. A dream he had…no, no. An idea, as he'd been falling asleep.

A potential way out.

With growing excitement, he retrieved the bolt from where he'd stuck it in the mattress after using it last time, ran his fingers along the wall until he reached the door, and sat on the floor.

Given that no one had come after him the last time he removed the vent cover, he decided it was unlikely there was a camera in the room, night vision-equipped or otherwise, so he didn't even bother concealing his actions as he removed his prosthetic leg. As soon as his stub eased out of the cup, he sighed with relief. He had worn the leg far too long without taking a break. Even toughened with calluses as his stub had become, it felt raw and worn. He allowed himself just a few seconds to rub his hand over it and massage the tissue.

Using the bolt, he removed the back frame of the vent again. This time he didn't tie any strings to the front. Without any light, it would have been a struggle at best to run them over the slats and snag them back so he could tie them off, but he wasn't worried. His previous experience had shown him the front wouldn't fall out.

Once the back frame was free, he set it on the floor, out of the way. He felt along the slats embedded in the front half until he found a loose spot. Taking extra care, he worked his fingers into the space until he was able to wrap them around the corridor side of the slat.

Next, he used his free hand to push forward on each corner in succession until the frame popped out of the hole. He laid it quietly on the corridor floor.

With the hole now unblocked, he shoved his arm as far through it as possible, and reached across the front of the door until his hand came in contact with the locking bar that ran up and down the outside. He moved his hand upward, already knowing the door handle was too high for him to reach, but giving it a try anyway. After confirming his limitations, he pulled all the way back inside the cell and grabbed his prosthetic.

This was where his whole plan lived or died. Holding the leg by the ankle, he fed it through the rectangular opening. It was tight, but he was able to squeeze the whole thing through.

Closing his eyes, he pictured the front of the door as he turned the leg so that it was vertical, and moved it toward the door handle. When he passed the point where he thought he should have reached it, he shifted the leg to the side, and pushed up. He met no resistance, so he tried again. This time the cup struck home.

Down and vertical meant locked. Up ninety degrees to a horizon, unlocked.

It took him three tries to get the cup setting just right against the handle. The first two tries resulted in the leg shooting out away from the door, both times nearly causing him to lose hold of the ankle. On the third try, he felt the handle turn and heard the long metal rods slip along the side of the door. When the handle stopped moving, he gave the door a tentative push. It gave at the bottom, but the top held firm.

He placed the end of the prosthetic against the handle and shoved again. There was resistance, then finally a soft *pop* as the top rod slipped free of its locking slot. Immediately, the door swung outward a few inches.

Nate quickly retrieved his leg and remounted it against his sore stub. As soon as it was securely in place, he exited his cell, closed his door, and reengaged the metal rods. He replaced the front frame of the vent in the hole. Though he couldn't see his handiwork in the dark, he was confident the door looked unchanged, and until someone opened it, there would be no reason to think he wasn't still inside.

To his left, the corridor led to the doorway he'd been taken through every time he left his cell. On the two occasions he'd been unhooded, he'd seen that the door was similar to the cell doors in its metal makeup, but that there was no corresponding locking rod on either side. To the right was the unknown.

He hesitated. Should he open the others' cells? Get them out, too?

He couldn't just leave them there.

Find the way out first, then get them.

He decided to go in the direction he'd never been taken. But before he took his third step—

"Who's out there?" a voice whispered.

Nate froze, sure a guard had quietly entered the corridor

and heard him moving around.

"I know you're there. Who is that?"

It wasn't a guard, Nate realized.

He turned the other way, and tiptoed until he was outside the occupied cell farthest from his own.

"Peter?" he whispered, leaning down toward the vent.

"Hello, Nate."

As Nate had suspected, Peter had figured out who he was the first time they'd spoken.

"How did you get out of your cell?" Peter asked.

"Creative use of limbs."

A grunt. "All right, and how are you getting out of the hallway?"

"I was about to have a look around. As soon as I figure it out, I'll come back and get the rest of you."

"Might be better if you get out and go for help."

"I'm not leaving you all here."

Peter was quiet for a moment. "They made a mistake bringing you here."

"And don't think I'm not going to let Quinn know about it."

"No. He would have been a mistake, too."

"What do you mean?"

"Residue of an old job neither of you were on, that's all."

"Then why the hell—"

"Doesn't matter. Go find the way out."

Nate wanted to know more, but Peter was right. Now wasn't time for a leisurely chat. "I won't be gone long."

"Good luck."

Keeping one hand in front of him, and the other on the wall, Nate made his way down the corridor as quickly as he dared. For the first thirty feet, he came across other doors he guessed led into rooms similar to the one he'd been in, but all their locks were open, so he knew they were empty.

A few yards past the last door, the passageway turned to the left. In the distance, he could see a thin glowing line low to the floor.

A door, he thought. Another way out. But did the light

mean there was someone on the other side?

Stepping lightly, he approached the light. It was a door all right. There was enough illumination for him to make out that much. But unlike the other doors, this one was made of wooden planks held together with iron strips at the top and bottom. It looked old, perhaps not as old as the building itself, but a century or two wasn't out of the question.

Instead of a knob, it had a ring, also iron. Unless it was locked on the other side, all he had to do was pull it.

He dropped silently down onto all fours, and moved his ear up to the gap along the bottom.

There was only the stillness of an empty space on the other side.

As he started to rise, a voice yelled out in the distance. He put his ear back to the gap, but instantly knew the noise was not coming from the other side of the door. It was coming from back down the corridor in the direction of the cells.

He rushed back toward where the hall made its turn, but just before he got there, the corridor lights came on. He jammed to a stop, feeling suddenly exposed. He looked back at the wooden door. It was still closed. Whoever turned on the lights had done so at the other end.

"Hey! Hey!" the voice yelled. "Can't I get some water? I need some water."

Now that he was closer, Nate could tell the yeller was Peter. What the hell was he doing? The guards were on their way in now. How was Nate supposed to get everyone out?

That bastard, he realized. Peter was purposely drawing the guards' attention so that Nate *couldn't* come back for him and the others.

"Might be better if you get out and go for help."

What choice did Nate have now? Even if he waited where he was, and tried to release the others when the coast was clear, he had a very strong suspicion that Peter would call out again the moment he knew Nate was close.

Damn you, Peter.

He returned to the door and grabbed the metal ring. When he heard Peter yell out again, he pulled the door open enough so he could peek through to the other side. Another corridor, empty. He opened it more, passed through, and shut it behind him.

Get away and get help. That was his mission now.

The sound of Peter's yells dropped to near nothing as he moved away from the door. The new corridor led him to a set of stairs that ended at a doorway two floors up. He listened for any sounds of life before opening it. He found himself in a small stone room, not much larger than the cell he'd been in. The difference was that this room had windows to either side, and another entrance straight in front of him. He could also feel a breeze, because there was no door covering the other opening, and no glass in the windows.

Looking out the window to the left, he could see the courtyard below, and realized the room he was in was on top of the wall that surrounded it. To confirm this, he eased over to the other entrance. Beyond it was a four-foot-wide walkway that ran down the center of the wall, lined on each side by a two-foot-high, one-foot-thick lip. To the left was the courtyard, and to the right a narrow sandy beach lining the ocean. He had to be in some kind of old sea fort that had been restored but hadn't held up so well.

The defensive wall curved around the courtyard and disappeared behind the bulk of the central building. Though the night was moonless, he could make out the dark shapes of trees and bushes in that direction. It had to be the land side. That was the way he needed to go if he had any hope of finding a phone or a radio.

He moved through the doorway, but stayed close to the building to cut down any silhouette he might make against the night sky. He checked the beach to his right. It was a good twenty-five feet down. Not a distance he wanted to jump, but he might be able to scale the stone wall if he were careful. Centuries of storms and sea air had eaten away at it, creating cracks and nooks he could use for his hands and feet. From there he'd have to walk around, fully exposed, until he reached the far side.

The quicker route, and the one that would get him to the

cover of the jungle sooner, would be to stay on top of the wall, then scale down it on the land side. He'd be able to get a better view of his surroundings from there, too. The drawback was that moving along the wall could expose him more than the longer walk along the beach.

He examined the courtyard, looking for any movements or indications that someone was there. It took him less than a minute to spot the guard standing next to one of the doors of the central structure. As he watched the man, he noted that the guard seemed to be paying more attention to the other courtyard entrances than to the wall.

If Nate stayed low behind the walkway's lip, he should be okay.

He crouched down so that he was on his hands and feet, and moved onto the walkway. It was an awkward way to travel, but no alarm was raised.

When he reached the point he was aiming for, he peeked over the lip, back into the courtyard, and relaxed. The angle was such that the guard was now out of sight.

Nate stretched his muscles, and stood up so he could take a quick look around before he started down. He'd been right—he had a much better view.

But what he saw was not even close to what he'd hoped for.

As he'd noted earlier, the fort was surrounded on three sides by water. He could now also see that the coastlines ran parallel to each other past the fort and along both sides of the jungle area before they disappeared into the night. The problem was, they didn't stay that way for long. Though he couldn't see where it happened, he knew they met back together just a few miles away, because in the distance, he could see starlight playing on the ocean.

He'd suspected he was on an island. He just hadn't realized how small it was.

Doesn't matter, he told himself. *You've still got to try.*

He looked at the jungle for another few seconds, then lowered himself over the edge of the wall and started climbing down.

CHAPTER
FORTY THREE

PUERTO RICO

IT WAS AFTER midnight by the time they landed in Puerto Rico. Earlier, while waiting for their connecting flight in Mexico City, Quinn had made a call to an associate living on the US territory. As arranged, Veronique Lucas was waiting for them when they exited the terminal.

"This way," she said, leading them across a suspension bridge to a Suburban waiting in the nearby parking structure.

Orlando, in the backseat with Daeng, broke out her laptop as they drove away from the airport, and set to work on some items she and Quinn had discussed on the flight. Since most of their trip had been over water, her ability to log on midair had been greatly reduced.

Quinn was sitting up front next to Veronique. "Any problems pulling things together?" he asked.

"Had to sub a few items, but think you'll be happy. Otherwise I took care of everything you wanted."

"Thanks, Vee."

"Is this something you need an extra hand on? If so, I've got some time."

"I think we're good. But if that changes, I'll let you know."

They drove through the sleeping city of San Juan, then west along the northern coast of the island. Quinn took advantage of the time to work his way through the Romero file. After a while he heard Orlando close her laptop. The look she gave him when he glanced back said she'd learned something she needed to tell him, but they both knew it was best not to say anything in front of Veronique. It wasn't that they didn't trust her. It was just always better to keep the information contained.

After forty minutes, Veronique turned down a two-lane road, followed it for a couple of miles, then pulled into the parking area for a small, private airfield. There was no terminal or control tower, just a runway with the appropriate strips of lighting for night operations, a cemented area for planes to park, and a windsock.

Tonight, there was also a Gulfstream G500 jet sitting there, ready and waiting.

The first thing Quinn did when they got out was to pull Orlando to the side. "Change of destination?"

"No," she said.

"All right. Give me the rest once we're settled."

Veronique led them toward the plane.

"Crew?" Quinn asked.

"Two," she told him. "Gogan's the pilot; Unger, co. I've used them a lot. They'll do what you need and not ask questions. You'll be happy."

Veronique's word was good enough for Quinn. She'd always been buttoned up, and he knew she wouldn't tolerate underperformers.

The intros were brief. Once done, Veronique held out her hand.

"I owe you a martini," Quinn said as they shook.

"Just one?"

"Maybe two."

She smiled. "Good luck." She said goodbye to the others, turned, and headed back to her car.

While Orlando, Daeng, and Liz were strapping in, Quinn told Gogan where he wanted to go, then joined his team in the back.

As soon as the wheels left the ground, Orlando said,

"Javier Romero was a very powerful man in Isla de Cervantes. It's not a large place, but its strategic location has meant a *lot* of money flowing in. Officially, the island is neutral, but unofficially the US Navy has used it for years as an alternate port when needed. Romero's family has owned most of the harbor since the 1800s. That was all fine and good when he stuck to business."

"But he didn't," Quinn said.

"No."

"Let me guess. Politics."

"Right on one. And you want to guess who he chose for a mentor?"

"Surprise me."

"Hugo Chavez."

"Great," Quinn said, meaning anything but.

Chavez was the egomaniacal, anti-anything-that-didn't-promote-him leader of Venezuela. A man who had basically made himself president for life despite the occasional election, and who relished seeing others follow in his footsteps, as long as they remembered he was the one giving them the hand up.

"At Chavez's urging, Romero decided to make a run for president. Some of the polls even had him comfortably ahead. How reliable they were, who knows? But apparently just the thought of him winning was something that couldn't be tolerated."

"Hence the termination order. CIA?"

"Not exactly, though I'm sure our intelligence community helped guide the decision."

"Who, then?"

"Basically from what I can tell, an unofficial subcommittee of the Organization of American States."

The OAS was made up of representatives from North America, South America, and the Caribbean. Their stated mission was one of supporting other member nations in areas such as human rights and democracy. Assassination, Quinn was sure, wasn't on their official list of good deeds.

"So they're the ones who hired Peter?" he asked.

"That's what it looks like." She hesitated, like there was something more.

"What is it?" he prodded.

"I, um, played a hunch. I'm not sure if it means anything, but the body on Nate's last job—Senator Lopez—he was serving in the Mexican delegation to the OAS four years ago."

Quinn felt a familiar burn at the base of his neck. "As what?"

"Special envoy for the president of Mexico."

"Isn't that what the Mexican representative to the OAS is supposed to be?"

"One would assume."

"What were Lopez's duties?"

"The few places I was able to check had no information. I've put out some discreet feelers, so maybe something will come back. But I don't think it matters."

"Why not?"

"When I found out about Lopez's tie to the OAS, I checked around to see if there were any other OAS or former OAS personnel missing or recently dead. I focused on people who would have access to the highest levels of their government." She paused. "I found three others for sure, all whose bodies have turned up in the last three weeks—a former ambassador in Chile, an economics expert in Brazil, and member of the Canadian parliament. There could be more, but it seemed unnecessary to keep searching."

If Orlando's theory was right, each was a member of a secret council of death who passed judgment on Romero, and then hired the Office to carry out the termination. That in and of itself was not surprising. They wouldn't have been any different than the clients on most of the other jobs Quinn had worked on over the years, but the fact that members of that council were now being eliminated was unusual. Especially when you took into account the kidnappings—or worse—of the people they'd hired.

"Any idea who's behind it?" he asked. "Could it be some of Romero's former colleagues carrying out revenge on those responsible for their friend's death?"

"Well, there's no actual proof Romero did die."

Quinn stared at her, wide-eyed. "Wait. What?"

"He was shot and severely injured, but he wasn't killed outright."

"Are you saying he's still alive?"

"I'm saying I don't know for sure. There were reports for a while about surgeries and hospital vigils. Then the election went on without him, and eventually he was no longer in the news."

Quinn leaned back in his chair. "Peter's notation in the file. The complication." Another thought clicked in his mind. "*Curson*. He would have been the shooter."

"Right. And since this was probably pretty high-profile, not fulfilling his mission wouldn't have gone down well."

"That's why he was blackballed. Has to be. And that's what Peter was noting. The screwup." He glanced over at her again. "No follow-ups with Romero? No 'victim goes home to die' or 'miraculous recovery'?"

"Nothing. Zero. No reports at all."

"Come on. Someone had to be keeping tabs on him."

"Maybe, but it's a small country, remember? While the international press shined its light in the island's direction for a little while after the assassination attempt, as soon as a bigger story came along somewhere else, they were gone."

"What about the local press?"

"State controlled. Not all democracies are created equal."

"What about the Office? If they failed the first time, Peter must have sent a second team in."

"I checked the file. Though it doesn't say anything about Romero surviving, there's a notation on one of the log sheets of a second team being put together after the date of the initial job. But the mission was cancelled before the team could leave."

"By who?"

"Client."

"My guess is that if Romero didn't die, he was messed up enough that the committee that ordered his hit had lost the taste for blood."

That must have pissed Peter off, Quinn thought. But as annoying as it might have been, Peter would have been hesitant to counter the people who had paid him.

So, Romero alive. An extremely ego-driven politician with designs on ruling for life permanently derailed. It sounded like more than enough motive for revenge.

"Here's another little tidbit for you," Orlando said. "David Harris is a former freelance soldier who did a lot of mercenary work in Africa and South America. Not always on the side our government would like."

"He's politically motivated?"

She shook her head. "The person I heard from said he never gave a damn what someone believed. If the paycheck was big enough, that's all that mattered. Said that as he got older, he branched out a bit, and eventually hooked up with Romero through some of Chavez's contacts."

"So, is Harris working for Romero to honor Romero's memory?" Quinn asked.

"I don't think this guy would honor anyone's memory but his own."

"Romero's alive, then."

"That would be my guess."

"Any leads on Harris's location?"

"Nothing yet, but if we find one, I have a feeling we'll find the other."

Quinn nodded. It was exactly what he was thinking.

THEY LANDED AT St. Renard International Airport, Isla de Cervantes's main entry point just outside the capital city of Córdoba, at three a.m.

After their conversation at the start of the flight, Orlando had taken a nap while Quinn sat silently, his eyes closed, but his mind unable to shut down. Romero, with the apparent help of Harris, had been having the members of the OAS committee who'd sentenced him to death killed, but the members of the ops team—at least in Nate's and Peter's cases—they'd kidnapped. Why the difference?

He considered the possibility that each was taken to someplace quiet where a bullet was put in their skull, but that didn't make sense. Peter was removed from his home, where he'd apparently been in bed. Why waste time dragging him out of the building, and possibly exposing themselves, instead of terminating him on the spot?

Of course. Romero wanted to be present as each member of the ops team was put to death. It was the only theory that rang true, and it also lent more credence to Quinn and Orlando's belief the man was still alive.

What about Nate? Now that he'd most likely been taken to Romero, were they already too late to save him?

As soon as the question entered his mind, he pushed it away. What-ifs like that could derail them. He needed to stay focused. They would find Nate.

They'd find him alive.

To do that, though, they needed to find Romero and Harris. And to find someone, you started at their last known location. Romero's public trail had gone cold a little more than three years earlier, at the Isla de Cervantes hospital where he was treated for his wounds.

That's where they would start.

As the plane taxied from the runway to the area reserved for private aircraft, Quinn got out of his seat and turned so he could talk to everyone at once.

"We need to track Romero down fast."

"If he's still alive," Daeng said.

"He is," Quinn said. "I'm sure of it."

"How do we find him?" Liz asked.

Quinn looked at his sister. "Orlando and I are going to pay a visit to the hospital where he was last treated, and see what we can turn up. You're going to stay here with Daeng."

Liz didn't look happy. Before she could argue the point, Orlando said, "He's right, Liz. We need to keep a low profile. The more people, the more chance we'll be discovered."

"I can wait in the car," Liz said.

"True," Quinn said. "But what will you say when a security guard comes out and asks what you're doing? It's the middle of the night. People don't just sit in their cars."

She looked at her brother, her fear for Nate written on her face, but then she nodded. "You're right. Sorry, I...just..."

Quinn reached over and touched her hand. "We're going to find him. Don't worry."

Liz tried to smile, but failed. "I know."

Two Customs and Immigration officials met them in the parking area and processed their documents. Once that was done, Daeng and Liz headed back into the plane with the two pilots, while Quinn and Orlando hitched a ride with the C&I guys back to the main terminal.

On the road, in front of the passenger arrival area, were two taxis, both drivers asleep in their seats. Quinn and Orlando woke the man in the first cab as they climbed in, and had him take them to Cristo de los Milagros Hospital, where Romero had been treated.

By American standards, the place was small for being the main medical facility in the biggest city in the country. Of course, size was relative. Córdoba only had thirty-five thousand residents, while the island as a whole boasted somewhere in the vicinity of a hundred and seven thousand. When viewed that way, the two-story structure that wasn't much larger than a grocery store back home was undoubtedly more than adequate for the people it served.

They had the cabbie drop them off at the entrance to the parking lot, then took a quick, wide walk around the entire place.

"CCTV," Orlando said, pointing out the closed-circuit security cameras as she spotted them.

Using the camera function on his phone, Quinn zoomed in to get a better look. "Reycons. Y23s," he said, citing the make and model.

They were decent enough, but not top of the line. Using his knowledge of their specs, he picked out a blind spot that would get them right up to the hospital next to a nondescript side door without being seen.

They walked across a parking area, not deviating from

254

the path, and reached the side of the building without incident. By the look of things, the door was used by hospital personnel in search of a smoke break. Butts littered the ground, and the aroma of stale tobacco and smoke lingered in the air.

Before leaving the plane, Quinn and Orlando had equipped themselves with some of the items Veronique had loaded onto the aircraft at their request. Quinn removed a set of lock picks from his pocket, and seconds later had the door unlocked.

Orlando ran a handheld scanner along the door, checking for an alarm. It vibrated once near the top. She hit a few buttons, put the scanner back over the spot, and held it there until the vibration stopped. Once she gave Quinn a nod, he opened the door.

The hallway they entered was well lit and deserted.

"That one," Orlando whispered, pointing at a door just ahead on the right.

From the name plaque mounted on it, it was clear that on the other side they'd find an office. And where there was an office, there would be a computer.

Quinn picked the lock and then shut the door after they were both inside. The room was cramped but neat—books on shelves on both sides, and a desk in the middle with the hoped-for workstation.

While Orlando delved into the hospital's network, Quinn perused the books. They were mostly medical text, a mix of Spanish and English. There were also several binders specific to the hospital—guidelines, standard procedures, employee handbook, and a facility directory.

After several minutes, Orlando sat back, her eyes still focused on the screen. "I need to get to another computer. This one's blocked."

"If this one's blocked, won't they all be?"

She paused. "I should be able to get around it in IT."

Getting them into an empty office in the middle of the night was one thing. Sneaking into the hospital's main computer room was something else entirely. While there wouldn't be a full staff on duty at this time, someone would be around in case any problems came up.

Quinn snatched the facility directory off the bookshelf. Inside was a map, followed by pages listing names and extension numbers by department. He first located the computer room. It was on the same floor, but clear on the other side of the building. He pulled the map out of the binder, and found the page with the extensions for the IT department and one listing all hospital department heads. He removed them also.

"Here," he said, showing her the map. "This is where you want to be." He gave her a moment to memorize it. "What's the extension here?"

She looked at the phone. "425."

"I'll scope it out and clear the way, then call you."

He turned for the door.

"Hey," she said, stopping him.

He looked back as she stood up and came around the desk.

"Don't do anything stupid," she said. She pulled his head down and kissed him.

When she finally backed away, he said, "We haven't been doing enough of that lately."

"You're telling me." She gave him a playful smirk. "Now go do your job. I'll give you another one when we get out of here."

"Always nice to have a little motivation."

CHAPTER
FORTY FOUR

IT WAS EVEN worse than Nate thought.

As he set out from the fort, he hoped to find a small village or, at the very least, some facility that might have a means for him to get a message out. But the journey to the far side of the island took only forty minutes, and in that time, the only man-made thing he came across was an empty blacktopped landing strip.

He circled around the beach, thinking there might be a fishing hut or a dock, but it was clear that with the exception of the fort, the island was deserted.

What made it even more frustrating was the glow on the horizon. It was too big to be a ship, so it must have been from a city, meaning there was another island—a *bigger* one—out there.

Nate stared across the water. It couldn't have been more than twenty or thirty miles away. But since he had no way to get there, it might as well have been a thousand.

He allowed himself a moment to sit and rest. Calling for help was apparently not an option. Neither was escaping the island. As soon as the other prisoners were roused from their cells and it was discovered he was gone, Harris's men would come looking for him. There wasn't far he could go, after all.

He knew he had only one course of action open to him. Do whatever he could to save the others. There was a good chance he'd be killed in the process, but he couldn't just hide away while they were being tortured to death.

He pushed himself to his feet and turned back to the jungle.

First order of business: Get a better idea of the fort's layout, and try to gauge how many soldiers Harris and the old man commanded.

After that...

Well, one step at a time.

CHAPTER
FORTY FIVE

ISLA DE CERVANTES

FROM THE HOSPITAL map, Quinn noted that the patient rooms were located along the back half of the first floor, and throughout most of the second. Those would be the areas with the highest concentration of personnel at this time of night, therefore places best avoided.

The second floor wasn't an issue. They had no need to go up there. It was the first floor patient wing that was the problem. The IT room was just down the hallway from it, near the far, rear corner building where, according to the map, a nurses' station was located.

He made his way across the building via a central corridor that led past several offices, radiology, and a medical lab. Two thirds of the way down, he needed to take a hall to the left, then another to the right that went all the way to the hall the IT room was located in. As he neared the first turn, he could hear the hum of a machine.

He peeked around the corner. About twenty feet away, right where he needed to turn again, an older man was heading away from Quinn while pushing a large motorized buffer across the tiled floor. He'd move the machine from side to side, then push it forward a few feet and repeat the dance. Quinn watched him, silently urging him to hurry up. Five more feet and he could sneak behind the guy and down the other hall without the janitor even knowing.

Just as he was about to make his move, someone stepped out from the hallway that he'd been targeting, the person's approaching footsteps having been drowned out by the buffer.

Quinn pulled back quickly out of sight and began retracing his steps down the hallway. As he passed the lab, he checked the door. Locked. He did the same at Radiology.

Also locked. The next door was too far away. He would never make it, so he pulled out his picks again and quickly let himself into the room.

"*Disculpe*," a male voice called out.

Quinn closed the door behind him and did a quick scan. He was in a small outer room that opened into a larger one where a table for patients and the X-ray machine were located. He moved all the way into the big room and off to the side, out of view. On the wall next to him were several wide files sticking out of wall-mounted trays, presumably X-rays that needed to be viewed or filed away.

The outer door opened a few seconds later. "*Oiga, oiga. Usted no puede entrar ahí*," the voice said. The door closed. "*Disculpe.*"

"I'm sorry?" Quinn called out in Spanish. He pulled a file from one of the trays and removed the X-ray from inside.

The man stepped into the main room. A security guard—just Quinn's luck. The guy was about Quinn's height, but at least fifty pounds heavier.

"You can't be here," the man said.

"I'm Dr. Chavez. Just picking up some records." Quinn raised the file a few inches so the man would see it.

The security guard's eyes narrowed. "I've never seen you before."

"That's not my problem," Quinn said, donning stereotypical doctor charm. "I've been here for a week. I'm the consulting surgeon from Puerto Rico. Dr. Fernandez assured me I would have full access to whatever I needed." The directory page he had ripped out had listed Dr. Fernandez as the hospital administrator at the top.

The guard looked unsure. "I wasn't told anything about

that. You should have been given a badge. Where is it?"

"I don't know," Quinn said defiantly. "I probably left it in the office. Don't tell me I have to go get it."

"I'm afraid we have very strict rules about that here. I'll go with you. Once I see it, you'll be free to do whatever you need."

"This is ridiculous." Quinn frowned as he stepped by the man into the smaller room, but then he stopped abruptly and turned back. Gesturing at the other room, he said, "There was one other record I needed. Can't I at least get that?"

Predictably, the guard turned to look where Quinn was pointing.

Though he was big, the takedown when quickly. With an arm around the man's neck, Quinn cut off the flow of blood to the guard's head until he passed out. He dragged the man to the back corner beyond the table and lowered him to the floor.

Never one to pass up an opportunity, Quinn relieved the guard of his badge and the ring of keys on his belt. He used a couple of electrical cords to bind the man's wrist and ankles in case he woke too soon. To ensure no one would hear him if he woke up and yelled, Quinn closed the door between the two rooms before exiting the other door into the hallway.

He hurried back to the end of the corridor and peeked around again. The janitor was much farther down now, still working back and forth. Quinn slipped around the corner and took the next hallway without being seen. He didn't pause again until he reached the hallway that ran along the far end of the hospital. The IT room was thirty feet to his left, with the nurses' station another twenty-five beyond it.

He took a look, and grimaced. As he'd feared, the station was occupied. Two nurses were talking to each other as they shuffled through a stack of files on the counter.

The best play was the old standby—act like you belong.

Before turning the corner, he clipped the guard's badge high up on his jacket so it would be clearly visible at a distance. Next he examined the man's keys, identified the three he thought would be most likely to let him into the IT room, and proceeded.

At first the nurses gave no reaction, but as he neared the door to IT, first one looked over at him, then the other. He smiled and gave them a friendly wave. Once they saw where he was going, they smiled back and returned to their conversation.

Quinn gave the doorknob a quick twist, checking to see if it was locked. It was, so he slipped one of the three keys into the slot. No go. Number two, though, worked just fine.

As he opened the door, he glanced back at the nurses, but neither seemed to even realize he was still there. He stepped inside and was enveloped by the hum of servers and routers. The room was about thirty feet long and fifteen feet wide. There was one row of machine racks along the back wall, and two more down the middle. Against the wall that ran adjacent to the hallway was a long workbench.

At first Quinn thought maybe he was alone. The workbench and the area he could see around the racks were empty. He walked farther in, looking between the rows, and finally spotted a young guy with a mass of curly hair sitting at a computer station in the back corner. He was wearing headphones, and his body rocked forward and back as it kept time with whatever music he was listening to.

Moving in behind him was a piece of cake. The kid didn't even know he wasn't alone until Quinn's arm wrapped around his neck.

As soon as he passed out, Quinn laid him on the floor, then picked up the phone and dialed 4-2-5.

"WHOA, WHOA, WHOA," Orlando said.

Quinn was standing several feet away, in a spot where he could keep an eye on the IT room door. "What is it?"

"A flag."

He hurried over. "What kind of flag?"

"One that's going to let someone know if I set it off."

"Hospital security?"

"No. This is third-party stuff, outside." She glanced down at the guy on the floor. "Don't think Mr. IT there or any of his colleagues know anything about it."

"Attached to Romero's files?"

"Not exactly," she said. "There *are* no Romero files. Everything must have been removed. There's nothing even in the backups."

"Then a flag on what?"

"Thought I'd give the hospital's normal search function a try, just in case my program missed something. I checked the code first so I'd know how effective it might be. That's when I found it. It's set to go off if anyone searches the name Javier Romero."

"Can you tell who gets notified?"

"A Gmail account. Probably a dummy address that forwards it on."

"What does it tell them?"

"The parameters of the search and the IP location of the computer used."

Quinn thought for a moment. "Can you manipulate what information it sends?"

She looked at him with distain. "Of course."

He grinned. "How about you try this. Grab an IP address from a room in a nearby hotel, then do the search using 'Javier Romero' and 'current location.' That should get a response."

Orlando stared thoughtfully at the screen for a moment. "If we want to guarantee a response, we should add *your* name to the search."

"Great idea," he said. "Do it."

CHAPTER
FORTY SIX

JANUS SMILED AS he walked down the hallway. Though he wasn't fond of rising before daybreak, he did love waking up the prisoners. And since there weren't going to be very many more opportunities, he wanted to relish each.

He let one of Romero's security force open the door to the hallway they'd transformed into a cellblock, and then he stepped through. All was satisfyingly dark and quiet.

"Turn on lights," he said.

Another soldier flipped the switches that illumined the corridor, and turned on the bulbs inside each cell.

"Wakie, wakie!" Janus yelled.

He moved down to the room that held the squat bald guy who'd upset Mr. Romero the night before, and pounded his fist against the door. "Get up! Time for more fun."

He pulled up on the handle, releasing the bars that held the door in place, and gave it a yank.

"Up, up, up!" he ordered as he walked in.

The guy was already standing up, his face impassive.

"Hood and cuffs," Janus told the guard who'd entered with him.

Once the prisoner's head was cloaked and his hands were bound, he was led out of the room. Janus and another guard visited Berkeley's cell. After that, it was Lanier, then on to the last two, Quinn and Curson.

Janus was surprised Curson had lived as long as he had. The shooter had put up a big fight when he arrived on the island, and had tried to escape when he was escorted to dinner with Harris. It had been Janus's job to remind the man he had no say in anything anymore. One more beating and he was sure Curson would never get up again. Or, perhaps, this morning's planned whipping would do the trick. That was, if he hadn't already died in his sleep.

But first—Quinn.

"Wakie, wakie!" he yelled at the door to the cleaner's cell.

As he did each previous time, he slammed his fist against it, then turned the handle and pulled the door open.

"Up, up, up!"

THERE WAS A loud knock on Harris's door. He pulled it open and found Janus standing there, panting like he'd been running.

"A prisoner is gone," Janus blurted out.

"What do you mean, gone? Dead?" Harris asked, knowing Janus's English wasn't always the best.

"No. Gone. Not in cell!"

A gentle poke, like someone in the back of his mind tapping a finger against a wall. *One small error.* "How the hell did that happen?"

"The vent, I think," Janus said.

"The vent? What vent?"

"In the door."

The vents in the doors weren't even wide enough for a child to crawl through. "Impossible."

"Come. You see."

Harris moved into the hallway and pulled his door closed. "Which one is missing?"

"Quinn."

Harris paused between steps. *Quinn? Jesus.*

He picked up his pace. "Show me!"

They ran through the old colonial fort, their footsteps echoing loudly off the stone. The door to the cellblock was open, a guard standing beside it. In the makeshift prison, four more guards were stationed in front of each of the occupied cells.

"I was getting them up for morning session," Janus explained, now that they were no longer running. "Already had three out when found his cell empty. Put all back in and come get you."

The door to Quinn's cell was closed. Harris examined it. The vent cover was in place and nothing seemed out of order. There was, however, an odd scratch along the side of the door handle, thin but fresh. Had it been caused by one of the guards, or Quinn in his escape? Or had someone come in and let him out?

When he opened the door, the first thing he noticed was the rectangular metal frame lying on the floor. He looked at the back of the door and saw that it had been part of the vent. Kneeling, he put his hand through the hole and pushed on the slatted front half. With very little effort, the frame and slats popped out.

All right, but it still didn't make any sense. Quinn couldn't have crawled through it. And there had been nothing in his cell he could have used to reach the handle.

"Who's looking for him? Please tell me someone is looking for him!" Harris demanded as he stood back up.

"Not yet," Janus said nervously. "I came for you right away."

"Check the fort first. If he's not here, send everyone we can spare out onto the island! There's no place for him to go, so he'll be close. Find him!"

"Yes, sir." Janus hesitated. "What about the others? And this morning? Mr. Romero will be—"

"Find Quinn first," Harris ordered. "The rest can wait."

THE CHAOS LASTED nearly half an hour before the noise in the corridor finally died down. None of the prisoners said anything for another ten minutes, each wondering if there was a guard standing just outside.

It was Lanier who broke the silence. "How did he get out?"

"Screw that," Berkeley said. "Why didn't he take us with

him?"

"They said he went through the door vent," Curson offered from farther down the hall.

"How could he do that?" Lanier asked. There was a thud and a bang. "If it's the same size as mine, no way he could get through it."

"I don't know. I just know he's gone," Berkeley said.

"What if this is another trick?" Lanier said. "What if they took Quinn out last night and shot him? What if this is just them messing with our minds again?"

"Why would they need to do that?" Curson asked. "They whipped us. They electrocuted us. Don't know about you, but my mind's pretty messed up already."

"I think they're trying to give us false hope," Lanier said.

No one responded to that.

"Hey, Jonathan," Lanier said. "What do you think?"

Peter was stretched out on his bed, trying not to listen.

"Jonathan. You there?"

With a sigh, Peter said, "I'm here."

"What do you think happened?"

"I don't think anything."

"Come on. You must have some ideas."

"Sure, I have one," Peter said. "Looks like we just got a few hours off."

HARRIS'S CELL PHONE rang as he was heading to Romero's room to deliver the news. He looked at the screen. It was Ryan Porter, Romero's point man on Isla de Cervantes.

"What?" Harris said.

"Mr. Harris," Porter said. "Sorry to bother you, but just a little while ago someone used the database at Cristo de los Milagros Hospital to look for info on Señor Romero."

Harris slowed his pace, surprised. "Who?"

"I don't have a name, sir. They used the IT department's log-in, but the IP is from a hotel a few miles away." There was a pause. "Sir, one of the terms they used for their search is on the hot list."

"What term?"

"'Current location,'" Porter said.

Son of a bitch, Harris thought. Crap was piling up on crap now. He closed his eyes and took a deep breath. He needed to concentrate on finding the cleaner. That was the most immediate problem. "Just see if you can find out who—"

"Sir, they also included a second name in the search."

A second name? He was almost afraid to ask. "What was it?"

"Jonathan Quinn. Does that mean anything to you?"

Harris froze where he stood.

"Sir?" Porter asked.

"Send the men to that hotel, find out who made that search, and eliminate them. Call me as soon as you know who they were."

CHAPTER
FORTY SEVEN

THE MARGUERITE HOTEL was located a block from the beach in the touristy west side of Córdoba. It had been an easy hack for Orlando to insert into the hotel's records that room 317 was occupied by a Mr. and Mrs. J. Quinn. That was also the room where the IP address she used in the search was assigned. In addition to room 317, she had claimed room 316 across the hall, and room 323 near the elevators.

Since they would need more than just the two of them to cover everything, they'd called Daeng and had him and, with some reluctance on Quinn's part, Liz join them. They stationed Daeng in 323 and put Liz down in the lobby with a newspaper. Quinn and Orlando took room 316.

"Don't do anything stupid," Quinn told Liz over the phone. She was their early warning system, tasked only with noting hotel arrivals.

"Don't worry, I won't," she said. "I'm just reading the paper. If anyone asks, I'm an early riser who didn't want to wake up her husband."

"All right. Just…be careful, okay?"

"I will."

After he hung up, he went over to the bed and sat next to Orlando. She was reading something on her computer.

"If no one shows up," he said, "we'll have to find another way to locate this son of a bitch."

"Yeah, I don't think that's going to be a problem," she said.

"What do you mean?"

She shut her computer. "A few minutes ago someone hacked into the hotel system, and checked on the occupants of room 317. I say they'll be here in fifteen minutes or less. How about you?"

THE TEXT FROM Liz came seventeen minutes later.

> 4 MEN IN SUITS W/BRIEFCASES.
> NOT TALKING. LOOK SERIOUS.
> HEADING FOR ELEVATOR.

"I should have taken the bet," Quinn said as he forwarded the info to Daeng, then moved toward the door.

"Did I not mention the plus-or-minus-three-minutes factor? I'm sure I did," Orlando said, walking up beside him and turning off the light.

Via the microcam mounted just above the frame of their door outside, they were able to monitor the door to room 317 on Quinn's phone. No one was there yet.

Quinn's phone buzzed with a message from Daeng that momentarily flashed over the video image.

> DING!

Daeng's proximity to the elevator meant he could hear when a car arrived. Apparently one just had.

Ten seconds went by before two men in suits walked past the room. Five more seconds and they came back, stopping this time at the door to 317, where the other two joined them.

They all set their briefcases on the floor and opened them. There was no question now why they'd come. Each removed a suppressor-equipped pistol.

Quinn shot Daeng a quick text telling him to be ready. He checked that his own sound suppressor was firmly attached to the end of his gun.

Veronique had supplied them with a variety of weapons. Quinn was holding his favorite SIG P226, while Orlando was carrying a GLOCK and had a vaccination gun full of sleep juice in her pocket. Daeng, too, was armed with a GLOCK.

One of the men pulled a small black box from his case and held it up to the electronic lock on the door. A light flashed green, he gently turned the handle, and began pushing the door open.

"Get ready," Quinn whispered.

Orlando was holding her phone in her free hand. On the screen was one of her many self-created apps. It displayed a simple green button that, when touched, would send a signal to the device now hooked to the fuse box controlling the lights on the third floor.

Across the hall, the first man entered room 317 and stopped a few feet inside. One by one the others joined him.

As the fourth started in, Quinn said, "Now."

Orlando's thumb tapped down on the green button and darkness descended, sudden and complete.

Quinn opened the door and raced across the hall in a crouch, reaching the fourth man before the guy had even turned around. He shoved the intruder in the back, pushing him farther into the room and knocking him into the guy just in front of him. Both men tumbled to the ground.

Muzzle flashes lit up the far end of the room. If Quinn had been standing, the bullet that smashed into the wall above him would have hit him square in the face. The other bullets flew through the doorway and into the hall.

Shooting first had been a mistake. Quinn and Orlando aimed at the flash points and pulled their triggers, once each. The two men who had entered the room first dropped dead.

Quinn heard the other two trying to free themselves from each other and join the fight. He whipped his gun down and positioned the end of the suppressor an inch from the closest guy's ear. The heat radiating from the muzzle was enough motivation for the man to freeze.

The other one continued trying to twist free. The shadowy form of the gun in his hand moved upward. Quinn was about to whip him on the side of his head with the SIG when Orlando stepped around him and kicked the gun out of the guy's hand. She then lashed out again, catching the guy under the chin.

His body went limp.

"Drop your gun," Quinn said to the fourth man.

"*No hablo inglés.*"

"Bullshit. Drop it."

The gun clunked to the floor. Quinn reached over and pushed it back toward the door.

"Orlando, some light."

There was a slight delay, and then the lights in the hallway came back on. A few seconds later, the room lights flipped on.

Quinn glanced back and saw Daeng standing just inside the threshold. "Door."

With a nod, Daeng closed the door.

Quinn returned his attention to the man on the floor. "Who sent you? Romero?"

A second of nothing, then, "Who Romero?"

Quinn grabbed his man by the shirt and pulled him up. He forced him to the back of the room, where his two dead colleagues lay. "Tell me what I want to know or you'll join them."

There was fear in the man's eyes, a particular kind of fear Quinn had seen before—the fear of an asshole who was used to being the deliverer of violence, not the receiver.

Quinn pushed the suppressor into the back of the man's head. "*Who* sent you?"

"Okay! Okay! Romero. Yes, yes. Romero."

"Where is he?"

"I don't know."

Quinn shoved the barrel forward again. "Where is he?"

"I don't know! Our boss just sent us here. Tell us to bring people in room back to him. I swear."

Quinn's eyes narrowed. "Back to where?"

RYAN PORTER WAS growing concerned. He should have heard from his security team by now. They'd had more than enough time to get into the room at the Marguerite Hotel and snatch whoever was in there.

The last he'd heard from them was that they were on site and getting ready to move in. That was nearly twenty minutes ago. They must have had some kind of problem.

He'd been monitoring the police bands, and all was quiet. So whatever was going on, at least the authorities weren't involved yet.

He drummed his fingers on his desk. *Ten more minutes, and I'll go check myself.*

He got up to fill his coffee mug, not that he wanted another cup. He needed to do something more than just sit there staring at his phone. He was halfway to the coffee maker when the intercom buzzed. He raced back to his desk and pushed the button.

"Yes."

"Mr. Porter. It's Felipe. We're back."

There was a small monitor next to the speaker. Porter turned it on, and a view of the entrance to the building appeared on-screen. The light over the door was enough for him to see Felipe's face, and the dark forms of the two men in hoodies behind him—Raul and Marcos, most likely. Between the two men was someone smaller. It looked like a woman. They were gripping her arms, and her head was bowed.

Porter pushed the button again. "Is that her?"

Felipe turned his face so he was looking directly at the camera. "Yes. She was the only one there."

"All right. Bring her in. I'll meet you in the storage room."

He pushed the button that unlocked the door. Feeling more relaxed, he filled his coffee and left his office. A little conversation, and then they'd get rid of her.

Problem solved.

"GOOD SO FAR," Quinn whispered once they were inside the building. "You keep it up, you'll stay alive."

The room immediately beyond the entrance was filled with large, old machinery. From the looks of things, it had been years since any of them had been turned on."

"Where is this storage room he wants us to go to?" Quinn asked.

"In the back," Felipe said.

"How do we get there?"

"Through there and all the way back." Felipe pointed between two of the machines.

"And then?"

"Um, we go left until we reach the white door. That'll be it."

"And you're sure he's alone?"

"Yes," Felipe said. "He sent all of us to the hotel."

Quinn gave Orlando a subtle nod. In a swift, silent motion, she raised the vaccination gun to Felipe's shoulder and shot an eight-hour dose of tranquilizer into his arm. Felipe turned in surprise, but before he could say anything, his eyelids began to droop, and they eased him to the floor.

Following Felipe's instructions, they headed to the back of the building, vigilant in case Porter wasn't the only one around. When they came in sight of the white door, Orlando moved into the point position so she would be the first one seen.

PORTER'S OFFICE WAS just down the hall from the storage room, so it wasn't a surprise he was the first one there. There was an old wooden storage box next to the wall. He dragged it into the middle of the room, right below the only light.

He took a step back, and smiled. Very intimidating. Whoever this woman was, she wouldn't last long. He was willing to bet he'd know everything she did before his coffee cooled.

He took a sip, and nodded. Perfect.

Behind him he heard the door open. He turned, a smile still on his face.

The woman came through the door first. She couldn't have been much more than one hundred and fifty centimeters tall. She was also Asian, which was a bit of a surprise.

"Well, hello," he said. "Please, have a seat."

Two of his men came in behind her, but Porter's eyes

remained focused on the woman, making sure she understood who was boss. When she got to within ten feet, she stopped, the look of despair on her face replaced by an eerily playful smile. Porter tried to maintain his own detached façade, but he couldn't stop his brow from creasing in confusion.

"Actually, Mr. Porter," one of the men behind her said. "You're the one who should take a seat."

CHAPTER
FORTY EIGHT

SO FAR NATE had counted eighteen soldiers leaving the fort and moving into the jungle.

They wouldn't send everyone out, he knew, but he felt confident, based on the yelling he heard coming from beyond the wall, that they would send the majority.

Under the cover of darkness, he had snuck all the way back to the wall, where he had momentarily considered climbing up and finding someplace within the complex to hide. But he felt he could control things better out here.

Surveying the wall, he spotted a heavy wooden door that, as far as he could tell, was the only ground-level exit to the complex. Choosing the location carefully, he dug a ditch between a couple of trees, just deep enough for him to lie in, and covered himself with dead palm fronds and other vegetation. The position gave him a perfect view of the door, with very little chance he'd be discovered.

That's where he was when the men had begun coming out.

Eighteen fighters.

He figured half that many were still inside. That would make twenty-seven total. Round that up to thirty, just to be safe. Add in Janus, Harris, and the old man. Thirty-three. Staff? Cooks? Medical personnel for the old man? That seemed likely. Figure forty people total, not counting the prisoners.

Looking at the whole number was a bit daunting, but one

by one, not so bad. Especially if Nate could get his hands on a weapon.

The door opened again, and a nineteenth soldier came out. Nate recognized this one. He was the jerk who'd come in with Janus and slammed the butt of his gun into Nate's back the first day. Nate could see the offending rifle slung over the guy's shoulder, and suddenly knew which weapon he'd like to start with.

As soon as the soldier passed by, Nate slipped out of his hidey-hole.

SOMEONE KNOCKED ON Harris's door. He opened it to find one of Romero's nurses.

"Yes?"

"Sorry to disturb you," the nurse said. "But Señor Romero wants to see you."

Harris wanted nothing more than to tell the nurse he'd come when he could, but he knew that would only enrage his employer, and the nurse would be sent back again.

"I'll be right there," he said, and shut his door.

Despite the early hour, he poured himself a whiskey and slammed it down. The alcohol helped mute the voices that were telling him everything was beginning to unravel. Of course, it wasn't. He still had control of the situation.

So what if one of the prisoners got away? So what if it was Quinn? He was just one person. And they would find him. He could only hide for so long. This was an island, for God's sake. A *small* island. If need be, they'd search it inch by inch.

What about whoever had been searching Romero's and Quinn's names at the hospital?

Porter will handle it.

No, everything was going to be fine. Things were too close to the end for them not to be.

He fought the urge to have another drink, and forced himself to head over to Romero's office.

"Have they found the cleaner?" Romero demanded as soon as Harris entered.

"It hasn't been that long. They need a little time."

"Unacceptable! They should have him by now." The old man fumed for a moment. "I want to continue as planned."

"You mean now?"

"Yes, now. Of course, now. We're wasting time."

"I'd be more comfortable once we have Quinn back."

"I will *not* let one person delay us. Do you understand me? Assemble the prisoners."

"We're understaffed at the moment," Harris said. "Most of the men are out looking for him."

Romero narrowed his eyes. "How many men to do you really need? The prisoners are beaten and weak. They'll be cuffed and hooded, too. We could do it with just Janus if we needed to."

Quinn is beaten and weak, too, Harris thought, *and look at what he did*. He knew there was no sense in arguing the point, though. "Yes, sir. I'll get things moving."

"Good. I'll be out in the courtyard in twenty minutes. They'd better be there."

THE GUARD DIDN'T know Nate was there until the rock slammed into his head, and even then, the realization probably lasted only a microsecond before he dropped to the ground.

Nate checked his pulse. Weak, and getting weaker. There was a very good chance the man wouldn't live for long.

Bummer. That was about as much sympathy as Nate could muster.

He grabbed the guard by the shoulders and dragged him into the brush, out of sight. A quick search netted him not only the rifle and some spare ammo, but also a GLOCK pistol, a five-inch hunting knife, and a palm-sized, handheld radio. Once he was geared up, he masked the marks he and the soldier had made in the sand, and went in search of number two.

IT WASN'T UNTIL Janus was hauling the prisoners outside that Harris realized he hadn't heard back from Porter. He tried calling him, but after four rings only reached voice mail.

"It's Harris. Update. Now."

CHAPTER
FORTY NINE

THEY DROVE SOUTH through Córdoba—Orlando behind the wheel, Quinn and Daeng in the backseat with Porter between them, and Liz up front with Orlando's computer.

"Here we go," Liz said, looking at the laptop's screen. "The island's called Duran, and is thirty-one miles south-southeast of Isla de Cervantes. Apparently, it was first spotted by Columbus on his final voyage in 1503. Says he didn't stop there, though. Not big enough, I guess." She began to read aloud. "'In the early 1600s, Charles Duran, one of the early Spanish governors of Isla de Cervantes, decided the much smaller Isla Helena, as Duran was first known, could serve as an early warning outpost, alerting the bigger island of approaching enemies by lighting bonfires at its highest point, a low-slung hill at the southwest end of the island.'

"'Over the years, the outpost's few buildings were renovated and added to until it became known as Fort Duran.'" She paused as she read on silently. "It does say the island eventually fell into private hands. Nothing about whose, though."

According to Porter, the private hands in question belonged to the Romero family, and they'd made Duran their private retreat for over a hundred years. Javier had apparently taken sole control of the island a year prior to his faithful run for the presidency, and had moved there permanently—with the blessings of the government he'd tried to oppose—when he was released from the hospital.

"Is there a map?" Quinn asked.

"Yeah, but it's small," Liz said. "Let me see if I can find something better."

A few moments later Orlando said, "Highway 3 south? Or is there another way?"

Ahead was a sign with an arrow pointing toward the entrance to the highway.

"Yes," Porter said. "Highway 3."

Orlando gunned the engine and transitioned them off the city street onto the faster road.

Their destination was a private marina just south of town, where Porter said there was a boat that could take them to Duran. Porter was more a behind-the-scenes guy, who became even more cooperative after a demonstration of how easy it was to dislocate a finger if Quinn wasn't happy with a response.

"I swear, I didn't know what he had planned at first," Porter had said. "It was too late for me to do anything when I did."

"Bullshit," Quinn said.

Porter looked nervous, but didn't push the point again.

"How did you get everyone's names?" Quinn asked.

"I don't know. Either Harris or Romero did that."

"The prisoners—you're sure they haven't been killed?"

"They were still alive last I heard."

"But the plan *is* to kill them."

Porter nervously licked his lips, then whispered, "Yes."

As soon as they'd extracted the information they needed, and learned about the boat, they packed Porter into the car, where Liz had been waiting, and headed out.

"Got one," Liz said. She raised the computer and flashed the screen at Quinn. On it was a map of the island.

"Perfect," Quinn said. "Nice and big."

Liz smiled, and lowered the machine back to her lap. "I'll save it to the drive."

"The turnoff's coming up," Porter said. "You'll see a sign for Córdoba Royale Marina. Just after that. The turn will be on the left."

There was a brief pause, then Orlando said, "I see it."

Quinn turned to Porter. "Tell me again, how many on the boat?"

"Only two."

"What about elsewhere in the marina?"

"Elsewhere?"

"Men on another boat, maybe? Or housed on shore?"

"No. Only the two guys."

"You know what happens if you're lying."

"You'll kill me."

"We'll kill you."

"I'm not lying. There used to be more, but Harris had everyone but a few who were still on the payroll moved out to Duran."

Quinn looked for signs of deceit, but saw none. Still, they wouldn't let their guard down.

As Porter had said, the unmanned marina gate was opened by entering a code on a keypad.

"Give me the number," Orlando said as she rolled down her window and pulled to a stop in front of the gate.

"Four, seven—"

"Before you finish," Quinn said. "I'd strongly advise you not to give us a code that will alert anybody."

Porter's chin began to shake. "I wouldn't do that."

"Then give her the code."

"Four, um, eight, two, two, nine."

"You're sure?" Orlando asked.

"Yes."

She punched in the numbers. There was a two-second delay, then the gate rolled out of the way. Porter directed them to a parking area in front of pier number eleven.

"That's it," he said, looking out the front window. "The one with the white top and dark blue side, tied up on the right."

The boat was a beauty—a Princess V57. Quinn was familiar with its specs, and knew once they were away from the island, as long as the water wasn't too choppy, they should be able to make thirty knots easy, getting them to

Duran in about an hour.

"Last chance, Porter. How many on the boat?"

"Two. I swear."

"Names?"

"Hansen and, um, Flores."

Orlando took Quinn's place in the backseat next to Porter, while Quinn and Daeng went to pay the men on the boat a visit.

No one was on deck. Unfortunately, the glass door to the cabin area was locked. Quinn explained to Daeng what he wanted to do. Once his friend was in position and ready, he knocked on the door.

"Hello? Anyone awake? Harris sent me. Hello?"

There was a thump somewhere beyond the door, then the sound of feet shuffling. Quinn knocked again.

"Hello? Where is everyone?"

Through the door, he could see a shadow come up the stairs from the below-deck living area and walk across the cabin. The door opened, and a man who'd obviously just crawled out of bed looked out.

"Are you Hansen or Flores?" Quinn asked.

"What? Who are you?"

"Look, Harris sent me. Are you Hansen or Flores?"

"I'm Hansen."

"Good. I've got something they want out at the island, but I need your help carrying it on board."

"No one told me anything about going out there today."

"Not my problem."

"I should call and check."

"Fine by me," Quinn said. "But help me get this on board first, all right? You're not the only stop I've got to make this morning."

Hansen frowned. "Let me put on my shoes."

When Hansen was finally ready, Quinn said, "It's over here."

As he led Hansen to the dock, Daeng moved in behind them, and gave the deckhand a quick shot in the arm from the vaccine gun.

Flores was even easier. He was still asleep in one of the beds below, and stirred only slightly as the tranquilizer entered his arm.

They put both men in the same cabin and locked the door.

Quinn returned to the car and pulled Porter out. Orlando followed right behind with the duffel bag full of equipment. When Liz climbed out, Quinn said, "You're not coming with us."

"But—"

"You're not coming, Liz."

"You might need me," she argued.

In the past, he would have gotten mad and told her she was staying, end of story. But this time, he put his hands on her arms and said, "I do need you. That's why you can't come. This is one of those not-safe situations. I can't do my job and worry about you at the same time. I swear I'll let you know the second everything is okay."

As she looked at him, he could tell she was trying to find something she could use to change his mind, but then the tension drained from her shoulders and she nodded. "Okay. I understand."

He pulled her to him, and she hugged him back.

"Find him," she whispered.

"We will."

When they parted, she said, "Be careful."

He smiled. "Go back to the plane. I'll call you there."

CHAPTER
FIFTY

CURSON WAS FIRST up.

Each crack of the whip was greeted with a scream, as the wounds from the day before were reopened.

Harris glanced at Romero. The old man's eyes were glued to Curson's back, and there was a satisfied smile on his face. With the exception of Peter, Curson drew most of Romero's attention. He'd been the shooter, the one who, while failing in his ultimate goal, had damaged Romero so thoroughly that it had taken over a year before the former presidential candidate could even take a step, let alone eat anything that wasn't prepared specifically for his surgically altered digestive tract.

The life Romero had lived since the shooting had been anything but pleasant and pain-free, and there were times Harris was sure his boss secretly wished Curson had done a better job. Death had to have been preferable.

But death hadn't been in his boss's cards, not earlier, anyway. It was coming now, though, the wounds Curson's bullets had inflicted finally doing what they had intended to do. A slow assassination. Mission soon to be accomplished, but not before Romero extracted his revenge.

Crack!

Curson yelled as he arced his back and then collapsed again, his weight supported only by the cuffs around his wrists.

A guard entered the courtyard through the far door. He

wasn't one of the men who had remained in the fort. They were all here with the remaining prisoners. He stopped just inside, and discreetly motioned to Harris that he needed to talk to him.

Harris checked Romero again. The man was rapt, his attention fully engaged in the proceedings, so Harris quietly stepped back and made his way around to where the guard was waiting.

"You found him?" he asked.

The soldier shook his head. "Some of our men have gone missing."

"Missing? How could they go missing?"

"I'm not sure, sir. We can't reach them on the radio and no one's seen them."

"How many?"

"Six."

Harris had sent out nineteen men. Six was nearly a third.

It.

Is.

Unraveling.

No! he wanted to yell. *No, no, no! That will not happen.* They were too close to being done. *He* was too close to the payday he'd stayed four years to collect.

Through clenched teeth, he said. "Are you sure?"

"We were all supposed to radio in every fifteen minutes. Two men have missed the last two check-ins, while the others missed the most recent. The commander has ordered everyone back here to regroup. He wants to go back out in pairs instead of solo. He sent me up here to let you know."

"Where is he right now?"

"Waiting for everyone in the anteroom by the wall entrance."

Without saying another word, Harris opened the door and left the courtyard. He found the commander, a man named Santos, exactly where the soldier said he would be. It also looked like most of the other soldiers were back.

When Santos saw Harris, he straightened in surprise. "Sir."

"I understand you are missing some men," Harris said.

"Yes. Seven."

"Seven? I was told six."

"There's another who should have been here by now. We've tried to reach him but no response. We're going back out in pairs. But don't worry. We'll find this bastard."

"You'll just be chasing your tail," Harris said. "I want you all to stay here. Post a few men along the wall. At some point Quinn will expose himself. *That's* when you all will go after him. Kill him the moment you see him." He knew Romero wouldn't be happy with that last order, but he was past caring. Quinn was a problem that needed to be eliminated.

"Sir, our other men out there—they might need help."

"We can't risk losing anyone else. Is that understood?"

"Yes, sir," Santos said hesitantly. "But I'm sure we can find him. The men are ready."

Harris glanced around at the gathered soldiers. There was determination in most of their eyes, but he could see fear in a few. "I'm sure they are. But we will do it my way. Now, assign the watch and have the rest stay down here, ready to move."

"Yes, sir."

NATE ROLLED HIS latest takedown against the rotting trunk of a dead palm tree. The man was still alive, though that status was contingent on his receiving medical treatment in the next few hours. Four of the other soldiers he'd removed were already dead or almost, while the last two were tied up and unconscious at separate locations.

It was clear a retreat was in progress. The man now lying against the palm tree had been headed back to the fort in a hurry. Nate had heard others, too, moving through the brush.

He took the man's weapons and dumped them under a bush thirty feet away, then returned to his hiding place near the wall. He was just in time to see two soldiers pass inside. After they were gone, he could hear no one else moving around, and soon guessed they were the last to return. The question now was, would the soldiers come back out again? Or were they going to remain in the fort?

Twenty minutes passed without the door opening again, then he noticed movement along the top of the wall. He crawled through the brush until he was far enough back to get a better look. Five men were spread out along the top.

It appeared as though they had decided to stay home for now. Too bad, but not the end of the world. He knew all he had to do was lure them out again.

He'd just give them a little time to settle in while he prepared.

CHAPTER
FIFTY ONE

DURAN ISLAND

THE MAP SHOWED that the fort was located on the southwestern end of Duran Island, so they came at it from the northeast, taking the boat in as close to the beach as they could get before dropping anchor.

Quinn held up the computer in front of Porter's face. The map of the island was on the screen. "This airstrip," he said, pointing at the lines indicating a landing area. "Is the cargo plane there?"

Porter raised his eyebrows in surprise. "What cargo—"

Quinn slapped him in the cheek. "Is it?"

"No. It's at St. Renard's in Córdoba. There's no storage or fueling facility on the island."

That was good news. No simple way for anyone to get off. "I assume there's a road or something to get from the runway to the fort without having to hack through the jungle."

Porter nodded. "A path. Starts right here." He touched the map and moved his finger, stopping it right before he reached the fort. "And comes out here."

On the ride over, Quinn had questioned Porter multiple times about the strength of Romero's force on the island. Porter said there were about twenty men. Quinn automatically doubled that number just to be safe.

Forty against Quinn, Orlando, and Daeng. Not exactly

the odds he would have liked, but odds, as he'd learned over the years, meant nothing. His little team would have the element of surprise, and that could easily tilt the balance in their favor.

"And how does anyone get inside?"

"There's a door in the wall." He pointed at the map again. "There."

Quinn closed the laptop. "Thank you, Mr. Porter. Now it's time for you to go to sleep."

A SMALL, QUICK-INFLATING landing raft carried the three of them and their gear to shore. On the beach, they divvied out the equipment and headed inland.

Walking through the jungle was not as hard as Quinn had feared. While there was plenty of vegetation, it wasn't thick enough to slow them down, and within minutes they reached the clearing where the airstrip was located. The deserted runway stretched for nearly the entire width of the island.

Double-timing it, they crossed the tarmac and entered the jungle on the other side. From there, they walked along the edge of the clearing until they reached the road Porter had pointed out.

It was wide enough for a small car, but not much else. Quinn could see where branches had been chopped away, and guessed that it was a constant struggle to keep the path from being reclaimed by nature. To avoid exposing themselves to anyone who might be using it, they stuck to the jungle a few yards off the trail, using it only as a guide.

Twenty minutes later, Orlando tapped Quinn on the shoulder. "Look," she said.

She was pointing ahead of them and up through a break in the trees. Just visible, maybe a quarter mile away, was a small section of the stone wall that surrounded Fort Duran.

Quinn smiled to himself. *Not far n—*

"Did anyone hear that?" Daeng said.

Quinn looked over and shook his head. "What was it?"

"I don't know. It sounded like—"

There was a loud crack of wood, followed by a groan

that was most definitely human. The sounds had come from the right and closer to the fort.

"That, I heard," Quinn said.

CHAPTER
FIFTY TWO

HARRIS WAS ONCE more standing next to Romero in the courtyard. The first three prisoners had received their lashes, and were hanging from their hoists, moaning in exhaustion and pain.

It was Peter's turn.

"Make this one extra special," Romero ordered Janus.

The blond man smiled. "My pleasure." He unfurled his whip again, and snapped it against the stone floor.

Romero looked back at the soldier manning the camera. "You are getting everything, right?"

"Yes, sir."

Facing forward again, Romero said, "I hope you're ready, Peter."

The hooded figure made no reply.

Romero nodded at Janus. "Commence."

Janus pulled his arm back, letting the whip drape behind him, but just as he was about to let it fly, a different kind of cracking noise came over the wall into the courtyard. It was followed immediately by a second, fainter noise.

"Stop," Harris said.

Janus had already paused, and turned to look at the top of the wall.

Harris was looking that way, too. "What was that?" he called up to the sentry nearest him.

"Don't know," the man answered. He gestured behind him, beyond the wall. "Someone's out there."

"You heard a voice?"

"Yes, right after the breaking sound. Sounded like they were hurt."

The only one it could be was Quinn. "See if you can spot him. I'm sending the others back out!" He turned to Romero. "Maybe we should finish this later."

"Absolutely not," Romero said. "There will be no finishing later. Janus can handle this fine. Go. Bring back Quinn."

CHAPTER
FIFTY THREE

NATE CREATED HALF a dozen weapons caches in places where he thought he'd need them. Each cache consisted of at least one of the seized firearms and two softball-sized rocks.

As he was doing this, he kept an eye on the fort in case anyone ventured out, but the door didn't open once. After he was set on the weapons front, he moved on to creating the lure.

He figured there were two ways to get their attention—visibly or audibly expose himself. A visible exposure was not very appealing. One of the soldiers might get off a lucky shot, and injure or even kill him. A loud sound, though, was different. He could control that.

He searched around for anything that could aid him in making the noise, and finally found something he thought would work. It was a tree, dead, but still standing. The branches looked brittle and easy to snap off. There was a large one, about the size of Nate's arm, halfway up. If he could break that off, the noise would be heard by the sentries on the wall.

He found the strongest vine he could, secured a stone to one end, tossed it up and over the branch, then did it one more time so that it had a good grip on the limb.

Tentatively, he gave it a pull and then let go. The branch was definitely ready to break, but he wondered if it would be enough. They might just think it was a natural occurrence, and he'd be wasting his efforts. He would have to reinforce it with a little human touch.

Grabbing both ends of the vine, he moved to the side, and set his legs so he could jump out of the way when the branch came tumbling down toward him. He gave it another test pull. This time, it let out a tiny *pop* that echoed faintly into the jungle.

He put his whole body into his next pull and jerked down on the vine. As he'd hoped, the crack of the branch as it separated from the tree was thunderous.

Just as the noise started to die down, he added the second part of his lure—an agonized groan. As soon as he was done, he sprinted into the brush and headed for his first cache of weapons.

He could hear a raised voice at the top of the wall, but couldn't make out what was being said. It didn't matter. His interest was on the door, and the soldiers that he was sure would soon be swarming out. He'd wait for them to pass and then cull them from the herd, one after another.

He settled into his hiding spot, his eyes on the wall. That's when he heard it. Faint. Just a brush of something on sand. But it wasn't the wind, or a palm frond falling to earth.

A step. He had heard a step, and it had been *behind* him, not in the direction of the fort.

Was a soldier still out there tracking him? Could Nate have missed him? Maybe the guy had hidden like Nate had, and now he was moving in for the kill.

Whoever it was, they were good, Nate had to give them that. After the first brush of sand, there had been no other sound. But Nate knew the person must've been moving toward the sound of the breaking branch.

He started to pick up the pistol, but then selected a stone that had an ax-like edge instead. If he shot off the gun, the echo could keep the other soldiers from coming back out.

With a quick glance at the still-closed door in the wall, Nate moved back into the jungle.

CHAPTER
FIFTY FOUR

USING HAND SIGNALS to communicate, Quinn told Daeng to circle left and Orlando right as they neared the spot where the noise had originated.

The groan had lasted about five seconds, and there had been no other sound.

Quinn eased forward, gripping his gun as he gently moved leaves and branches out of his way. He saw the top of the dead tree first. As he got closer, he spotted the branch that had broken off lying on the ground. He paused and scanned the area carefully, looking for the person who had cried out. No one was there.

The groan *had* been human. No question. So whoever made it had already moved off.

Quinn was about to go round up Orlando and Daeng when his gaze strayed back to the branch. There was something odd about it. He moved in a little closer. There was a vine wrapped around the middle. Maybe it had naturally grown that way, but his instincts told him no.

He took another few steps forward. The way the dirt was freshly kicked up around the branch, he knew it was definitely the thing that had made the noise. He grabbed the vine and gave it a tug. The end that was not wrapped around the branch was heavier than it should have been. He pulled again, and saw that it was tied to a rock.

Son of a bitch!

"Back!" he whispered harshly. "Everybody back!"

It was a trap of some sort. The branch had obviously been pulled down on purpose. And the groan? Just the cherry on top.

This close to the fort, it had to be meant to get the attention of the people inside, but why someone would want to do that was something he'd have to figure out later. Right now, he needed to get away.

Crouching, he ran into the cover of the brush, and then oriented himself so he was heading back to the point where he and the others had originally split up.

He ducked below several branches and went the long way around a dense thicket, taking the quieter path.

He sensed motion a split second before he heard the near-silent step. As he started to turn, someone wrapped an arm around his neck. He grabbed it with one hand, and tried to pull it off while twisting his gun around with the other so he could shoot his attacker, but the person behind him rammed a knee into the side of the gun's suppressor, and slammed it upward again, this time into Quinn's fingers.

Quinn tried to hold on, but the gun slipped from his grasp and fell to the ground. Around him, the world was starting to go black as the blood to his brain was being cut off.

In a last-ditch effort, he staggered forward and then thrust himself back, hoping to throw the attacker off balance. Though the man didn't let go, the move did loosen his hold around Quinn's neck, and brought Quinn back from the brink of unconsciousness.

He grabbed the man's arm with both hands and yanked down hard. He could feel his attacker lose his balance, so Quinn dropped to a crouch. The guy rolled over his back, sprawling to the ground on the other side.

Quinn snatched up his pistol, pointed it at the man. "Don't move."

CHAPTER
FIFTY FIVE

THOUGH NATE DIDN'T have a very clear view from his position, he was able to make out three soldiers as they moved off in different directions.

How the hell did I miss three?

Clutching tightly to his rock, he moved in as close as he dared and waited for one of them to pass by.

A minute passed, then two.

Suddenly a voice cut through the silence. It was a whisper, hard and decisive, but too low for Nate to make out the words. For a second, he heard someone run, then all went quiet again.

Come this way, he thought. *Right here. I'm waiting.*

He closed his eyes and listened intently.

The noise was slight—the branch of a bush, maybe, its leaves rubbing together for only a second.

Someone was close.

A light step. It could be heard only because it was just a few feet away.

As Nate opened his eyes, a man passed his position and started walking away. Oddly, he wasn't wearing fatigues like the others, but he had to be from the fort.

Another one lost from the herd.

With the guy's friends probably close, Nate had to be careful about drawing their attention, so he set the stone on the ground. For this one, he would use his hands.

Three steps forward.

On the fourth, he knew the man had heard him. He threw his arm around the man's neck and squeezed.

CHAPTER
FIFTY SIX

"NATE?" QUINN SAID.

Nate, dirty and bruised and beaten, stared up at him. "Quinn?"

Quinn reached down and helped Nate to his feet.

"What are you doing out here?" he asked.

"What are *you* doing out here?" Nate shot back.

"What do you think we're doing here? We came to get you."

"The others with you...?"

"Orlando and Daeng."

Nate closed his eyes, his head lolling back, relieved.

"Are you all right?" Quinn asked.

Before Nate could answer, Daeng emerged from the bushes to the left. He pulled to a sudden stop when he saw Nate. "Well, that was easy."

Quinn rubbed his neck. "Not quite as easy as you think."

Orlando joined them a moment later. "Oh, thank God," she said.

She threw her arms around Nate, but he instantly winced and pulled back from her grasp.

"Sorry. Just a little sensitive," he told her.

She moved around behind him, and lifted the back of his shirt before he could stop her. "What the hell?"

Quinn stepped over so he could see. Nate's back was lined with bright red welts and open wounds that could have only been caused one way.

"You need to sit down," Quinn said.

"I'm okay. Really, I'm going to be fine."

"No," Orlando said. "You won't be fine if we don't do something. These wounds are going to get infected, if they're not already."

"It's fine."

"We need to take him back to the boat," Orlando said to Quinn.

"No," Nate said.

Ignoring him, Orlando went on. "The sooner we get him to a hospital, the better."

"No!" Nate repeated. "Not yet. There are others still being held."

"We know," Quinn said. "Peter, right?"

Nate wrinkled his brow. "Yeah. And three more."

"Lanier, Berkeley, and Curson."

He smiled in genuine surprise. "You figured it out?"

"Pullman got us started, then we had a nice chat with your friend Burke."

"That bastard," Nate said, his eyes narrowing. "He set me up."

"That, he did."

"Did you kill him?"

"Thought that was a choice you should make. He'll be easy to find, though."

Nate nodded, but said nothing.

"I'm serious, Nate," Orlando said. "We've got to get you out of here."

"Not until we get the rest of them. They're going to be killed, probably sooner now that I've escaped."

"And exactly how did you do that?" Daeng asked.

"I'll tell you over a beer later." He looked at each of them. "With your help, I think we can do it."

"What's your plan?" Quinn asked.

"I've been picking them off one at a time. Have seven of them out of the picture already."

Quinn was impressed. "The tree branch and the groan was your attempt to get the rest to come out."

"Yeah. Shouldn't be much longer. If we get into position, we can start getting rid of them a lot faster."

"Now that there are four of us," Quinn said, "maybe we don't need to worry about them at all."

QUINN, ORLANDO, NATE, and Daeng watched from the brush as eight soldiers exited the door in the fort wall, and moved as a group into the jungle toward where the noise had occurred.

As soon as they disappeared, Quinn and the others jogged over to the door.

"Everyone ready?" Quinn whispered.

The three others pressed themselves against the wall, off to the side, holding their guns in front of them.

"All set," Nate said.

Quinn raised his fist and knocked. In Spanish, he said, "Open up. I found one of the missing men. He needs help!" He knocked again. "Hurry, hurry! He needs medical attention!"

Something that sounded like a bar moved on the other side. The latch turned.

A soldier opened the door and looked out. "Where is he?" he asked. He then seemed to realize Quinn wasn't who he expected. "Who are you?"

"We've come to pick up our friends."

"What?"

The other three stepped out to where they could be seen, their guns pointed at the soldier. The man's eyes widened. He reached for the rifle on his shoulder, but before he could pull it off, Quinn stepped inside and twisted it free.

The man seemed to suddenly find his voice, and started to yell as he ran toward the interior door. Quinn jabbed with the rifle, knocking the man down and cutting off the warning. He rolled the guy over with his foot.

"You open your mouth again, it'll be the last time. Sit up against the wall. Hands on your knees."

While Quinn dealt with the soldier, the others stepped inside. Daeng immediately closed the door and dropped the locking bar in place.

"You down here all by yourself?" Quinn asked the soldier.

"Go to hell," the man said. He spat at Quinn.

Nate came up next to Quinn. "I know you. You were one of the guys who helped escort me to your boss's office yesterday. Bet you also helped take some of my friends out of their cells."

The man's look of defiance slipped. "I...I was just doing what I was told."

"Did you watch as they whipped us?" Nate asked.

The man blinked and looked away.

"Maybe you were the one who hooked my hands up."

"No. That wasn't me."

"But you were there."

A slight nod.

"And you did nothing."

"What could I do?"

Nate placed the end of his suppressor against the man's forehead. "I guess we'll never know."

"No! No! Please!"

There was a *pop*, only it wasn't from Nate's pistol. It was from the vaccine gun Orlando shoved against the man's arm.

"So which way from here?" she asked Nate.

"Up."

CHAPTER
FIFTY SEVEN

HARRIS RETURNED TO the courtyard just as Janus finished whipping Peter. Leaving the prisoners dangling from their hoists, he escorted Romero back to the old man's suite.

"When Quinn is found, I want him whipped fifty times," Romero said once they reached the room.

"Whatever you want," Harris said, though in his mind, Quinn would be dead the next time either man saw him.

Romero turned his wheelchair toward the bed. "I'm going to take a nap. Don't bother me until it's time for the prisoners to have their electroshock."

"Yes, sir." Harris walked out of the room.

Unraveling, the voice said in his head. It repeated the word over and over.

"It's *not* unraveling," he whispered.

But what if it does unravel?

The question made him pause. If it did, what about the money Romero promised him? The money he'd been waiting for?

You can't spend money if you're dead.

That wasn't going to happen. If things truly spun out of control, it would be time to think about his own skin.

The boat.

Yes. Right. Romero's boat. It was tied off to a small covered dock behind the fort. He'd take that.

When he got back to his room, he'd gather the cash he'd been stashing away and put it in a bag by the door, easy to grab. It was nothing compared to the amount he was due, but it would hold him over for a while.

I won't need it, though. It's just in case. Everything is going to be fine.

He headed toward his room, his pace quicker than normal. As he neared his door, he saw two soldiers farther down the hall, walking away.

"You, there," he called out.

The soldiers kept going.

"Hey, I'm talking to you."

They finally stopped and one of them turned.

"Tell your commander that I'll be in my room and am to be notified the moment the fugitive is brought in."

"Yes, sir," the soldier said.

Once inside his suite, Harris poured himself another whiskey, this time savoring it as it went down.

To surviving, he thought. *One way or another.*

CHAPTER
FIFTY EIGHT

A QUICK SEARCH of the room at the base of the wall revealed a separate storage area filled with extra gear for the soldiers.

The men each donned one of the spare uniforms. None was small enough for Orlando.

"You two stay here while Daeng and I do a recon," Quinn told Orlando and Nate.

"You don't know the place. I do," Nate said. "I should go."

"I'm guessing you're a pretty hot commodity around here right now. As much as I'd like you to come, best if you stay under wraps as long as possible."

"Don't you dare cut me out," Nate said.

"Not cutting you out. Just making the smart play."

Nate locked eyes with him for a moment before he reluctantly nodded. "Okay, okay. I'll stay for now."

Daeng's Asian features would be impossible for anyone to miss if they got too close. But at a distance and with the bill of his cap pulled down far enough, his dark skin and black hair would actually be an asset.

They took a stone stairwell up to a hallway on the next level, and, after a few minutes, located the hallway with the rooms where Nate and the others had been held. Since there were no guards around, it seemed a pretty good guess that the prisoners weren't around either.

Just to be sure, Quinn made a quick trip down the block, while Daeng stood guard outside, and checked the cells.

Though it was obvious they were being used, all were empty.

Quinn and Daeng followed Nate's directions on how to get from there to the courtyard. A few times, they heard footsteps down intersecting halls but had yet to cross paths with anyone.

Upon reaching the courtyard door, Quinn eased it back a few inches and peered out. He realized why they hadn't seen anyone else. Most everyone who was still in the fort was in the courtyard. He could see a portion of the top of the wall. There were three soldiers spread out along it, and in the actual courtyard were four more. There was also a big blond guy sitting in a chair, soaking up the sun. He had to be Janus.

"Watch out for him," Nate had said as he briefed them. "He's a tough son of a bitch."

The most shocking sight was the four figures with black bags over their heads. They were dangling in the air by arms hooked to chains. Their backs were the worst part. They were even more chewed up than Nate's. It was clear from the blood dripping down that they'd just been whipped again.

Peter, Lanier, Berkeley, and Curson.

Quinn watched each man for a moment to be sure they were all still breathing, then moved to the side and let Daeng take a look. When the Thai man was done, they shut the door.

"Back downstairs," Quinn whispered. "We need the others."

On the way back to the stairs, they made a wrong turn and ended up in a hallway they hadn't been in before. Realizing their mistake, they turned around and started back they way they'd come. A moment after they made the U-turn, they heard a door open. Footsteps in the hallway behind them.

There was a part of Quinn that wanted to pick up the pace and get out of there as quickly as they could, but he knew doing so would bring unwanted attention, so they continued on at a purposeful, but non-rushed pace.

"You, there," the man behind them yelled.

They kept moving, pretending like they hadn't heard.

"Hey, I'm talking to you."

"Stop," Quinn whispered. "But only I will turn."

Quinn faced the man who'd called them. He had expected the speaker to be another soldier, but instead he was looking at Harris, the bald former mercenary himself. Quinn kept his expression neutral.

"Tell your commander that I'll be in my room and am to be notified the moment the fugitive is brought in."

"Yes, sir," Quinn replied.

Harris opened a nearby door and passed inside. Quinn marked the location in his mind, and told Daeng who he'd just seen.

"If Harris is here," Daeng said, "then Romero's got to be somewhere nearby, right?"

"One would think so."

WHEN THEY BROUGHT us back, Janus and one of the guards would come into the cell with me," Nate said. "I couldn't see what was going on with the others, but it sounded like the same thing."

Nate told them that so far, after every torture session, they would leave the prisoners outside for a while before taking them back to their cells to await the next event. That was good. Quinn had been worried they would just be left in the courtyard. Making an assault there would have been a quick way to get one or most of the prisoners *and* themselves killed. The guards on the wall would quickly pick everyone off before Quinn and the rest had a chance to do much of anything.

When they finally settled on a solution they all thought would work, Quinn said, "From this point forward, if someone's in your way, kill them. Understood?"

It wasn't a hard sell. Though none of their job descriptions was that of professional killer, they had all killed before. Given what had been happening at Fort Duran, none of them would take issue with doing so again.

They checked their comm-gear, got into their positions, and waited.

THE POUNDING OF feet echoed down the hallway, signaling

the imminent arrival of the prisoners back to their cellblock.

"Daeng, are they to you yet?" he said into the radio.

Daeng was in a room down the hall with the door open but lights off. His would be the first position they passed.

"Seconds away," Daeng whispered.

Quinn and Orlando were in the same hallway, but on the other side of the door to the cellblock, hidden by the curve of the corridor. Nate was in the cellblock itself, at the far end, tucked around the elbow turn of the hall he'd used to escape.

There was a click over the radio—Daeng letting them know the soldiers and prisoners were outside his door. A few seconds later, he whispered, "Four guards and that big blond."

"Copy," Quinn replied.

"Copy," Nate chimed in.

The footsteps kept coming, until it almost seemed as if they would pass the cellblock entrance and head right around the curve of the hall to where Quinn and Orlando waited. But then, not quite in perfect synchronization, the prisoner detail stopped.

The door to the other hallway opened with a creak, and the ragtag march started up again as the prisoners were led inside. As soon as the door closed, Quinn and Orlando came around the corner and stepped over to it. Daeng joined them a few seconds later.

"In position," Quinn said into his mic.

A single click from Nate. *Message received.*

Quinn grabbed the door handle, ready to pull the door open as soon as Nate gave them the two clicks that meant *go*.

NATE STOOD AS close to the corner as he could possibly get, waiting for the preplanned moment. It wasn't hard to imagine what was going on. In front of every cell, a soldier-and-prisoner pair stood waiting until Janus deemed it was their turn to go in.

A door opened, then three sets of steps—Janus, a guard, and a prisoner. As they passed into the cell, the sounds of their movements diminished.

Janus's voice drifted down to him. "Do not get too

comfortable. You will not be here long." This was followed by a laugh, and the sound of Janus and the guard exiting the cell and closing the door.

One down.

Nate continued to listen as the second prisoner and then the third were put back in their rooms.

When the door to the third cell shut, he clicked his radio once. *Be ready.*

The fourth cell opened. Janus and one of the guards took the last prisoner inside.

Click-click.

As soon as the message was sent, he stepped out to where he could be seen. "Hey, I hear you're looking for me."

QUINN COUNTED OFF five seconds after the double click before he pulled the door open as quietly as he could.

"...looking for me."

As expected, the three guards in the hallway had all turned in Nate's direction and were not paying attention to the door. Quinn, Orlando, and Daeng moved inside and spread out.

The guards, all eyes still on their escaped prisoner, began unslinging their rifles.

Quinn's target was the farthest guard, Orlando's the middle, Daeng's the nearest. Within a second and a half, they each pulled their triggers. Like dominos, all three guards fell to the ground, dead.

The open cell was the one nearest Quinn and the others. The guard who'd been inside stepped out to see what was going on. A bullet to the forehead from Quinn's gun sent him crashing back inside.

Nate jogged down the hall, stopping fifteen feet on the other side of the open door. "Janus! Come out!"

A scuffling of feet, then nothing.

"Janus!" Nate yelled again. "Give it up. Come on out. This is done."

"Nothing is done. I think you will let me go."

"You think wrong."

A laugh, then Janus appeared in the doorway. But he wasn't alone. He had Peter in his arms, and was holding him high enough to protect his own head and chest.

Peter grimaced. "Just shoot him."

Janus peeked around Peter at Nate. "Well, Quinn, you *are* pretty good. You bring help?"

"Put him down," Nate said.

"Go over with your friends or I break his neck. You know I can."

"I don't care if you hit me," Peter said. "Shoot him!"

No one pulled the trigger. Peter was—if not quite a friend—someone who'd been an important part of their lives for a long time. They weren't about to shoot at him if they could help it.

Quinn motioned for his old apprentice to join them. As soon as Nate did, Janus eased out of the room, turning to keep Peter between them and him at all times.

Quinn searched for a shot, anything that might disable Janus and allow them to get Peter free, but Peter was unintentionally doing a pretty damn good job of shielding the other man. Quinn might be able to shoot Janus in the foot, but it was iffy at best.

Janus started backing down the hallway in the direction Nate had been hiding. Nate took a step forward to follow.

"Don't," Janus said. "I *will* kill him."

"Kill him and we'll kill you," Nate said.

"Peter here will still be dead, and I might still get away."

Janus took another step back. This time Nate didn't move.

"Good boy," Janus said, not stopping.

"Shoot him!" Peter yelled.

Janus momentarily freed up a hand and punched the former head of the Office in the face. There were no more outbursts.

"What's going on?" Lanier called from his cell.

"Yeah," Berkeley said. "What's happening out there? Are you here to get us out?"

"Everyone shut up," Quinn said.

...

THE COLLECTED

"Come on, man," Berkeley said. "What's going on?"

"What's going on is that we're going to leave you here if you say another word."

Janus had reached the turn in the hall. "Don't follow me," he ordered, and then disappeared.

Quinn and Nate immediately ran after him. As they neared the corner, they heard a grunt and a thud. Then running feet, heavy and fast.

They sprinted the rest of the way to the end, and whipped around the corner, their guns ready.

Peter lay motionless on the ground about halfway between the corner and the far door, but Janus was gone. They raced over and knelt down. Quinn checked Peter's pulse.

"He's alive," he said.

Nate glanced at the hallway beyond them. "Janus can get to the top of the wall that way. If he does, he'll warn everyone. That could be a problem." He stood up. "I'm going after him."

"I'll be right behind you."

With a nod, Nate took off.

Quinn put Peter over his shoulder in a fireman's hold, lugged him back to the others, and transferred him to Daeng's shoulder.

"Get the others out," he said. "Take everyone to the room downstairs and lock yourselves in. Nate and I are on cleanup."

"You two can't do it alone," Orlando said.

"If we need help, I'll let you know." He took off down the hall.

NATE KNEW THERE was no way he would catch Janus in time. The son of a bitch had too much of a head start, but he had to try.

He grabbed the wall just before he reached the stairs so he could propel himself around the corner and up. The around-the-corner part worked. The up, not so much.

Janus was standing three steps above him, waiting. Nate

smashed into the man's chest and fell back onto the ground, his gun skittering off to the side.

The welts on his back screamed again, but he ignored them.

Janus jumped down, his feet heading straight for Nate's ribs. As Nate rolled to the side, Janus kicked out in an attempt to change direction, but Nate slammed his elbow back, hitting the big man in the calf.

Janus toppled over, his arm slamming the stone floor with a giant *thwack*. As the big man lay there, momentarily stunned, Nate popped up onto his feet and scanned the ground for his gun. He tensed when he finally spotted it five feet to Janus's right. All Janus had to do was turn his head to see it, then reach out and grab the barrel.

"Get up!" he yelled at his former tormentor, egging him on. "What are you, scared of me?"

Focus returned to Janus's face. His gaze narrowed, and he pushed himself up. "You big problem."

Nate moved to his right. "Yeah, I am."

Countering him, Janus went left. *Perfect.*

"I take care of problems," Janus said. "That is my specialty."

"Well, you haven't taken care of this problem yet, have you?"

"No. But I am not done yet."

The gun was only a few feet behind Nate now. If Janus had seen it, there had been no indication.

"I don't know. You seem kind of done to me."

Janus smiled. "You try to provoke. I provoke not so easy."

Nate took a half step backward. "It was worth a try, wasn't it?"

"Trying is for the weak. I never try. I do."

"I don't believe that's how the quote goes," Nate said as he slid back a little more.

"What?"

"Yoda."

"Huh?"

Nate's foot touched the end of the barrel. "Never mind."

What he really needed was for Janus to take a swing at him, so he could duck down and grab the gun without being obvious. If Janus knew what he was doing, he could put a stop to it before Nate would be able to get the muzzle trained on him.

"You problem. But now I make you not."

Nate urged him forward with a Bruce Lee-style wave of his fingers.

Instead of taking a swing at him, though, Janus charged, roaring. Nate dropped anyway, one hand hugging his chest to his knees, while the other searched for the gun. As his fingertips touched the suppressor, Janus's massive thigh whacked into his shoulder.

Nate tumbled onto his side, the gun under him and digging into his ribcage. Janus stumbled over him, then twisted back around and lashed out with his foot. His instep connected with the rear of Nate's skull, sending a shockwave of blinding pain through Nate's head.

"What's going on down here?" The voice came from behind them somewhere.

Nate forced his eyes open. A soldier was standing near the base of the stairs. Nate guessed he was one of the watchmen from the wall.

"Help me with him," Janus said.

"Yes, sir," the man said.

The moment Janus looked toward the other man, Nate wrapped his hand around the grip of the gun and yanked it out from under him. The soldier was the first in his sights. He pulled the trigger and his bullet hit center mass, neutralizing Janus's would-be helper.

Janus twisted around and tried to grab the gun from him, turning Nate's hand back and forth, but Nate wouldn't let go. When the barrel started arcing toward Janus, Nate let off another shot.

Janus yelled angrily as a splotch of blood appeared in his upper right chest. He made another try for the gun, and Nate pulled the trigger again. This time the bullet only grazed the other man's ear.

Someone was running down the hall from the direction of the cells. Janus looked over, shoved himself away from Nate, and sprinted for the stairs. Nate got off another shot just before Janus moved up out of sight, but missed.

As he started to stand, Quinn ran up and held out a hand. "Here."

Back to his feet, Nate said, "He's mine."

CHAPTER
FIFTY NINE

"I KNOW WHERE Harris is," Daeng told Orlando.

They had just finished moving everyone to the room at the bottom of the wall. The three op agents were in pretty bad shape, but were at least able to walk. Peter, on the other hand, was still unconscious and had to be carried, though he was showing signs of coming out of it.

"What about Romero?" she asked.

"Him, I'm not sure, but he's probably in the same area."

She thought for a moment. Her concern was that while Quinn and Nate went after Janus, Harris and Romero might escape.

"I don't want them to get away," she said.

"No. That would not make me happy."

She looked around the room. If the men they'd just rescued were civilians, no way would she and Daeng leave them. But they weren't. They were professionals. Damaged professionals, yes, but that didn't mean they'd forgotten how to fight.

She pointed at the dark-haired man sitting on the floor next to Peter. "You. Lanier, right?"

He looked over. "Yeah."

"Think you can handle a gun?"

"I'm not dead, am I?" he said.

QUINN WAS FIVE steps from the top, Nate just in front of him, when they heard Janus yell.

"Intruders inside! Coming up the stairs now. They have taken the prisoners! Someone call back men who are out searching!" Then, not quite as loudly as before, he said, "Give me your gun."

Son of a bitch! It was exactly what they wanted to avoid.

At the top of the stairs were a stone room with two windows and an open doorway on either side. Through the far doorway, Quinn could see Janus and four other men on top of the wall. Janus had a rifle, taken, no doubt, from the now unarmed man standing behind him.

The rifle was trained on the stone room, and as soon as Quinn and Nate stepped out of the shadows of the staircase, it barked to life.

The bullet whizzed between the two of them, sending them both diving to the side. They crawled through the room to either edge of the outside door.

There were several more shots, the bullets smashing into the building, both outside the room and in.

Quinn motioned for Nate to stay where he was. He pointed at himself and the window that overlooked the beach. Next, he pointed at Nate and mimicked shooting.

Nate gave a nod.

"On my signal," Quinn mouthed. He went over to the window and looked out. There wasn't much of a ledge there, but it was enough.

It took him ten seconds to work his way along the outside of the room to the front corner. Once he was set, he gently tapped the wall with the butt of his gun.

From inside came the *thup-thup-thup* of bullets passing through Nate's suppressor. Four rifles returned fire. Quinn gauged their position, and as soon as Nate started firing again, he peeked around the corner and let off four rapid shots.

Two were direct hits, sending a pair of soldiers tumbling backward over the wall. The third shot went wide, and the fourth hit Janus in the arm, knocking the rifle out of his hands. Instead of picking the gun back up, Janus lowered himself over the courtyard side of the wall.

While the man was now mostly out of sight, Quinn could

still see one hand holding on to the top.

He took two shots at it, but both missed by a few inches.

A bullet hit the wall six inches from Quinn's face, forcing him to focus on the remaining armed soldier. Make that two. The man that Janus had taken the rifle from had reclaimed it.

Quinn took a quick shot, readjusted his targeting point, and shot again. This time he got his man.

There was another shot from inside the room, and the remaining soldier went down.

Quinn looked back to where Janus had been hanging on, but the hand was gone.

He leaped around the corner of the room onto the walkway, and looked down into the courtyard. Janus wasn't there, either.

"Where is he?" Nate said, coming up beside Quinn.

"Don't know."

Nate turned back toward the stairs and began to run.

HARRIS LOOKED UP from his desk.

Someone was yelling, the sound coming down the hallway and through the door to his room. With a spark of hope, he rose to his feet, thinking the search party had finally returned with Quinn. He started across the room, anticipating a knock on his door from a messenger sent to tell him just that.

But it wasn't a knock he heard next. It was the boom of a rifle. As he jerked to a stop, another shot went off.

Unraveling.

He glanced at the bag next to the door holding his money. Was it time?

Perhaps the watch had spotted Quinn beyond the wall and they were shooting at him. That could have been—

More gunfire. Not just from one weapon, but several.

Run!

He sprinted toward the bag, and was reaching for the strap when someone knocked on his door.

"Yes?" he said without opening it.

318

A pause. "Sir, we have a report."

"Come back later. I'm busy."

"We were told to give it to you now."

He stared at the bag for a moment, then left it where it was and turned for the door. He had to get rid of whoever it was. He couldn't have anyone see him leave and try to get to the boat before him.

He pulled the door open. "What is it?"

The soldier standing on the other side smiled oddly at him. "Told you I knew where he was."

Harris had never seen this man before. He was Asian, not Latin, and though there was something familiar about him, he definitely was not on Romero's payroll.

Harris shoved the door shut in the man's face, dropped next to the bag, and pulled at the zipper so he could get at the gun inside.

Behind him, the door banged loudly as it was thrust back open.

"I wouldn't, if I were you," the soldier who wasn't a soldier said.

Harris glanced back, the zipper half open.

The man had a gun aimed at his Harris's head.

Harris had waited too long. He should have left the moment things had started to go wrong. Hell, he should have left years ago.

A small, Asian woman walked in behind the man. She was also armed, her weapon also aimed at Harris. Her gaze moved down to the satchel at his feet. She smiled.

"Do I see a bag full of money?"

"HERE?" DAENG ASKED.

It was the fourth room they'd come to since hauling Harris out of his suite. Though Daeng had asked the same question every time, Harris had yet to give him an answer.

While Daeng pulled the man out of the way, Orlando tapped on the door with her gun. "Mr. Romero?"

Nothing.

Staying to the side, she undid the latch and let it swing

open.

Storage room filled with cardboard boxes.

"This one?" Daeng asked when they reached the next door.

"Go to hell," Harris said.

Daeng slammed Harris against the wall and wrapped a hand around the man's neck. "That's not very polite." He locked eyes with Harris. "Do you know who I am?"

"I don't care."

"You cared enough to trick me into going back to Bangkok by killing two people I knew."

Harris's eyes widened.

"Yeah, that's right," Daeng said. "I guess you couldn't keep me away, though." Daeng let go of the man's neck and pushed him down the hallway. "I *will* kill you before this is over. Count on it."

Orlando knocked, then opened the door when no one responded. It was an empty room.

They came to another door and stopped.

"So?" Daeng asked.

Harris was back to his silent game.

This time when Orlando knocked, they heard someone on the other side. The door opened a foot, and a young man wearing hospital scrubs looked out.

"Can I help you?" he asked in Spanish.

Answering in kind, Orlando said, "We need to see Señor Romero."

"I'm sorry, but he's taking a nap.

"Oh, what a shame."

She pushed the door open.

"Hey! You can't—"

His words died in his mouth as he caught sight of the gun in her hand.

"I'm sorry. You were saying?" she asked.

He backed a few feet away. "Please. I'm only a nurse. I don't know anything. I'm just here to monitor Señor Romero's health. Please. Please don't hurt me."

"If that's true, then we won't have any problems."

They joined him inside. The room was large, with a desk and work area at the near end, and hospital bed at the other. In between was a living area, with a couch, chairs, and tables.

Her eyes on the nurse, Orlando motioned to the couch with her gun. "Sit over there."

He immediately complied.

"And don't move," she told him. "If you do, I'll assume you're a problem. Trust me, you don't want that to happen. Tell me you understand."

"I won't move. I swear."

Orlando, Daeng, and Harris walked across the room to the bed.

Romero was indeed asleep. Though it had been only four years since the assassination attempt, he looked decades older than the picture of him in the file Misty sent.

"Time to get up, Mr. Romero," Orlando said in English.

The old man didn't move.

Orlando pinched his nose and covered his mouth with her palm. It took only a second for Romero's eyes to fly open as he gasped for air. She held on for another second, then let go.

He took in several rapid breaths. "*¿Quién demonios es usted?*"

"I'm afraid we're the bearers of bad news," Orlando said, still using English. "Your little torture fest is canceled."

"What are you talking about? Who are you?" He looked at Harris. "Who are these people?"

HARRIS KNEW HE had to forget about the money bag now. It was strung across the woman's shoulders, and there was no way he could get it without taking a bullet first. The *only* thing he needed to concentrate on was getting out of the fort and off the island.

He'd remained hyper-alert as they led him down the hall, searching for Romero's room. But then the man in the fatigues had revealed his identity, causing Harris's mind to spin yet again.

Daeng. The man from Thailand. Quinn's preferred

assistant.

Harris had thought he played that one so well, and that he'd effectively taken Daeng out of the picture. How in hell was he here?

The next thing he knew, they were standing in Romero's room next to the old man's bed.

Focus! he scolded himself. *Get out of here and get to the boat.*

"I'm afraid we're the bearers of bad news," the woman said to Romero, Harris's money bag still hanging over her shoulder. "Your little torture fest is canceled."

Romero looked both annoyed and confused. "What are you talking about? Who are you?" He focused on Harris. "Who are these people?"

Harris hesitated, then said, "These, Señor Romero, are associates of Quinn's."

As the cleaner's name left his mouth, he could see that Daeng's and the woman's attention was fully on Romero.

His inner voice screamed, *Now!*

BOTH ORLANDO AND Daeng knew it wasn't a matter of if, but *when* Harris would try something.

The man must have thought it was a surprise move when he swung his elbow at Daeng. If he hadn't telegraphed it by tensing his shoulders, it might have worked. But by the time his elbow reached the point where Daeng's gun had been, Daeng had already taken a step back, out of the way.

Harris didn't give up, though. He whirled around, his fist flying out and catching the tip of Daeng's chin. Leading with his shoulder, he knocked Daeng to the side and started running for the door.

Orlando's shot went wide but Daeng's flew true, his bullet puncturing Harris's back before exiting the other side.

Momentum carried Harris forward another few feet before he toppled to the floor.

"*¡Dios mio!*" the nurse cried out.

Orlando gave him a quick look. "Remember what I said about moving."

The nurse nodded rapidly as he pulled his arms and legs toward his chest, trying to make himself as small as possible.

Daeng reached Harris first and shoved him over onto his back. The man's breathing was ragged, but his eyes were open.

"That's a nasty wound," Orlando said as she moved in next to Daeng. "Good thing we don't need him for anything else, because he's not going to be around much longer."

"Still too long, I think," Daeng said.

"True."

"May I?"

"Absolutely."

Daeng stepped closer so that he was looking directly down at Harris. "Look at me."

Harris's gaze jumped around.

"Here," Daeng said, pointing to his own face. "Look at me!"

The man did so.

"You killed my friends and have been torturing another. That's why you are on the floor now. That's why you can barely breathe. And that's why I am the last thing you will ever see."

Daeng's gun, already aimed at the man's head, fired.

The nurse let out a yelp, but quickly covered his mouth with his hand.

"You all right?" Orlando asked Daeng.

He nodded and headed back to the hospital bed without saying a word. Orlando followed.

Romero had barely moved, his face even paler than before.

"There are consequences for every action, Mr. Romero," Orlando said once she was standing beside him again. "You understand this because you were trying to pay back the men who attempted to kill you. I can sympathize to a point, but the problem is, those you went after are our people. No one goes after our people without consequences."

"If you are going to kill me, fine. Kill me." He tried to pump his chest out as if he were making it a target.

"Whether we kill you or not isn't up to us."

"Who, then?"

"The man you've been calling Quinn."

QUINN AND NATE raced down the stairs, back into the cellblock. Quinn was glad to see all the cell doors open, the rooms empty.

"Janus is probably trying to get out of the fort," Nate said. "Which means he'll probably head down to the wall exit."

"The others are there. They won't let him through."

Nate threw open the door at the end of the block, and started to step into the intersecting hallway. "Yeah. We can trap him between—"

A loud crack echoed down the other corridor and through the doorway.

Nate yelled out in pain as he thrust himself back into the cellblock, hugging his left arm to his chest.

At first Quinn thought it had been a gunshot, but then he saw the wound on Nate's forearm—a long red mark, not unlike those on Nate's back.

A whip.

"He's not downstairs," Nate said through clenched teeth.

Quinn moved around him so he was closer to the threshold. "Which way?"

"To the left somewhere."

Nate lowered his arm, fighting the pain.

"You going to be all right?" Quinn asked.

"Fine," Nate answered quickly.

Keeping the suppressor tight against the wall, Quinn thrust his gun through the doorway and aimed it roughly in the direction the whip had come from. He let off three quick shots, spreading the fire from side to side.

There was a *whoosh* as the whip lashed out again. The tip hit his gun, missing his finger by less than half an inch. He shot again before pulling the pistol back.

"Together," he told Nate, as he popped the nearly empty mag out of the gun's grip and shoved in a new one. "I'll take high."

This time, they both swung their guns around and opened fire. When they heard the *whoosh*, they pulled their guns back. As soon as the whip cracked, Quinn rushed out into the hallway.

Janus was twenty feet away, using the corner of another passageway to stay out of line of fire. He was pulling the whip behind him, getting ready to strike again.

"Drop it!" Quinn ordered.

The whip flew out, and Quinn pulled his trigger.

Instead of a *whoosh* and a *crack*, there was a *whoosh* and a *thud* as the whip fell to the ground. Clutching his hand where his middle finger had been a moment before, Janus disappeared around the corner.

"Come on!" Quinn said to Nate, and started after the big man.

The narrow hallway Janus had been hiding in went back only fifteen feet before jogging right, so the big man was already gone when Quinn rounded the corner. At the next turn, Quinn slowed just in case Janus was waiting there to jump him, then stepped around it, his gun held ready.

What he found was a well-worn staircase leading down, but no Janus.

Quinn turned on his mic. "Orlando, Janus is heading your way."

"My way?" she said after a short delay.

"We think he's going for the exit in the wall. Send Daeng out to—"

"We're not in the room."

"You're not? Then where are you?"

Another delay. "On our way there now."

"What about the others?"

"The others are there and armed. And I'm pretty sure they'd be happy if Janus suddenly showed up."

"Okay. We'll meet you there."

Though he wondered why Orlando and Daeng weren't with the freed prisoners, there was no time to think about it at the moment. Still taking point, he and Nate ran down the stairs, and followed the passage until they came to the widened area outside the room Peter and the others were waiting in.

Janus, bloodied but obviously not broken, was trying to pull the door open. He raged and pounded against it when it didn't budge, and yanked the handle again.

Quinn and Nate stopped a few feet into the room and raised their guns.

"I believe it's locked," Nate said.

Janus whirled around, panting like a bull in a ring, his eyes angry and wild.

"Calm down there, buddy," Quinn said. "Nothing you can do now."

Janus shifted his gaze from them to the door and back. "Let me out! Let me go!"

"That's not going to happen," Quinn told him.

Janus roared, and pounded on the door again. "Open!"

"Not going to happen, either," Nate said.

Janus turned back. "Let me go!"

"No."

A frustrated scream filled the space. At first, the big man just stood there, shaking, then something seemed to snap in his mind, and he sprinted toward them as if he were going to rip them apart, piece by piece.

The first bullet slowed him, but didn't stop him.

The second, the same.

The third brought him to his knees.

The fourth sailed over his head as he collapsed onto the floor.

Quinn and Nate heard steps running down the stairs behind them. They turned quickly, ready to shoot again.

Orlando appeared first.

"Just us," she said, holding up her hands.

The two men lowered their guns.

Daeng showed up a few seconds later, carrying an old man. Romero, Quinn realized.

"You two had your hands full," Orlando explained. "So we thought we'd get him while you were occupied."

"What about Harris?" Quinn asked, worried that the bald man had gotten away.

"No longer a problem," Daeng said. The look on his face left no question as to what had happened and who had pulled the trigger.

A silent moment passed, then someone yelled from the other side of the door, "Everything all right out there?"

Quinn walked over and said, "You can open up now."

The hinges creaked as the door swung inward. Lanier looked out, Berkeley and Curson right behind him. Grins broke out when they spotted Janus on the floor, then full smiles at the sight of Romero.

CHAPTER
SIXTY

QUINN, ORLANDO, NATE, and Daeng made a sweep of the entire fort to make sure there weren't any more of Romero's soldiers hiding out.

The only other people they found were two other nurses, and the three men who had been handling the cooking and the housekeeping. After a quick discussion, they locked the five of them and the nurse from Romero's room in the kitchen, where the group could wait for the officials who would descend on the island after they'd been notified.

Once the fort was secured, Quinn and the others made their way up to the top of the wall. Keeping their bodies below the walkway lip, they spread out along the walkway. Quinn turned on the radio they'd taken from one of the soldiers.

"I've got a message for the group outside the fort," he said in Spanish. "Can you hear me?"

Static.

"I'm calling the security force that was sent out to look for the man who escaped. Are you there?"

More static, then, "Who is this?"

"You don't need to know that. What you *do* need to know is that your bosses are no longer in need of your services."

"What are you talking about?"

"I'm talking about Mr. Harris, who is now dead, and Mr. Romero, who I'm sure wishes he was. They are not in control of this fort anymore."

A long pause. "Why should we believe that?"

"I assume you're close to the wall. Am I right?"

No response.

"Doesn't matter. I think you'll get the message." Quinn clicked off the mic. With his voice raised enough for his friends to hear, he said, "Now."

As one, they angled their guns toward the jungle without exposing more of themselves than necessary. They let off two shots each.

Quinn keyed the mic again. "Hope we didn't hit anyone."

"What do you want?" The man's tone had done a one-eighty.

"It's not what *we* want. It's what you probably want. To get off this island."

"You'd let us go?"

"Sure, we'll let you leave," Quinn said. "Or we could continue hunting you down and killing you off."

The man took a moment before he spoke again. "Are we supposed to just *swim*?"

"There's a boat at the other end of the island. We'll give you thirty minutes to get there and shove off. Anyone left after that will be eliminated. Do we have an understanding?"

DAENG WAS TASKED with shadowing the remaining soldiers and making sure they all boarded the boat and left. While he did that, Quinn called Gogan, the pilot of their private jet, and gave him the coordinates of the island's airstrip. Then he, Orlando, Nate, and the other former prisoners—with the exception of Peter—moved the bodies of Harris and the dead soldiers into the downstairs room. They decided to leave Janus where he was, his bulk more than any of them wanted to deal with.

When they finished, Orlando retrieved the bag she'd brought downstairs. "For your trouble, gentlemen," she said as she unzipped the bag and flashed the contents at Lanier, Berkeley, and Curson. "Doesn't necessarily make up for what happened, but it's something." She zipped it back up and tossed it to Lanier.

A little while later, Daeng radioed in that the soldiers had all left. Shortly after that, Gogan called to say he was getting ready to take off and would be there in no more than twenty minutes.

When Quinn hung up, he walked over to where Peter was sitting with Romero.

"We need to head out. Are you ready?" he asked.

"Our friend here is being a little close-lipped," Peter said. "Doesn't want to say how he came into possession of our names or found out where I lived."

"Unfortunate," Quinn said. "You need a little more time? We could spare maybe another few minutes. You could hook him up to that electroshock machine."

Peter frowned. "That would only kill him. Rather he died on his own at this point. It's going to be painful." He stood up. "Besides, I have a pretty good idea where the leak came from."

"Well, if you need our help plugging it, you let me know."

Once the others had all moved outside, Quinn took a last look around to make sure everything was just right.

The weapons the soldiers had been carrying were in a pile against the wall, and the bodies were laid out on the floor in a line. Directly behind them, strapped to a wooden chair, sat Romero. In his office, they had found digital movies of the whippings, with Romero clearly visible, watching the proceedings. Orlando had copied the videos onto two separate memory cards. One she kept. The other was in a plastic bag taped to Romero's shirt, the words WATCH ME written across the plastic.

Everything in the room looked fine. Once Quinn and the others were in the air, a call would be placed to the Isla de Cervantes state police. The authorities would be told of a gunfight at Fort Duran, and of a band of the surviving rebels racing toward the main island in a speedboat at that very moment.

It wouldn't provide complete satisfaction for what had happened, but it would do.

Quinn stepped outside and closed the door.

JANUS KNEW HIS end was near, but it hadn't quite arrived yet.

He had regained consciousness to the sounds of voices. He recognized one right away. It belonged to the prisoner Quinn, who had escaped and ruined everything.

Without opening his eyes, he tried to follow their conversation, but it was hard to focus. He had been shot— how many times, he didn't know—but his body refused to die.

Finally the voices stopped, and a door closed.

They're gone.

He lay there for a moment, just to be sure, and then pried his eyelids apart.

With effort, he pushed himself into a sitting position before rising painfully to his feet. He had to pause and grab the wall. He thought he was about to pass out again, but then the haze cleared and he was back.

He looked around.

I'm downstairs.

Right. That's where he'd been when they shot him again.

To his left was the way back into the fort. To his right, the open door to the antechamber that housed the fort's exit. Through the doorway, he could see something odd on the floor, something his mind was having a hard time processing. He walked over for a closer look.

Bodies. All wearing uniforms.

No, not all. Harris was there, too. Dead.

"Huh," he said, feeling no emotion whatsoever.

"Janus?"

If Janus had been able to, he would have jumped in surprise. Instead, his head slowly turned to the voice.

Strapped to a chair directly behind the bodies was Señor Romero, looking even more frail than usual.

"Janus. Untie me. Now!"

Janus staggered into the room, and stopped beside

331

Romero's chair.

"Come on!" Romero said. "Quickly!"

He looked at the old man, and glanced at the straps holding Romero down. They looked like the same straps that had been on the electroshock machine upstairs. Thick and strong. A good choice.

"Hurry! Get me out of this chair!"

Janus walked over to the pile of weapons, awkwardly lowered himself to his knees, and hunted around.

"What are you doing?" Romero asked. "Get over here!"

Janus found a knife and pulled it out.

"If that will make it faster, fine. Now cut me out."

A knife was fine, but there was something that would do the job even better. Back on his feet, Janus raised the rifle he'd grabbed and shot Romero in the chest. No sense in letting the old man outlive him.

He stared at his work for second. His bullet had gone right through the letter A of the word WATCH that was on a piece of plastic attached to Romero's shirt. Why it was there, he had no idea, nor did he care.

For a moment, he lost focus, his mind drifting off. When he snapped back, he was looking toward the door to the outside.

Yes. That's it.

Using the rifle as a cane, he made his way outside.

There was one other person who needed to die before he did today.

THEY MADE IT to the airstrip five minutes before they saw the jet descending toward them.

"You broke the first rule, you know," Quinn said to Nate as they waited.

"Never get caught," Nate said with a nod.

Quinn put a hand against his forehead to shade his eyes as he tracked the plane's progress. "I've never been caught."

Nate's face scrunched up on one side. "Is that true?"

"It's what I'm telling you."

"So it's not true."

332

"It might be.

"And it might not."

They fell silent for a moment.

"Thanks for coming to get me," Nate said. "You know I'd do the same for you."

"Whether you would or wouldn't have before, you have to now. You owe me."

"Oh, good Lord," Orlando said. "Are you boys finished? The rest of us don't want to hear this."

"I was just thanking him," Nate said.

"And I was just accepting that thanks," Quinn added.

She rolled her eyes.

Seconds later the plane swooped in, its tires emitting a rubbery screech as they touched down. Before the jet had even stopped moving, the group headed down the clearing beside the tarmac to meet it. They were about a hundred feet away when the door opened, and Liz hopped down the ladder.

"Nate!" she said, running toward him.

Nate paused for half a second. "Liz?"

"I knew there was something I forgot to mention," Quinn said, allowing himself a playful smile. "And by the way, you and I need to have a talk about what you're allowed to tell my sister and what you're not."

JANUS COULND'T SEE the plane, but he could hear it. Afraid they'd know he was following them if he moved any closer, he'd stayed within the cover of the jungle, a dozen feet from the clearing.

The walk from the fort had drained all but the last bit of his energy. Each step now felt like he was moving through a vat of mud. His eyesight, too, had become problematic. Though he could see the others standing together near the landing strip, he had to use all his concentration to pick out the one he was pretty sure was Quinn.

He was the one who had to die.

The roar of the jet increased. Putting a hand on the tree next to him, Janus leaned forward so he could see the end of the runway. A plane appeared over the island, and seemed to hover in the air for a second before landing. He watched as it raced down the runway, passed the group waiting for it, and stopped near the other end.

He thought it would come back this way, but instead Quinn and his friends were walking toward it.

No!

He knew he couldn't go much further. His body had given him all it had and more already. But he couldn't let Quinn get away.

He weaved unsteadily out of the brush, and forced himself to follow the troublemaker. Halfway there, he knew he wouldn't make it. Worse yet, Quinn was at the front of the group, greeting someone who had just come out of the plane. He was too far away.

Janus wanted to scream, but he held it in.

Do what you can.

The rifle felt like a thousand pounds as he raised it to his shoulder. He steadied himself as best he could, pointing the weapon at the back of the pack.

"You all go to hell," he whispered, then pulled the trigger.

To SAY QUINN was getting used to seeing his sister and Nate embrace would have been stretching reality. But this time there was a certain satisfaction.

There'd been moments over the last few days when he wondered if the two of them would ever have the chance to be together again. But here they were, arm in arm. It was a sight to be cherished, not frowned upon.

"All right, everyone," Quinn said, turning toward the others. "Let's get on—"

The word stuck in this throat as he saw Janus standing seventy yards behind the group, not only alive but pointing a rifle in their direction.

As he pulled out his gun, he shouted, "Down! Everyone!"

But his warning was drowned out by the *bang-bang-bang-bang-bang* of the semiautomatic rifle.

Quinn saw movement at the back of the group. Someone going down.

He ran to the side and let off five quick shots. Four more shots came from off to his right, Daeng circling the other way and mirroring Quinn's course.

Janus took two steps backward, his rifle tilting up in the air.

Quinn emptied the rest of his magazine.

As Janus went down for the last time, his finger jerked on the rifle's trigger, sending a final hail of bullets flying high over the jungle.

As Quinn ran toward Janus, he released the empty mag and jammed in his final one.

He and Daeng reached Janus at the same time.

The man's chest was full of entry wounds, and his eyes had the empty death stare Quinn had seen so many times before. But there was only one way to make sure the man never got up again. Quinn aimed his gun at Janus's forehead and pulled the trigger.

"Quinn!" Nate called out.

Quinn whipped around, thinking maybe there was another attacker somewhere. But Nate was at the back of the group, kneeling on the ground. There were two people lying to either side of him.

"Hurry!" Nate yelled.

The hair on the back of Quinn's neck stood on end. He ran as fast as he'd ever run, trying to keep his mind blank.

The closest person on the ground was Peter, and Quinn instantly knew the former head of the Office would never get up again. A bullet had caught him on the side of the head just above his right ear.

Then he twisted around and saw the other person Janus had hit.

ORLANDO HAD NO idea what happened.

She'd been standing, she was sure of that, but now she seemed to be lying on the ground.

Why can't I get up? Why can't I move?

THE COLLECTED

Voices. Hollow. Distant, but not distant.

"Quinn...Hurry..."

I'm tired. Why am I so tired?

The ground shook under her. *Thud. Thud.* Then something bumped against her arm.

She could feel it. She couldn't move her arm, but she could feel it. That was good, right?

"No, no, no, no, no!"

Quinn?

"Orlando. Orlando, can you hear me?"

I can hear you.

"Orlando? Come on, baby, stay with me!"

It was strange. Though she knew he was right beside her, it sounded like he was a million miles away.

"Do you hear me? Baby, please, stay with me!"

Growing farther and farther.

"You're going to be okay. You're going to be fine. Just stay with..."

ACKNOWLEDGMENTS

As always, any book is a team effort, and I am very thankful to my Team Quinn members, and to all the readers who continue to enjoy the adventures of Quinn and his friends.

This time, special thanks go to: Ivonne de Cervantes for helping me with my Spanish (any errors, as much as I always hate to admit it, are mine); friend and fellow novelist Robert Browne, not only for the long conversations about plot, books, and basic BS, but for creating the fantastic Quinn covers; and, of course, Elyse Dinh-McCrillis, whose expert eyes find the errors, both easy and deceiving, that I never catch. You have my undying gratitude.

Finally, my thanks and love to the three people who make doing this even more worthwhile than I could have ever thought possible—my kids: Ronan, Fiona, and Keira. The future is yours, and I can't wait to see what you do with it.

X

16967782R00181

Made in the USA
Charleston, SC
19 January 2013